JERRY COX

ON THE LIP

A NOVEL

Touching Covers, Inc.
Washington

Touching Covers, Inc.
Washington
Please visit *www.WebSurferUSA.com*

Library of Congress Cataloging-in-Publication Data
Cox, Jerry
1. Surfing – United States - Fiction
2. Businessmen – United States – Fiction
3. Electronic Commerce – United States – Fiction
Title: PS3603.O9.O585 2011
ISBN: 978-0-6151-4937-0

SECOND PAPERBACK EDITION

For Victoria, forever

Near
Langley, Virginia
September, 2001

TOM REY TOLD PEOPLE all summer he was killing himself in the tech business. Now, he means it, for real.

He stabs the key into the ignition of his spanking-new Porsche 911 and sucks in a deep breath. Knowing it's one of his last, he lets it escape grudgingly.

How will the media play it, he wonders, accident or suicide, and who will mourn a twenty-five-year old, self-styled "King of the Internet" after his tank of ultra-premium gasoline fills his cavernous, five-car garage with carbon monoxide? With no suicide note, much less a Last Will, who will inherit the megabucks he made from his stock in Fred Hanson's radical Internet invention?

Perhaps his casual, collegiate clothing and un-moussed hair will give them a clue. He had to push aside all the new Bosses and Hilfigers and Zegnas in his professionally-designed walk-in closet to find his old Abercrombies and his Pumas. They are loose and a little ragged, just like the life he had already left behind.

His buds often teased him that he would make a perfect Abercrombie & Fitch model, but that doesn't matter now. If he doesn't kill himself right now – tonight – he figures he'll wind up in a federal penitentiary. An orange jumpsuit won't help fend off unwanted attention and his innocence will be finally and completely irrelevant.

His in-dash CD player taunts him. The Nirvana song, "Rape Me," pops up on random play. He cries, then laughs and sings along with Kurt Cobain.

He'll have to belt out the lyrics *"waste me-e!"* a lot louder if he wants to drown out the muscular hum of the engine under the rear hatch, but oxygen is already getting preciously thin. Instead of screaming the final chorus, he rasps it.

He keeps nodding and his forehead bounces off the leather-wrapped steering wheel a couple of times. It doesn't smart as much the second time and he wonders why his short life isn't passing before his eyes, like in the movies.

After a couple minutes, a weird dream puts him in the movie *On the Beach*, which he once checked out at Blockbuster, mistaking it for a surfing video. He's in Australia with a bunch of other sorry jakes. They have everything to live for until a nuclear war forces them to make a choice. They can let radiation sickness torture them to death or they can drink the Kool-Aid to avoid the agony. It's not just the end, but *"the* end," as in *"game over, Dude."* He is the debonair guy with a cool ride, a Ferrari, and he kills himself in it.

"If you gotta go, it might as well be in a great set of wheels," he tells himself, then immediately reverses his decision. A great set of wheels can carry him back to Southern California, back to his old life, far away from the greedy tech gurus and the shadowy guys from Langley. He *can* take his life back.

There's only one problem. His hands weigh a ton all of a sudden and can't move from his lap to shut off the engine. His head rolls side-to-side as his ears fill with a piercing noise. At first, he thinks he has slumped over the steering column and is laying on the horn. He knows that can't be right when his forehead takes a final dive into the steering wheel. This time, it doesn't hurt a bit.

FRESH AIR CUTS INTO HIS LUNGS. The Porsche's in-dash CD player is silent, but the engine is still running.

"Get out, you dumbshit!" Or something to that effect, his home security system screams at him. Nobody told him it featured a carbon monoxide sensor, much less that it was designed to pop the garage doors the instant it went off.

"*Fucking* technology!" He swears and laughs at the same time. He staggers out into the driveway and draws in the warm, dry, late-summer air. It reeks of recently-felled pine trees from the half-acre lot across the street. A motion detector fires a spotlight directly into his face.

"Nature takes its course! *Nature takes its course!*" he shouts into the light, over and over, louder and louder, until he coughs so hard he falls to his knees. When he catches his breath, he realizes there is only one thing to do, go to every ATM, max out on cash withdrawals. He lays all the large bills on his California king-size bed, counts and stacks them and makes plans. He flip phones an "800" number, buys a one-way ticket, First Class, and charges it to his corporate American Express card.

He has only one option now: *to survive.*

PART ONE
DOG WISH

"Man is troubled by what might be called the dog wish, a strange and involved compulsion to be as happy and carefree as a dog."

-- James Thurber

Start-up

I N THE SUMMER OF THE YEAR 2000, Fred Hanson finally was catching a wave. The new "dotcom" he founded, an Internet start-up named "WebSurferUSA," was making the whole, jaded, mega-hyped tech world sit up and take notice. His sparsely decorated corner office in Cambridge, Massachusetts, makes him look and feel more like a tech entrepreneur, less like a twenty-seven-year old with a Ph.D. dissertation run amok.

The space just outside his door is more a chute than a hallway. Software engineers, web designers, geodesy experts, lawyers, bankers and anxious investors have no choice but to queue up. This enables Fred to deal with them one at a time, never in any logical order.

Fred always halts the frantic parade whenever his lawyer calls from the New York office of Kohler and Kray.

"Everybody signed off on the final paperwork for the new angel investment round!" James Foster Bass Jr., Esquire, known as "Jamie" back in college at the University of San Diego, can barely contain his excitement.

"The additional *twenty million dollars* will be deposited in the bank within ten to fourteen days," the newly minted lawyer announces with great fanfare, his voice so full of excitement, it almost sounds like laughter.

Fred's butt cheeks unclench for the first time in three weeks. Negotiations over the new cash infusion made the black semicircles under his eyes darker and deeper every day. WebSurfer has never produced a penny in revenue, much less a profit, but he allows himself to look toward what Internet analysts call "the profit horizon." His guts flip the moment he catches sight of it. At the company's anticipated "burn rate," this new wad of mad money from a group of private investors in Washington, D.C., will cover expenses for only a few months.

AS HIS LAWYER coldly recaps the latest investment round, Fred ignores the building-wide smoking ban, rips a match from a Harvard Faculty Club matchbook, strikes it and fires up an ultra-light. His wireless headset magnifies the noise and Jamie wonders if Boston has just been nuked. Fred the California surfer-dude never smoked – not tobacco, at least. Fred the East Coast entrepreneur began sprouting embarrassing love handles on his middle the minute he got back to Massachusetts.

"We're still on track for taking WebSurfer public within the year?" Fred realizes his company can turn overnight from "dotcom" to "dotbomb."

"Let's say within the next twelve months, not necessarily within this calendar year." Jamie selects his words carefully. "Much depends on Sammy Schwartz."

"Sammy Schwartz?" Fred has to stop and think. He remembers that one of the partners in Jamie's firm, a middle-aged Princeton graduate, used an old school tie to convince one of the hottest "New Economy" investment banking firms in New York to consider "taking WebSurfer public." Samuels and Schwartzman Partners, Ltd. – everybody called it "Sammy Schwartz" – had a Midas touch. Success was assured if these Wall Street hot-shots decided to round up brokers and investors to buy stock in the company and give it the "market cap" it would need to function in the intensely competitive Internet marketplace. They would, of course, skim off hefty fees.

When they finish discussing preliminary plans for the "initial public offering" or "IPO," the securities law procedure that will transform WebSurfer into a publicly traded company and Fred into a mega-millionaire, Jamie adopts a more casual tone.

"Almost forgot something, Bro! You remember Tom Rey, don't you?"

ON THE LIP

Fred is startled to hear Tom's name in the same breath with the good tidings about WebSurfer's new capital infusion. Tom never made it easy to keep their tight personal bond alive. He had no computer at home and never bothered to set up a personal e-mail account.

"Shore dew," Fred drawls. "Raised that boy from a pup." He mimics the Texas accent Jamie brought with him as a scarcely eighteen-year old freshman at USD, but which evaporated quicker than his farmer's tan.

"Have you forgotten all those weekends, when you got stoned out of your mind and played that sappy REM song, 'This One Goes Out to the One I Love,' for the whole crowd that was hangin' at our place in OhBee?" Fred almost asks, but he bites his tongue when he realizes Jamie is on speakerphone. Surely, Fred trusts, Jamie still nurtured enough undamaged brain cells to remember living with him and Tom in a ramshackle house on Ocean Beach a few miles south of the USD campus, before Jamie went to law school and Fred went home to Cambridge to get a doctorate in engineering from the Massachusetts Institute of Technology.

"You won't believe this, Dude!" Jamie's lawyerly demeanor evaporates completely. "Word is, our old Dog is gonna be on *Animal Planet* tomorrow night."

"Isn't that out past Uranus somewhere?" Fred inquires, deliberately using the long "a" pronunciation.

"Nah, you know, that cable show!" Jamie is sure Fred is jerking him off again, just like in their college days.

Fred sucks hard on his low-tar cigarette. Pangs of guilt mix with his nicotine rush. He should never have let a 3,000-mile separation make all those beach romps, impossibly wild parties and reckless, occasionally dangerous, adventures seem like dreams, fantasies, vapors, ghosts of an entirely different person's existence.

After an awkward pause, Fred asks Jamie, "got ol' TeeRey's phone number handy, by any chance?"

Jamie already wishes he hadn't mentioned Tom.

Roasting

WEBSURFER'S NEW CORPORATE HEADQUARTERS sits atop a five-story, brick and glass structure in the heart of Cambridge. The employees look like a collegiate golf outing that took a wrong turn, but everyone's nose is glued to one of five huge, state-of-the-art, flat panel computer monitors.

Before the ink was dry on WebSurfer's incorporation papers, Fred moved his thirty-six employees from five different suites scattered around the Harvard and MIT campuses. Fred was physically exhausted from trying to keep up with his growing gaggle of geeks, many of whom had eagerly abandoned well-paying jobs in bio-techs and other established brick-and-mortar companies across New England. Most of them got paid a combination of burger-flipping cash wages and shares of WebSurfer stock, each of which had roughly the same par value as a week-old New England Lottery ticket. Self-consciously like the sainted and despised Bill Gates before them, some dropped out of Harvard, convinced that college was an impediment, not a springboard, to megabucks and geek sainthood.

After five joyful years of oneness with the beach, Fred can't help thinking of the business in surfing terms, and he runs WebSurfer exactly the way he surfed. Tom Rey taught him everything he knew about the sport, but Fred developed his own personal style.

From the moment they met, Fred was fascinated with Tom's extra sense, something like the precognition dogs in California show just before a major earthquake. He could always *feel* a good wave before it emerged from open water, what surfers call "the fetch."

Fred, however, missed too many good waves. He worried about making a mistake, "going over the falls," getting caught up in curling water he couldn't handle and "drilled" face-first into a reef or slammed into hard-packed sand. He "clucked" often enough, some of the Phi Delts started calling him "Freddy the Swish."

On the beach, Tom was everybody's hero. He mastered almost any wave PeeBee, OhBee or Redondo could throw at him. His excellent balance and timing allowed him to maneuver about halfway up the surging wall of water and do "cutbacks," jerking the board left or right instantly to keep the ride alive.

"Surfers can do *anything*," Tom told Fred soon after they met. He learned to wait however long it took for a manageable wave and went straight into "the pocket," the tube of air inside a curl. Eventually, Fred found "the glide," those fleeting, transcendent moments when a surfer becomes convinced that *he* is the only thing in the universe that is not in motion. His new-found reputation for good, long, elegant rides helped his sex life immensely.

Fred returned the favor. Without Fred's intense tutoring and enough dog-eared back issues of *Swank* to obviate the need for dating until after exams, Tom could not have passed all the courses he needed as a solid-B English major at USD. As soon as Fred returned to Cambridge and got his hands on the postage meter in his department chairman's office, he started mailing Tom MIT T-shirts.

"It stands for 'Many Intelligent Twits,'" according to one of Fred's accompanying notes. He stopped sending them almost a year ago.

The happy memories are not the only reason Fred's pulse quickens when he thinks about Tom. For two weeks running, Tom has starred in Fred's recurring dream, more a repressed recollection than a nightmare. It jolts Fred bolt upright in bed, hyperventilating, icy sweat cascading unobstructed down his nearly hairless chest, around three o'clock every morning.

TECH HAPPY HOUR is starting at the eVillage Restaurant and Bar, but Fred Hanson does not look happy. His elbows are propped on the heavily lacquered top of a massive bar with mahogany paneling that looks like it was ripped out of his uncle's private library back home on Beacon Hill. In Fred's troubled mind, he is not clinging to a bar. He is stranded on a desert island or marooned on a planet out of its orbit, lost in the ocean of space that made up eVillage's high-tech barn of a barroom.

After his rugged day in Herndon, Virginia, the incongruously sleepy exurban capital of the World Wide Web, Fred's downcast nose and chin form similar angles, classical lines. He is morose, even though he began his afternoon meeting at UOL.com, the world's second-most-popular Internet service provider, full of confidence. He repeated his "pitch" for the one hundredth time and thought it tripped smoothly off his tongue. Now, it just replays on a continuous loop inside his throbbing head.

As he waits for the last possible moment to tuck his tail between his legs and catch his flight back to Boston from Washington's Dulles International Airport, Fred wonders if his plane home also will crash and whether he would really mind if it did. He refuses to think about the last time he felt so apprehensive, but he never forgets that he descended from a long line of Yankee heroes. Many of his ancestors threw themselves into the breach. He is beginning to think he will be the first to fall on his own sword.

The bar, located just a few miles east of UOL, off a different Dulles Toll Road exit, got a cleverly-written, if not especially favorable, write-up from a rising young business reporter for the Boston *Globe*. The bar owner planted a couple of glowing reviews in some of the infotech magazines Fred routinely stole from the doorstep of another tech company in WebSurfer's building on the way into his office.

"Five bucks after five o'clock!" the bartender, a woman with ragged blonde hair, tries to cheer her slumping customer. The first two beers were $6.50 a pop, but the price went down at five, when Tech Happy Hour started.

Cold beer and a gathering crowd usually pumped Fred up in no time. The tech types popping into eVillage look young, even in Fred's twenty-seven-year old eyes. He can tell they are the local worker bees, buzzing in from the honeycomb of cubicles in the new high-rise office buildings spreading all over Tysons Corner, Virginia, just two miles away.

Fred pretends to pay no attention as the cubicle kings clump together on all four corners of the rectangular bar, ordering happy hour-priced domestic beers and third-rate Argentine white wines. Hard liquor was out of the question, or perhaps just out of the budget. The young white men certainly weren't drinking anything that might put hair on their chests, having spent their first month's salaries to laser all productive follicles into submission.

The clump closest to Fred, which includes cheerful, WASPy, preppy women and nerdy, East Indian men in expensive casual clothes, called themselves the "Early Adopters" because they convinced their employers it was smart business to post a delegation at eVillage *at the beginning* of every Tech Happy Hour. This was not "getting buzzed" on the job; it was "building the buzz."

A decidedly slick-looking guy, clad in black from head to toe, appears out of nowhere and begins an animated conversation with the Early Adopters. A New Yorker, Fred concludes from the image in the corner of his eye. Among the skills Fred picked up in California, he was most grateful for his ability to judge people by their appearance.

The guy is Fred's age, perhaps a little older, but Fred can't make out his ethnicity. He seems too short to fit in with the preppy women and his complexion is too pasty white to fit in with the Indians, yet all the Early Adopters seem anxious to speak to him.

The stranger mounts the backless barstool next to Fred and orders a Rolling Rock.

"Man, you look like you got the weight of the world on your shoulders!" he tells Fred earnestly.

"Naw," Fred replies. He identifies the Brooklyn accent but detects some education behind it. "Just everything above ten degrees latitude, north."

The stranger chuckles as his long, delicate fingers slip a business card into the pool of condensation rolling off of Fred's fourth beer.

"Bill-ee Ship-ee, Editor, ee-Zyne," Fred reads the card out loud.

"It's Billy Shippe, actually. The 'e' is silent."

"So, what's a zyne?"

The stranger chuckles again, patiently.

"It's 'ee-zeen,' as in 'electronic magazine.' It's the oldest online publication about the tech business. 'The Voice of the New Economy,' we call it. Been on the web for almost eighteen months. You in the game, Bud?"

"That remains to be seen." For once, Fred does not want to talk about WebSurfer. Instead, he tells a perfect stranger about his sixteen hour workdays, seven days a week, and complains about not getting laid since the government issued his patent.

FRED HAD ALREADY BLOWN the whole day by flying to Washington and trying to explain WebSurfer to a half-dozen look-alike UOL executives. They spent the entire session fondling their cell phones and hand-held computers, as if desperate to get called out to something more important. The execs dashed in or out of the room, round-robin, shouting unnecessarily into their dangling microphones, with their young faces pinched in urgent concentration.

"In the new millennium, addresses will derive from a digital, user-friendly, grid-based system instead of confusing street addresses or measurements of latitude and longitude," Fred began. "Not even pilots and surveyors can write down or type degrees, minutes and seconds of 'lat' and 'lon' coordinates into a computer accurately. One little mistake and they end up in a completely different hemisphere!"

"With its patented reference system, WebSurfer will power a new Internet-based search engine for the real world. It offers *unique* and *revolutionary* functionalities over a wide range of platforms. It was designed to be an *infrastructure* solution, a whole new platform from which Internet businesses can operate, not just another would-be supplier to the endless cyber-Wal-Mart."

Fred's audience, UOL's princelings-of-the-week, were hand-picked by Mike Culver, Universe Online's publicity-hungry founder and CEO. Fred could see why the media called them "Culver's Clones." The blond crew cuts right out of the 1950s looked bored throughout Fred's PowerPoint presentation. If they were trying to hide their athletic builds behind their folded arms and identical coral hued designer golf shirts, it was not working.

The post-presentation give-and-take turned out to be more of a give-and-give and give some more. The consensus around the table seemed to be that UOL had no use for the strategic partnership Fred had in mind. At most, one of Culver's clones allowed, they might be willing to take the whole big mess off of Fred's hands by assuming all of his brainchild's bank debt. Mysteriously, the clone had calculated it to the penny.

Fred was exasperated. As the majority shareholder, he would make a killing if his company ever managed to "go public." The preliminary valuation study, done by the best in the business, suggested an initial $15-a-share offering price. Fred's WebSurfer stock would suddenly be worth more than $15 million. His personal revenue from the patent license could eventually mean millions more.

Culver picked absent-mindedly at a hangnail the whole time and said nothing. When he finally looked up, a chill seized Fred from the crown of his head to his toes. He saw shark eyes, and that made him think about his darkest moment with Tom Rey, his old surfing buddy. A couple of the clones could not resist smirking when they saw Fred shudder and squirm in his ergonomic guest chair.

Animal Planet

THAT SAME LATE SUMMER AFTERNOON, Tom Rey struts into Orville and Wilbur's Surf Bar, the most notorious hook-up joint in Pacific Beach, California. He is dressed for a celebration – baggy linen shorts in place of his usual tattered and faded board shorts, canvas deck shoes instead of flimsy rubber flip-flops (no socks, but at least the toes are intact) and a solid blue-green polo the color of his eyes.

When Tom appears, a bartender vaults onto the bar and stands up. His shoulder-length, dark brown hair barely fits under the fake thatched roof canopy that runs the twenty-foot length of the bar.

"D-u-u-u-u-u-u-des!" the barkeep shouts over dozens of lively conversations. Young patrons at the far end of "the O&W" get a good look at his loose, blue and gold Hawaiian shirt. It is already splattered with cheap beer and brownish soap scum.

"D-u-u-u-u-u-u-de!" roars the reply from the regular cast of rowdy frat boys, white-nosed lifeguards and mellow surfers. Clad in faded board shorts, tank tops and rubber flip-flops, they are fluent in the local tongue, Teenage Mutant Ninja Turtle.

Sun-burned bleach blondes sit on barstools in twos or threes, with dainty tattoos beckoning between thong straps and butt cleavage. It is unusual for the crowd to gather indoors on such a crystalline July evening in the San Diego beach town. A hundred or so revelers ignore the ocean-view deck and the crimson slice of sun slipping behind gentle Pacific waves. They are stoked for a major television event. All four of the bar's ancient, beaten-up, 1992-

vintage TV monitors are tuned to a single channel. For the first time in O&W history, ESPN is out of sight.

The bartender stretches both arms in front, as if he plans to dive headlong into the chattering crowd. "This is Tom Rey's big night! *Animal Planet*! How totally *radical* is that?"

"TeeRey! TeeRey!" Tom's Phi Delt fraternity brothers from USD start chanting.

The lean, not-quite-six-footer strikes a relaxed pose near an open, roll-up patio door and keeps one eye on the sunset. Seen from the bar, Tom cuts a glowing silhouette into the fading light, which refracts through his bushy blond hair.

A skinny guy with pitch-black chin pubes and a baseball cap crammed backwards on his skull throws Pretzel Stix at him. He hits an Asian woman standing next to Tom, an obvious stranger to the beach in a form-fitting, off-white dress and matching high-heeled shoes. The diminutive *Animal Planet* reporter seeks shelter by inserting two fingers into the pocket of Tom's wrinkled linen shorts.

"Our Tom is goin' *fuckin' global* tonight!" the bartender, Corey Collins, exults. His friendly, unaccented voice makes him sound like a professional master of ceremonies. He dropped out of USD after being too stoned to remember attending more than a handful of classes during his first and only semester of college.

"Tom will be on the tube in about twenty minutes. So-o-o-o-o – who's for a brew?" Collins performs a sure-footed athletic dismount, knocks open three beer taps at once and starts passing empty plastic pitchers under them.

EVERYONE AT ORVILLE & WILBUR'S SURF BAR downs a couple more rounds. The visiting television reporter takes her fingers out of Tom's pocket long enough to signal Collins to turn up the volume by shaking two fists high above her head. Collins finds two remotes and pounds the volume controls with his calloused thumbs. The conversational rumble dies down just enough to allow the baritone voice-over, in an Americanized British accent, to break out over an aerial shot of the Zoo.

"Here, at the world famous San Diego Zoo," the announcer intones, "they know all about the birds and the bees."

The crowd groans quietly. Over the next few minutes, viewers watch several breeds of birds mate. It is less erotic than *Animal Planet*'s perennial ratings-booster, two wild orangutans performing jungle love, as only apes can do it.

Suddenly, Tom's perfectly lit face fills all the screens. He is classically handsome, but there is more to it. This healthy-looking, quintessential California surfer-dude would make any channel-skater put the clicker down. Even after they realized they hadn't landed on the latest MTV reality show, people would stay tuned, if only to see if anything intelligent could possibly come out of that face.

The caption across the bottom introduces him to the world as "Tom Rey, Expert on Animal Reproduction." The "TeeRey" chant degenerates into chortling almost before it starts. Tom's momentarily serious television image recites a textbook description of how emus, large flightless birds from Down Under, fertilize their eggs. The details get drowned out by laughter when Tom reveals that the males often approach females on their knees and then peck them in the head when they ejaculate.

"On your knees!" the Phi Delts chant as they drop to the sand-scraped wooden floor.

"If the female is especially receptive," the televised Tom instructs matter-of-factly, "the males will line up behind her and wait their turn."

The frat boys drag their bare knees across the floor and form a line at the feet of a notoriously receptive brunette on a barstool. She struggles desperately to ignore them.

The reporter appears on-screen and purrs, "what does the male emu do after he pecks the female?"

Tom remembers the rest of her question – "light up a cigarette?" – but he notices it got edited out.

Tom's onscreen face breaks into a seductive grin.

"*Shoot'n'scoot!*" he tells the entire world with a jaunty, sideways cock of his head.

≈≈≈≈≈≈≈≈≈≈≈≈

"*SHOOT AND SCOOT!*" Tom's brothers mock him, and Pretzel Stix fly again.

"Hey! You promised you wouldn't air that part!" he says, genuinely embarrassed. Tom knows his little joke will cost him dearly at work.

The reporter grabs his hands and pulls him down. Her tiny Japanese lips brush his right ear as she speaks. Tom makes a mental note to check for lipstick there in the morning.

"Sometimes, I just can't help myself!" She blinks as another pretzel stick bounces off her forehead.

A bright halo surrounds any guy basking in the afterglow of his fifteen minutes of fame, so everybody in the bar crushes toward Tom. It was their right as fellow Californians to share the experience.

"D-u-u-u-de! *D-u-u-u-u-u-u-u-de*!" is the only thing several of the guys can think to say while they give Tom a customized soul-shake. No higher form of flattery could come from a single syllable.

When Collins restores ESPN on the monitors, he also cranks up some classic Beach Boys on the O&W's sound system, which made up in decibels what it lacked in frequency range. People who want to hear each other talk wander through the patio door, onto the deck outside. Those inside start gyrating to the beach party classic, "Catch a Wave" and otherwise normal, all-American males sing along in nut-crunching falsettos.

Collins usually switched to the only Doors album in the O&W's collection late at night, after his droopy-eyed loadie friends floated in. Tonight, Collins starts Jim Morrison crooning "LA Woman" a little early.

"Mo – jo – rye – zinnn!" he belts into the air microphone in his right hand and shoves full pitchers of beer across the bar with his left. Tom walks casually out the front door, one hand weighing lightly on the "talent" from *Animal Planet*, the other holding his cell phone up to his ear as its message counter goes berserk, trying to keep up.

Collins flashes two upraised thumbs and an exaggerated, full-face wink. He knows Tom won't be back to prowl the O&W tonight. His former roommate was always a dog, never a pig.

≈≈≈≈≈≈≈≈≈≈≈

Dog Wish

≈≈≈≈≈≈≈≈≈≈≈≈

THE REPORTER FROM *ANIMAL PLANET* called all the shots in bed. The sex was methodical, engineered for efficiency. Tom thought she was a lot like that Honda Civic he test drove, but couldn't afford: tight getting in, but gets you where you want to go. She was back in her twenty-second floor condo on Wilshire Boulevard in LA before midnight.

Shoot and scoot. Tom knew he would not hear from the reporter again, but he surely would get an earful from his boss at the San Diego Zoo. The dour son of Cuban immigrants, who insisted upon being addressed as *Mr.* Menendez, was disappointed to discover, too late in the hiring process, that Tom's Spanish surname was adopted by his Polish immigrant father when he first moved to California.

Tom's beachwear was always casual to perfection, but his dad, known as Dojlidy Zywiec when he arrived from Gdansk, had notoriously bad taste in clothes, spotty English and nonexistent Spanish. His Hispanic co-workers at the dock thought he was trying to emulate Elvis Presley, so they started calling him "El Rey" – "the King." The elder Zywiec liked it so much, he changed his name to Don Rey. Tom was twelve years old before he learned how grateful he should be for his Dad's cultural melting-pot bankshot.

Wired

eZINE'S EDITOR, Billy Shippe was present at every eVillage Tech Happy Hour. His talent for drawing people out landed him a secret deal with the ever-so-obscure owner of the ever-so-chic bar. He got free drinks, first dibs on scoops hot enough to attract paying subscribers to his tech newsletter and a modest percentage of the illegal trading gains. The tainted money was disguised as the exorbitant advertising fees eVillage paid for pop-up ads on *eZine*'s website, including the sexy, full-motion video spot promising lurid Bangkok vacations to those who attended Tech Happy Hour and threatening life-long obscurity to those who spent Thursday afternoons grinding in their cubicles.

Shippe made it his business to arrive for Tech Happy Hour promptly at five o'clock every Thursday. He pumped the crowd for two hours and, well ahead of the next day's opening trades on Wall Street, fed the bar owner a full report on all the mergers and acquisitions the young and loquacious guests were legally bound not to discuss with anyone.

Usually, all Shippe had to do was spring for a few rounds. To loosen up young eVillagers who were too hip to get sloppy drunk at these working-world fraternity parties, Shippe was always ready to lay out a short but potent line of cocaine on the small, mirrored shelves he made sure got installed inside the floor-to-ceiling door of each stall in the men's room. An easily flushed paper straw ensured an efficient, surreptitious snort.

The wily owner of eVillage knew that "secret" and "privileged" information was the stock-in-trade of Northern Virginia corporate law firm junior associates, who fancied themselves as the hired guns of the Wild Wild Web, and young software engineers, "code slingers," in desperate need to impress somebody, anybody.

The bar's web advertisements offered "great opportunities to meet new people and perhaps the contact you're looking for with the *inside information you need!!*" Then came the kicker: "Remember, it is *who you know!!*"

Despite the self-congratulatory hype, a lot of what passed for hot intelligence around eVillage was bullshit. After traveling full circle around the room, many of the steaming turds were still recognizable by the puffing poseurs who dropped them in the first place.

The women, mostly lawyers, dropped hints about mergers. The guys, mostly techies and bean-counters, were more likely to leak some bogus quarterly earnings figures, especially if they thought their demonstration of "insider" status would get them a job interview with their employer *du jour*'s biggest competitor or, better yet, some coital interface-time with a Wild Web Wench. Only a fraction of the "insider" intel was real, but it was worth a fortune to anybody with a bit of risk capital and a modern disdain for those vague and inconvenient laws against insider-trading.

Shippe usually wore a body wire. Sometimes, he had to replay an afternoon's worth of recordings four times before he could reliably separate all the infoturds from the bankable insider tips. He put together a puzzle made of bits and bytes of audio. Like an optimistic kid confronted with a room full of horseshit, he started digging eagerly, confident there *had* to be a pony in there *somewhere*. Shippe found one often enough.

Shippe described his profitable little sideline as "stock analysis," even though the Securities Exchange Commission had banned him for life from the financial services industry as part of the settlement in a scandal that drove him off Wall Street two years earlier. Shippe got nailed because he got chummy with an informant but, despite his best efforts, never quite intimate enough to get under the guy's shirt and discover that he was wearing a wire. He avoided prison by the skin of his way-less-than-Hollywood-quality teeth.

After commuting for weeks between WebSurfer's offices in Cambridge and UOL's headquarters in Northern Virginia, Fred Hanson had become a regular at Tech Happy Hour. Now that he had overcome his reluctance to buck himself up with a quick snort whenever he thought he would drown in gloom, a wire was going to make Shippe rich.

BILLY SHIPPE AND FRED HANSON silently sip on their beers and pretend to study an electronic ticker-tape zipping across a screen that seems to float in mid-air over the bar. Beyond it, highway billboard-sized posters for tech companies, some already defunct, cover a massive expanse of wall.

The posters defined different parts of eVillage's loft-like space, as did the crisscrossing bare girders and exposed air ducts. The building housed a bar, a restaurant and a party room on an open platform suspended in full view over the main space. Fred, for once, hatches an optimistic thought. A "private" party on what amounted to a stage would be an effective place to "build the buzz" among the e-nebriated e-gos.

eVillage erected not just a poster but a mural, an obsequious *homage* to America Online, an Internet acorn that took root in the mid-Nineties just a few miles away. From his early vantage point in Boston, Fred watched it suck digital steroids out of the ground and help turn Washington's Dulles International Airport into an East Coast O'Hare.

Fred also notices a massive billboard for AOL's rival, Universe Online. The portion with the company name hadn't been glued on yet, but their logo – a full-color painting of a quintessential hunky surfer dude riding an awesome wave, toes clutching an oversized notebook computer – made Fred wonder whether the Internet upstart might be violating one of the WebSurfer trademarks Jamie set up a few weeks after he incorporated the company.

UOL's real-time market share numbers were giving AOL founder, Steve Case, a peptic ulcer. Culver knew he was jeopardizing Case's top-secret plans for a blow-your-socks-off merger with some "old media" company, but he had not yet figured out which one.

The iconic surfer dude stands too erect on the "board," Fred decides, not crouched the way a real surfer must to maintain control and keep a "ride" going. The guy in the drawing looks so much like Tom Rey, Fred does a double-take. He stifles a grin, afraid his face might break, and points at a television monitor just below the billboard.

"Hey, switch the channel to *Animal Planet*, willya?" Fred orders and the bartender complies.

Billy Shippe notices how quickly the lines crossing Fred's face disappear the instant Tom fills the screen. Shippe keeps one eye on Fred and the other on the television.

"Impressive," Fred declares, as Tom explained how seasonal changes in the photoperiod affect the production of the emus' reproductive hormones, especially the plasma concentrations of luteinizing hormone and testosterone. Tom even covered the inverse effects of prolactin concentrations, Fred notes.

"In the Northern Hemisphere, winter is the normal breeding season," Tom added with a sly grin, "but emus have been known to *do it* in the summer *just for fun.*"

Tom's next line hits Fred like an early-morning splash of aftershave on a nick in his pointed chin.

"Shoot'n'scoot!"

Fred is stunned. In his dreams, he hears Tom utter those exact words every night, right after he pulls Fred's nuts out of the fire, where he finds them roasting, slowly and painfully, just before three o'clock in the morning.

He dials Tom's cell phone number and ends up voice mail number thirty in Tom's "messages waiting" queue.

Nuts

DAWN PATROL, Tom's early-morning run and surf reconnaissance mission, is over. With a sweaty MIT T-shirt halfway over his head, he manages to answer his phone on the third ring.

"Hey, Tomcat!" Tom immediately recognizes the voice of his old housemate and savior of his grade point average, but the Boston accent is thicker than any Tom had ever heard. "I *need* you, Bro."

"I need you, too, Kahuna." Tom pants farcically as he holds the phone up to his wet, red face. "What are you doing up so early on a Saturday? Not even close to noon in Boston, is it?"

"Let's just say the early bird gets the worm."

"I thought we weren't supposed to talk about TeeJay."

"That's not the kinda worm I'm talking about."

"So, what's on fire, Fred?"

"It's a long and twisted story."

"Hmm. Long and twisted. Sorta like your dick."

"Just tell me you'll come talk to me about it."

"About your dick? That'll make for a short conversation."

The frat house semantics put Fred totally at ease.

"Nah, about the business I started. Surf's up, Dude, but I'm shreddin' to stay on the board. I'm gonna be on the lip before I know it, Man, and I need your help, big time. Tell me I can count on you, Bro."

Tom is shocked to learn that Fred has already arranged for an all-expense-paid flight to Boston.

"I promise to make it worth your while, Bro." Sensing Tom's hesitation hardening into refusal, Fred resorts to begging. "Please? *Please*? I *gotta* see you, Man. It's a *fucking emergency*!"

TOM'S FLIGHT TO BOSTON is only the third time he goes airborne with anything bigger than a longboard. The flight attendants are sturdy, tough-looking veterans. He stretches his legs and chats up the only one under age forty to keep her topping off his wine glass. Tom watches the pilots at work through the cockpit door, which stands open while they get their mid-day meal.

"Gnarly buncha buttons, Dudes," he congratulates them, and the two aging fighter jocks roll their eyes and smile and raise their thumbs.

On the ground, Tom fears asphyxiation from the fumes choking the Callahan Tunnel. After a lengthy ride over a short distance, he steps inside the exclusive Hotel Marlowe, in the heart of the "new" Cambridge, toting a small, hastily packed canvas gym bag. He walks across the marble lobby floor, done up in a tan-black-and-white compass-point pattern, toward a wood-paneled podium. Tom feels under-dressed in his leather mocs, no socks, chinos, white dress shirt and preppy blue blazer. These were the clothes he wore to the most important meetings and events at the Zoo, except that the only dress shoes he ever owned were still tucked neatly underneath his desk.

Fred comes up behind Tom and embraces him with both arms, like a brother feared lost at sea, back home again, safe.

"Hey, hey, hey! You made it, Man!"

Tom turns and unselfconsciously hugs him back. He is relieved and amused to see Fred in a professorial, gray tweed jacket, less formal than Tom's blazer. Fred's slight weight gain is apparent in his face, which Tom reckoned to be about four shades whiter than the day Fred left California.

Keeping one arm around Tom's shoulder, Fred steers him into a spacious hotel dining room and speaks quietly and seriously into his left ear, as a bellman runs Tom's gym bag up to his room.

"Listen, Tom. There's a guy here tonight – name's Simon Keith – who's just raised a ton of cash for my company. He's going to join the Board. Whatever he says, go along with it for right now, OK? You won't *really* be committed to anything, I promise. We can iron it all out over a coupla brews after he leaves, OK?"

Tom grins at him.

"Trust me?" The question mark is unmistakable in Fred's voice.

"What's the name of your company again?" Tom keeps grinning.

Before Fred could answer, Tom finds himself in the surprisingly firm grip of a white-haired, square-jawed, ruddy-faced man in his mid-sixties. He wore an expensive, tailor-made business suit and a shirt containing more starch than a hot German potato salad.

"Simon Keith." The older man surprises Tom with a granite handshake. He keeps Tom at a distance of about a foot and slowly looks him up and down, twice. Tom couldn't tell what Keith was looking for, or whether he found it.

"Glad to meet you. I'm Tom Rey." He is not even tempted to say "wazzup."

The trio sit down to an expensively set table, with china and crystal and a wider phalanx of knives and forks than Tom had seen outside of some of his fraternity brothers' wedding receptions.

"I can see you gentlemen have a lot of catching up to do tonight, so I'll get straight to the point. Mr. Hanson insists you're a good man to have around when there's a lot hanging in the balance."

Tom's pulse quickens and his cheeks burn. Surely, despite Keith's peculiar choice of words, Fred never told this stranger the *real* reason he felt that way? He glances at Fred, who keeps a poker face.

Keith elevates his nose, stretching remarkably taut skin above the knot of his Armani power tie. "Your salary will be just a small part of the compensation package. I'm sorry, but a majority of the Board insist it be limited to $160,000 a year. Fred tells me you make a good deal more as the Zoo Director, but the pay cut you are taking will be made up to you in other ways – ways that are performance-based."

Tom brings one hand to his chin, keeps his jaw from hitting the table. Fred must have known that the Zoo did not pay him half that amount, and he was several rungs below Zoo Director.

"You're taking on one hell of a responsibility," Keith continues. "This is against my better judgment, but I'm afraid Mr. Hanson has the entire Board over a barrel. He enjoys reminding us that he is the sole owner of the WebSurfer patent, and the company is practically worthless without the license. Also, if he wants to *give* you almost half a million of his own personal shares outright, that's his business."

"Sounds kinda tough to argue with, Mr. Keith," Tom thinks out loud.

"Please. Call me Simon." Keith leans forward and trains his steel blue eyes on Tom. Charm seeps from every pore. "We'll be seeing a lot of each other, so you might as well start now."

Keith bows stiffly from the waist, shakes hands again and disappears into a chartered Lincoln Town Car.

Tom and Fred re-take their seats. Fred wears a satisfied grin.

"W – T – F?" Tom abbreviates. It would be rude to shout "what the fuck?" over the elegant place-settings.

"Yes, W – T - F, indeed," Fred says, as he summons the waiter and pays him fifty dollars for the two Perriers and small appetizer he shared with Keith.

"Time for brewskis!"

FRED FINALLY SETTLES DOWN TO BUSINESS after each of them drained two black-and-tans. By midnight, the Cambridge brewpub is so crowded and noisy that they can barely hear each other. Fred sits up straight on his barstool and holds both arms out to his sides, as if he were about to begin a formal oration. The third black-and-tan sloshes from the heavy English pub glass in Fred's right hand and ashes float from the cigarette in his left.

"I'm in worse trouble than in TeeJay."

Tom knows there can be no such thing as "worse trouble than in TeeJay," a nearly-disastrous spur-of-the-moment pilgrimage the two of them made to the raunchy border town of Tijuana, Mexico, in the early Fall of Tom's sophomore year. At the time, they dubbed it "Tom and Fred's Not So Excellent Adventure," and left the lurid details to other guys' porn-fed imaginations.

"I got no choice, Man, gotta sell stock," Fred continues, "shitloads of stock. And you're the best damn salesman I know, Bro. You could sell lobsters in Maine."

There was that accent again, "lobstahhs."

After a long pause, Fred adds, "and I *know* you won't fuck me, like Keith and his bunch will, if I turn my back on 'em for a second."

Tom also is getting a little disoriented, but not from jet lag or beer. The sight of his old buddy, his mentor, the dude who saved him from flunking out of college, who dared him to try new and sometimes regrettable things, at once the same and changed, pleading with him to take a salary bigger than Tom ever imagined, sets his mind reeling. Tom is certain this is the same guy only because the two-armed embrace in the hotel lobby felt so familiar, so reassuring that they could pick up their friendship, their brotherhood, right where they left off, as if they didn't have two years, a whole continent and some totally wicked shit between them. Yet here they are, in a Boston brew-pub decorated with coral and turquoise walls, leopard-print carpets and rococo chandeliers, an altogether weird introduction to Fred's new, high-tech world.

IN HIS HOTEL ROOM, Tom finds a check, made out to him and marked "sign-on bonus," on top of a half-inch thick legal document. As he tosses his clothes onto a velvet chaise, throws the jaguar-print bolsters from the bed to the floor and slides between Frette linen sheets, Tom turns the number embossed into the check over in his mind. It is $60,000, equal to his entire annual salary at the Zoo.

Tom is accustomed to beds other than his own, so he sleeps soundly and relatively late for a Sunday morning. By eight o'clock, he is on a jogging path the hotel concierge recommended. As the sun decreases its angle on the Charles, Tom marvels at the pleasantly incongruous sight of the Back Bay brownstones and high-rise office buildings and hotels directly across the river.

Fred greets him in the marble lobby as Tom returns, sweat swamping his Pumas. In the room, Tom strips off his sweat-laden T-shirt, shorts and jockstrap, selects at random one of several bars of designer soap the maid laid out and dodges into the shower. He leaves the bathroom door open so they can start their conversation. The two lived together in close quarters for two years but Fred, now at home in Puritan New England, feels a little embarrassed, averts his eyes and takes in the riverside view.

"You know, Bro, you're out of your fucking mind?" Tom shouts over the steaming hot shower. "I don't know jack shit about your business."

"Yeah, well, you don't know jack shit about *emus*, either," Fred yells back. Still facing the window, Fred goes on. "*Nobody* knows anything about my business. It's ground-breaking stuff. That's why the Government issued me a patent. That's why it's gonna make me mondo money, Man."

"What do you need *me* for?" Tom washes rosemary mint-scented shampoo out of his hair quickly. The smell is making him gag.

To pull off a successful IPO, Fred knew, someone would have to do a major sales job on the stock, meet with analysts and financial reporters and live out of a suitcase for weeks on end. Ultimately, a lightening-fast, transcontinental "road show" would capture the cash and prestige that would make WebSurfer a household name and make everybody involved with the company stinking rich. Fred could not personally do everything at once.

"I need help projecting a reality distortion field," Fred mutters, amused by the terminology his best geeks used to describe his efforts to make WebSurfer and its vaporware look like a no-brainer investment.

"Wazzat? Hang on a sec, Bro."

"Somebody has to make investors *comfortable*," Fred shouts back.

Tom steps out, naked and dripping, and starts working his curls with a plush hand towel.

"I'll hold a table in the restaurant downstairs," Fred excuses himself abruptly.

TOM, DRY AND DRESSED TO FLY, joins Fred in the middle of the dining room, near a steaming table of heart-healthy breakfast foods and an omelet chef, who furiously works four skillets at once. The guys' faces are as fresh as the salsa, premium cheeses and exotic vegetables flying high over the omelet bar.

Tom silently slides the thick envelope across the table. His eyes tell Fred, "no thanks, Bro."

"The check's inside," Tom says before Fred can respond.

"You don't understand." Fred's jaw stiffens. "The bonus and the salary are sure bets. Those are guaranteed. The stock's the kicker."

"I never owned a share of stock in my life, Freddy. What good is it?"

"We're planning to take the company public in a few months. The shares I'm giving you could be worth millions." He fails to mention the legal complications and market risks – for example, the lockdown period that could force Tom to wait six months before cashing in. Newly public tech company stock was infamous for starting out lofty, then collapsing within weeks.

"I have several mega-deals in the works, and as soon as they get inked, the stock's got no place to go but up-up-up."

The last time Tom encountered numbers with so many zeros was in his freshman math class. Without Fred's help, he would have flagged it.

"Keith wants one of his stiff-dick cronies down on State Street," Fred confesses. "The guy is such a complete barney, I swear to God. We'll be over the falls within six months. The stock certificates won't be good for wipin' your ass. The bank debts won't go away. I'll be *axed*, Man, laid low, and so will a lot of the dudes who put their faith in me. Bet a shitload of money on me. Dropped *everything* and came to work at WebSurfer."

Ravenous after his morning run, Tom attacks a freshly made Spanish omelet. As Fred pleads with him, Tom chews thoughtfully, rolls his eyes and sits back in his chair, not knowing what to think or say.

"I know it's a monster decision for you, Tom, but I *know* this will work. Just give it one year. I mean, what's one year to guys our age? After our ship comes in, you can go back to PeeBee, tackle Waimea, go on surfari until you're forty, have Endless Summer, whatever you want. Word of honor, Man. You'll be set for life. Just say yes – *please*, Tom. *Don't leave me like this, Bro.*"

Fred's words give every hair on the back of Tom's neck a major hard-on. It was more intense than the tingle Fred got, watching Tom advise males of every species across the world to "shoot'n'scoot." A loud "click" explodes inside Tom's head, so sharp and real that it nearly makes him jump out of his chair. His mind's eye focuses on rivulets of sweat rolling over a glistening steel blade. Tom perspires and his stomach churns, but it's not from the hot peppers he sprinkled over his omelet.

"Déjà vu all over again," he mumbles, as Fred stares deeply, fearfully, into Tom's eyes.

"Freddy," Tom wipes his mouth with a linen napkin, "this is nuts."

"Nuts. Yes. Good choice of words, Bud." Fred turns a shade paler and smiles sheepishly. "You saved them before, that night in TeeJay. I'm counting on you to do it one more time. Only this time, you will be rewarded with something a hell of a lot better than half of a fuzzy worm. *I swear.*"

Tom agrees to take the envelope and the check back to PeeBee with him and think about it. Fred's nuts would have to roast for at least a couple more weeks. The Summer Longboard Challenge was coming up at Tourmaline and Tom had missed a whole weekend's surfing practice.

FRED WAS ON FIRE the day after Tom flew back to California. The "three F" investors – founder, friends and family – were mostly Boston Brahmins and lawyers from the non-identical twin towers of downtown's International Place. They had grown bored and weary trying to get rich on hourly billings. Internet plays made them feel young and hip and made for good cocktail party one-upsmanship, but their generosity had its limits.

At first, his "angel" investors – rich people looking to make a killing off of a technology startup business without ever having to run it – seemed Heaven-sent. Simon Keith, a retired Washington, D.C., super-lobbyist, led a private investment club, the George Town Angels, pretentiously spelled out as three words. It included former members of Congress, a former Assistant Secretary of Defense, a former Deputy Director of Central Intelligence and some dodgy businessmen from South Korea who avoided being physically present in the United States.

Two of Fred's cousins warned him to steer clear of Keith, a Nixon White House functionary in ages past. They found subtle ways to work into the conversation Keith's notorious taste for much younger men. They hinted that Keith might also be dangerous somehow. Fred chalked all of it up to their Ivy League disdain for Keith's ultra-conservative politics.

They turned out to be right, Fred discovered too late. Keith made a play for control of the company, but Fred used his legal ace in the hole to beat him back. Fred personally owned outright the patent on the geographic reference system and wisely made the corporation's fundamental technology license contingent on his continuing ownership of a majority of the stock.

Keith insisted that Fred must stop deluding himself about his surfing buddy and hire an investor relations guy immediately. He wanted a certain baby-faced preppy from one of the big capital management houses on Boston's State Street. No way could Fred ever trust any guy his age who wore Savile Row suits on "casual Fridays," ties that cost more than a three-mil wetsuit and had a standing weekly appointment for a professional manicure from a flamboyantly gay Vietnamese guy named Charlie.

Really!

TOURMALINE SURFING PARK is a stretch of ocean and sand on the north end of Pacific Beach, reserved exclusively for serious surfers. The Summer Longboard Challenge was a week away, but it's Saturday morning, when parking was always tough. Gwen Stephens, a pushin'-thirty downtown San Diego lawyer, is on the verge of giving up when she finds a spot barely big enough for her classic Alfa Romeo convertible.

She catches up with Mary Bly, the slightly younger office manager at the law firm of Jacobs and Johns, on the beach with two of her still-unmarried, thirty-something girlfriends. They stop ogling males in skin-tight "shorties," summer wetsuits that hugged everything between their bulging biceps and their knees, long enough to exchange quick introductions.

Gwen, who was the most ambitious and aggressive woman in her law class at the University of Chicago, hears the other women's body clocks ticking loudly in proximity to so much good-looking and athletically endowed genetic material. She figures the guys for dolts. The only difference between surf dogs and football players, she assumes, is that football players drag their knuckles in Astroturf instead of seawater.

Tom was one of her husband's fraternity brothers and Bly picks him out of the lineup as soon as he paddles out. She catches Gwen studying Tom, passes her a too-full plastic cup of pink chablis and whispers that she should "keep an eye on that guy." Gwen is uncertain whether Bly intends a warning or a preview of coming attractions.

Before she hits "the big 3-0" next year, Gwen planned to hang her shiny brass nameplate outside one of the partner offices with a panoramic view of the ocean from the twenty-third floor. She counted on having an additional eight or nine years to marry a rich man – a doctor always sounded like a good idea, but she was open-minded about a specialty – and pop out a couple of stunningly attractive and highly-intelligent kids.

In grammar school, the future lawyer developed the habit of writing numbered lists of pros and cons, using as many Latin words as she could muster. To her critical eye, Tom had the following four things going for him *ab initio:*

1. The way he looked in a form-fitting wetsuit rang her chimes like a church bell on Easter Sunday. The boys she grew up with in Bloomfield Hills, Michigan, were always cocooned in multi-layered preppy regalia. The few she unwrapped were clammy and deadly pale, and fewer still were well-built where it counted. During her first year of law school, she found Edgar, who grew up on a Kentucky horse farm and was hung like one of their prize stallions. She took him for a ride every weekend until he graduated from the law school, bought a penthouse in New York's Chelsea neighborhood and announced he was gay. After that, she derided him as *"Homo Erectus."* California boys seemed a more predictable species.

2. Tom was a longboard surfer. The longer, nine- or ten-foot board was considered "old school," compared to the more maneuverable six-footers that became popular when millions of "stus," beginners, started chasing the craze in the Sixties. All those short-term hedonists with low frustration tolerance demanded boards that could give them at least one decent ride during a week-long surfing vacation. Gwen could appreciate a man who was willing to take the time to do it right, and she knew bigger and longer were better in all things. *Res ipsa loquitur.*

3. Tom's stance on the board, with his right foot forward, was known as "goofy foot." Gwen was never particular about whether a guy used his right hand or his left, but she figured that a man who would let the world call him "goofy foot" was not likely to be

intimidated by a professional woman of superior intelligence; herself, for example. *Ecce femina.*

4. Tom was from another planet, light-years away from her world. She never met a lawyer, male or female, who could do more than *talk* about surfing, so this guy, while physically proximate, appeared socially distant from everyone in her professional life. *Terra incognita.*

Gwen watches closely when Tom gets his chance to strut his stuff. Sunlight pierces deep into the water. It glistens, except where it churns itself into whitecaps and spray. As a swell rises, Tom turns the big board toward the shore on a dime and paddles furiously, his whole body stretched out face-down on the board. Just when Gwen thinks he will be overtaken by the wave curling on his flank just a few feet away, Tom pops up as if his head were self-propelled. Spectators on the beach hoot louder as he moves forward on the board, still keeping its three tail fins planted halfway up the face of the wave.

"That Tommy Rey!" Bly shouts to Gwen over the cheers and whistles as Tom quickly shuffles his feet all the way forward and grips the "rails," the edges, of the board with all of his toes.

"Noserider! Noserider!" Bly and her friends taunt. Gwen passively sips her wine, squints over her sunglasses and looks puzzled.

"He's hanging ten!" Bly explains. "He'd win more competitions if he'd stop showing off."

Tom tries to perform an "aerial," a highly sophisticated board maneuver that involves launching off the "lip" of a wave – the seam between an ocean swell and a wave, where the rotating seawater first begins to trip on itself and curl under. The trick is to land upright, on the face of the wave. An aerial is hugely difficult to pull off with a longboard. Tom landed the board successfully once, but it didn't count under California rules. No one was there to share the experience, so it didn't happen. This time, he fails, comically.

THE LEARNING CURVE for surfing is longer and steeper than most people realize. Considerable physical stamina is needed just to keep paddling out to the "lineup." That's where a surfer is close enough to shore to catch a wave and far enough out to sea to take to his feet and ride what he's caught. A real surfer lays flat on the board, face down, paddles furiously to the lineup, then sits up tall, straddling the board, watching, waiting, feeling the water, smelling the wind, anxious to sense the overwhelming, incomprehensible, undeniable power of the world's largest ocean.

Experience helps, but it really comes down to a divination, a sixth sense, a feeling, like a bone, broken years earlier, announcing it's about to rain, a tingle in the spine that signifies danger, the first flutter of sexual arousal. It can't be taught. It's inside you, just waiting for you to tap into it, or it isn't.

People who don't have it or are too lazy to look inside themselves for it become "ho-dads," wannabes, not surfers. They just paddle out to the lineup, pose for a while, then prance back onto the beach with their boards under one arm, hoping a babe in a thong will go all Gidget on them.

TOM TUCKS his ultra-light epoxy board under one arm and carries it onto the beach. He plants it nose-first in the sand, just twenty feet from Mary Bly and her friends. When he unzips and peels the top portion of his black wetsuit down to his waist, all of them, including Gwen, giggle like schoolgirls. Tom ignores them at first, until he recognizes Bly and trots over to her.

"Where you been hidin', Babe?" Tom always uses pet names, even for women he knows well, to avoid the unconscionable disaster of calling out the wrong name in the middle of an orgasm.

Tom offers each of Bly's friends a wet handshake, as seawater drips heavily from hair recently cropped to a length that still failed to satisfy his boss. Gwen grips his wet hand firmly and holds onto it longer than the other three. She giggles again when he greets her with a simple "Wazzup?"

"How 'bout lunch at the O&W – on me!" Gwen insists, so Tom and Bly agree. Tom sets off down the beach toward his apartment, the top floor of a two-story house, surrounded since the Sixties by tacky ocean-view motels, for a quick change of clothes. He disappears under the huge Crystal Pier, where tourists spent $300 a night to sleep in rows of blue-and-white cottages on a boardwalk fifty feet above the surf.

He intends to ditch the law ladies but changes his mind while he is blow-drying his hair.

LIQUOR ALWAYS ARRIVED QUICKER than food at the O&W. After two mid-day margaritas on an empty stomach, Gwen is already beginning to throw caution to the steady Pacific wind. When Tom gets up from the table for the third time to slap skin and trade war stories with a parade of surfing buddies, Bly catches her measuring him with her eyes.

"Listen, Gwen, this guy's really *not* your type," Bly licks salt off her right index finger and wags it at her favorite lawyer as she shakily gets up from the table, after a third margarita, and announces she is heading home.

"What are you, the voice of experience?"

Bly blushes.

"Oh, God, Mary, does your husband know?"

"It was before we got married!" She places her hand over her mouth and laughs, "but after we got engaged!"

Bly pumps Gwen's hand formally as she leaves the table.

"Attorney-client privilege!" the two agree in unison. Bly blows Tom a drunken, provocatively friendly kiss on her way out, nods toward Gwen, then winks at Tom.

When he returns to the table, Tom takes Bly's chair, next to Gwen. The afternoon sun gently toasts the backs of their necks.

"How do you know everybody in this place?" Gwen asks, halfway to the bottom of her fourth margarita. She never guessed that Corey Collins spiked the women's drinks with double shots of tequila, to help his old roomie. Whenever Tom scored, Collins counted it as an "assist."

"Biblically," Tom answers Gwen's question in a matter-of-fact tone. He looks penetratingly into her eyes to see whether she gets his little joke. Tom saw her doubt it was entirely in jest.

"Really?" Gwen brushes a wind-blown strand of strawberry-blonde hair out of her eyes.

"Really." Tom looks deeply into her gray eyes until she shifts them out to sea.

"My place is just around the corner," he says matter-of-factly, "and I make a bitchin' margarita for a whole lot less than six bucks a throw."

"Really?" She says, stuffing the credit card slip into her pocket Daytimer, wondering which client's billing code she would use.

"Yeah, *really*."

She brings her eyes back to *terra firma*, sighs and lets Tom's blue-greens swallow her whole.

Balance

AFTERNOON SUNLIGHT streams into Tom's Spartan bedroom and Gwen Stephens discovers something entirely unexpected about herself. She is a moaner. Not a whimperer, a heavy panter or a groaner, but a full-throated *"ohGODohGOD harderHARDER ohyesohYES ohmoreMORE!"* screamer. It comes as a pleasant surprise to Tom, too, who hadn't hooked up with a woman with such a high verbal score since junior year.

At first, Tom fears he is hurting her, so he withdraws. Her breathless, urgent instructions make him feel truly appreciated. Tom gets increasingly stoked and his pace grows even more deliberate as Stephens' decibel level rises. He goes faster and slower and stops, then slow, then fast again.

Tom thinks about his high school guitar lessons, taken for the express purpose of impressing the ladies. It was more fun to practice making this kind of music, he decided long ago. The necessary instrument was always at hand, and he never had to worry about losing his pick.

Guests at the motels surrounding his second-floor apartment go about their touristy Saturday afternoon business, pausing to listen only long enough to make sure no one is getting murdered. If his landlord's daughter is downstairs, Tom assumes she is dead drunk and capable of sleeping through the Northridge Earthquake. He has no idea she's gone clean and sober.

ON THE MOTEL BALCONY directly across from Tom's bedroom window, a half dozen teenage boys squeeze past a young man with slicked-back hair. They snigger at his too-short, too-tight swimming trunks and bare legs so pale that the California sunshine bounces off with a blinding flash. When the teens and their cloud of boisterous laughter pass, the man lifts his New York Knicks T-shirt, pulls a steno pad out of his waistband and continues taking notes.

Before long, as creaking bedsprings become the predominant sound from across the way, business turns to pleasure. He holds the spiral binding to his lips, then bites into the pad's cardboard covers until the feeling pumps all the way through him. Billy Shippe looks at his wrist, where his watch usually covers its own whiter-than-white shadow, and decides there's time for a quick swim before he catches his overnight flight back to Washington – after he changes his shorts.

TOM IS STARTLED by the figure bolting through his apartment door.

"Who is *he*?" Gwen demands, as she dives under a bedsheet. She realizes the intruder is a tall, wiry woman, a little younger than Tom, with close-cropped blond hair and a deep tan.

Tom confronts his landlord's daughter, Carly Bonner, at the bedroom door. Despite living in her house, Tom has rarely seen her up close. He caught a little wood off of her one day, shortly after he moved in, as he searched his apartment for something, anything, clean to wear. From the half-window in his closet, he spied her sunbathing topless in the little garden behind the house. He enjoyed eyeing her lithe, runner's body and firm breasts until she reached under the lawn chair, raised a fifth of cheap vodka, the kind of rotgut he hadn't touched since high school, to her lips, took in a mouthful and replaced the bottle, all in one motion. At ten in the morning, the sight deflated him in a heartbeat.

"Sounds like an episode of *Animal Planet* up here," Carly says, pretending not to notice that Tom is naked, but for a leather string around his neck and a doughnut-shaped jade stone that dangles an inch below his Adam's apple. Tom's tan lines divide an exceedingly milky complexion and a lightly toasted Wonder Bread tan.

Tom is surprised to learn Carly watched his global television moment. He shoots her a sheepish shrug, then walks her to the apartment door and turns the lock.

He returns to the bedroom to find Gwen carefully studying a wall covered entirely with photos of Tom and his beach buddies. A teenaged Tom, heavy, brine-soaked blond curls nearly touching his shoulder blades, grasping a surfing trophy. Tom spiking a volleyball, his bare toes pointed straight down to the sand, a full meter below, his fist almost as far over his head, his face showing a killer instinct. Tom in Mexico, looking silly and completely wasted under a cartoonish sombrero. Tom jovially locking arms with half a dozen frat brothers on the deck at the O&W. She noticed no family photos, no photos with girlfriends.

A large, squishy ball, nearly the size of an old-fashioned bean-bag chair, lay on the floor at Gwen's feet.

"Interesting décor," Gwen says, as soon as she sensed Tom watching her from behind.

"It's called a balance ball," Tom offers. "Surfing practice. Helps me balance on the board."

Wasting no time, Gwen deftly guides him by the hand across the room, seats him on the balance ball and, in one motion, deploys the necessary precautions while lowering herself onto him. Tom finds it challenging to compensate for her lack of balance, even with both of his feet planted on the floor in front of him and under her long, flapping legs.

Tom's habit during intercourse is to concentrate on something else. He could last a lot longer that way, a talent well-known in PeeBee. Gwen does not notice that Tom's mind is on something else he plans to enter, the high-profile surfing competition coming up at Tourmaline.

CARLY SITS in front of her old, fourteen-inch RCA television, a lukewarm can of Diet Sprite in hand. As she watches the VHS tape she made of Tom's appearance on *Animal Planet*, the revealing encounter upstairs re-runs through her mind.

The scratched-up TV with a built-in VCR has been Carly's faithful companion for eight weeks, ever since she gave up the bottle. She couldn't hang out in any of her favorite bars, even the few she hadn't been thrown out of, or with any of her motley group of drinking buddies. She got sloppy drunk with some of her friends almost every other day after she turned seventeen. Now twenty-three, she could see the toll it was taking every time she summoned the courage to confront her sallow, rail-thin visage in the mirror. She tried many times and it never seemed to get any easier.

At last, she asked herself a crucial question. "Do you want to live, or do you want to die?"

Carly established a rigorous exercise routine and drank enough Diet Sprite to disprove any connection between artificial sweeteners and cancer. Running kicked up juices in her that seemed to replace the alcoholic buzz. It made her horny for the first time in years.

Sobriety also made Carly more conscious of events going on around her – and above her. She began noticing the back staircase creaking and clattering around ten o'clock several nights a week under two sets of footfalls, then Tom's bedposts tapping with an almost mechanical rhythm on the uneven floor above. She had been around the block enough times to suspect that every guy in the world makes a unique sound when he comes.

Tonight, there is no tapping. At the beginning of her seventh replay of Tom's *Animal Planet* interview, Carly's frustration boils over. She blasts the volume up as high as it will go.

"Shoot'n'scoot!"

Her ceiling emits unmistakably orgasmic moans, one high, the other a familiar, rapid-fire *"unh-unh,"* then unrestrained laughter, then the sound of two conjoined bodies splashing sweat against the wall, then onto the floor, as the balance ball rolls to the middle of Tom's bedroom.

AYURVEDIC MEDICINE was Carly's latest fascination. According to this ancient East Indian practice, every person has seven major energy centers or "chakras" in the body. Each chakra is a spinning wheel or vortex of life-force energy that flows into and emanates from the other chakras. Every one of the wheels operates at its own frequency, characterized by a certain color, sound and range of emotions.

Carly was certain it was no accident that she caught Tom in the buff with Gwen Stephens. The circumstances allowed her to connect with the source of Tom's orange or *swadisthana* chakra, located four finger-widths below his belly button. That must be why her eyes were drawn there! Carly was only sensing the imbalance between his "sex" chakra and his *anahata* or "heart" chakra! Tom was the surfer-dude equivalent of a stream overrunning its banks. The next morning, she checked out every self-help book she could find in the public library.

Longboard Challenge

TOM URGENTLY NEEDS to put everything related to Fred, especially any lurking memories of their TeeJay adventure, out of his mind. Nothing must get in the way of winning the Summer Longboard Challenge.

Surfing is the only thing on Tom's mind when he hauls his board to Tourmaline that late-summer Saturday in 2000. He is barely twenty-four. He still has time, maybe, to go all the way, if he can just stop showing off.

For once, his consciousness is as clear as his conscience. He still doesn't know what WebSurfer is, much less what it can do for him or to him. For the moment, he doesn't care. After the competition, he will find a hook-up. If he actually manages to win, a smorgasbord will await him at the O&W.

Tom is so focused on the rhythm of the sea, so determined to get in sync with the surf, so in the moment, he hardly notices when his landlady, Carly, stakes out a spot just beyond the water's reach. She looks remarkably sober, bright-eyed and cheery that morning and totes a Thermos of boiling-hot coffee to keep herself that way.

The O&W was a principal sponsor of the Summer Longboard Challenge. It attracted strong surfers, even a few semi-pros, to Tourmaline. The purse was small – just a thousand dollars – but the bragging rights for a good showing were huge.

Nobody seems concerned about the bank of dense, gray clouds that collapse to the ground the moment they roll to the shoreline, obscuring the horizon and putting a chill into the bones of optimists who showed up dressed for the more-typical, toasty California sunshine. Carly gathers her windbreaker around her throat as a chilly wind picks up and the ocean spray stings her face. The waves suddenly get bigger and more powerful, she notices, and their crashing noise gradually drowns out quieter conversations among the gathering fans.

Tom and his rivals work hard to paddle out. Confronted by successive, breaking waves, they all have to turtle-dive, roll over sideways and let the wave break over the bottoms of their boards, to make any headway toward the lineup. Smack in the middle of the beach, the judges scramble to keep hold of loose papers when the wind gusts and the canopy over their heads threatens to rip loose of its metal frame.

Carly tightens the chin strap on her Headhunter surf cap and pulls out a small pair of antique opera glasses she inherited from the grandmother who built the house in which she and Tom live. She rotates a wheel to focus on Tom, just as he turns his board to shore and prepares to catch a wave.

When Tom pops up on the board, Carly zeroes in on his face. She spies incontestable determination, unlike anything she has ever seen in Tom. Even at a distance of a hundred yards, it is obvious nothing else is on his mind. His blue-green eyes seem so deadly intense, so lit by the ocean itself, Carly shudders.

THE SPECTATORS CHEER loud enough to drown out the wind and waves, but the voices seem to fade as Carly focuses on Tom. When she notices competing chants of "TeeRey" and "RayMond," Carly lowers her opera glasses and sees that both Tom and Raymond Chu, another local favorite she knew from one of her Eastern Medicine classes, both launched on the same wave. Suddenly, this surfing competition is a horse race.

The wind dies down, but the wave suddenly rises into an "overhead," Tom's height, in a perfect, gentle curl. Both riders work hard to stay in front of it, crouching, turning and pivoting to keep their boards on the face, to avoid getting dumped or left behind on the powerless, back side of the wave.

Carly keeps the opera glasses glued to her eyes as she stands up and joins the "TeeRey" cheer. Almost a full minute into the ride,

Tom still looks strong, elegant and completely in control. She could see Chu's board drifting higher up on the face, closer to the curl. As Chu picked up speed, he finds it much tougher to control his board. He gradually slips above and behind Tom, his feet engulfed in the white water curling over his board.

Tom, farther down the face of the wave, has the right-of-way. Chu is experienced, knows that, but gets carried away, first by the moment, then by the wave. His body shoots backward, over the lip, with such force that the Velcro-strap "leash" that attaches him to his board snaps at the plug. The board, a ten-footer with a high rocker, rockets forward through the air, an unguided missile.

Carly watches in horror as the turned-up nose of Chu's log glances over Tom's shoulder. Tom is crouched on his own board, so Chu's glides over his trapezius muscles. She sees the board's three tail fins rake Tom as he goes headfirst into the water. Tom's board follows him in, hardly makes a splash.

Carly cannot believe her eyes. She drops the opera glasses so hard that they swing down on their cord and bounce off her rock-hard belly. All she can see is the wave, losing little strength, rolling toward her. She studies the fetch behind it closely, looking for any sign of "tombstoning," a board bobbing over a submerged surfer.

The two-person safety patrol on jet-skis buzz around Chu, some twenty feet away from where Tom went under. Chu waves to them that he is uninjured and able to swim ashore.

No sign of Tom. The "goat boats" leave Chu in opposite directions, which convinces Carly they have no clue where to look.

As Carly runs to the water, her opera glasses, windbreaker and shoes fly off in every direction. One of the event security staff, a brawny, goateed guy who worked as a bouncer at a bar on Garnet Avenue, and who threw her out of the place twice during her drinking days, blocks her way. When he tries locking his arms around her, she punches him in the nuts with her left fist and leaves him doubled-over in the wet sand until a wave knocks him on his back and washes his swearing mouth out with salt water.

Carly dives headfirst into one wave, then another, until the water is deep. As she treads water over a small swell, Carly spies

Tom. He is lifeless. His head bobs just a foot under water. His left leg is still tethered to his board.

A bolt of lightning seems to shoot down Carly's spine, but she doesn't allow it to paralyze her. She dives straight for the strap, grabs Tom's calf with both hands and rips the Velcro open with her teeth. She abandons the board, which somehow lodged in the sand, nose first.

With one arm locked around Tom's neck to keep his head above water, Carly kicks furiously to shore. She got fired from her lifeguard job the third time she showed up drunk, but she remembered her CPR training as if it occurred yesterday. She lays Tom out on the first flat spot of wet sand she comes to. The rescue squad, obviously caught off guard, is dashing over from a tent behind the judges' stand. One of them stops to help the stunned bouncer to his feet.

Tom is not breathing, but he *has* to be alive. His color is OK, despite his having been plunged into the cold water for such a long spell. Carly straddles him the way Gwen Stephens once did, but sex is the farthest thing from her mind. She puts her hands together and shoves them hard into his chest. His rib cage does not yield much, but a little seawater gurgles out of his nose and mouth. She lays into him again, much harder, and the brine spews out. Tom chokes and struggles when she thrusts into his sternum a third time. As the remnants of a wave lap up, two inches deep, around them, Carly cradles Tom's head. By the time Carly jumps off Tom and tips his head back, the Rescue Squad arrives.

"Not yet!" Her command is just short of a scream.

She holds his nose, parts his lips and blows deeply into Tom's lungs. He is still choking and gasping for air when she finally yields custody to two stretcher bearers. Carly is relieved to hear him make any sound at all.

While they load him into an ambulance, Tom drifts in and out of consciousness. He remembers Carly's face hovering over him, then her fervid lips on his. He lapses into a dream, in which Carly suddenly morphs into a Mexican in a white coat, blasting away on a police whistle, not blowing air into his lungs, but pouring tequila down his throat. This half-dream gives him a warm feeling. It starts in his breastbone and works its way down.

"Will he be OK?" Carly anxiously demands of a forty-ish female med tech with hair as jet black as her skin. She was closing the back doors of the ambulance.

"Oh, yeah, Girl, I think you got his blood circulatin' jus' fine," she assures Carly, looking back over her shoulder at the healthy woody she discovered when she deftly sliced off Tom's blood-soaked board shorts with surgical scissors. "He be up'n'at'em in no time, I 'spect."

TeeJay

T OM NEVER IMAGINED "TeeJay" would be the only episode in his life to flash before his eyes during his near-death experience at the Summer Longboard Challenge, but that was what he remembered when the anesthesia wore off.

At the start of Tom's sophomore year, he moved in with Fred, still a senior, and Jamie Bass, who was a junior. Their house in Ocean Beach, a few miles down the Coast from PeeBee, had a leaky roof, weather-beaten gray wood shingles and a small front garden overrun with unkempt yuccas and twisted cacti. Its frontage to a side street two blocks off Newport Avenue was narrow, but the house was long, like a trailer.

On weekdays, the three housemates commuted to campus, usually in Jamie's old but reliable BMW 633i. On weekends, brothers bearing beer bongs commuted to OhBee.

Tom took up residence in the OhBee house to help Fred take advantage of the town's rent control. It could never be rented by a group consisting entirely of seniors because at least one tenant's name had to carry over into the next year's lease. Given the substantial risk of somebody flunking out, the incumbents tried to make sure they always had at least one sophomore.

Fred was the closest thing the beach pad ever had to a permanent resident. It was Fred's fifth year at USD, his second senior year and his third living in the OhBee house. It was also the first year he got laid regularly.

Fred never lacked his share of the rent. His father, a heart surgeon and professor at Harvard Medical School, married money and then became wealthy in his own right. When Fred was eighteen, they coerced him into applying for undergraduate admission to Harvard University. To their never-ending horror, he spurned the Ivy League in favor of USD.

The elder Hansons told white lies to their creamy-white, white-shoe friends when Fred started his fifth year of undergraduate studies – "he has an internship," "he's getting a double major" – anything to deflect suspicion that Fred kept up his excellent grade point average only by re-taking courses that drowned in a sea of beer foam or disappeared into an impenetrable cannabis haze. The true reason for Fred's second senior year was something he could barely admit to himself, much less understand. He wanted – no, *deserved* – another year with Tom. Fred shared none of this with his parents, and that suited them fine.

Dr. Hanson was forever too busy to worry about Fred, who demonstrably had a lot going for him upstairs. Mrs. Hanson, a buttoned-up tool company heiress, considered her son bright enough, but terminally impetuous. She assumed the worst about Fred's indecorous behavior in California.

"Just don't bring any of it home with you, Frederick Dear."

She had the will, in every sense of the word, to enforce her opinions. In the end, it was enough that Fred came home without a giggly beach-bunny bride, expensive drug addiction, incurable social disease, grotesque body piercing, permanent tattoo or obvious, disfiguring injury. Most of Fred's surfing scars were on his scalp, hidden under his thick, perpetually-unruly mop of chestnut-brown hair.

Fred and Tom were in symbiosis from the moment they met. Fred rescued Tom from the permanent purple haze surrounding his cannabis-crazy freshman roommate, Corey Collins, and Tom rescued Fred from self-abuse. Fred was not a bad-looking guy, but the advantages in hanging out with Tom were manifest. The New Englander's aquiline nose and slightly pointed chin gave Fred a fox-in-the-henhouse mystique that he was only beginning to figure out how to use. Some women found him striking, but his in-born New England reserve made the dark-haired Yankee seem aloof, even shy, around women and he was a frustrated keg-hugger at frat parties during his first two years.

All those years of ballroom dance lessons and Forties swing-dancing at prep school mixers and East Coast coming-out parties rarely proved useful in San Diego. In Fred's first two years at USD, that meant not hooking up much. The dry spells left more time for serious study but, Fred thought woefully, had he wanted studies instead of sex, he would have gone to Harvard.

From the day he arrived on USD's majestic hilltop campus, Tom had females buzzing around him, between classes, at the freshman dorm, on the track by the athletic field, at the Phi Delt house. When the opportunity arose for a liaison, Tom got in the habit of asking the intended bedmate to get a friend for Fred – not necessarily to bed Fred, but to at least keep him pleasantly occupied while Tom was doing the deed. One woman, a Brit, called them "the fox and hound."

Jamie Bass had his own distinctive approach to sex. He talked about sex and talked about it and then talked about it some more. As best anyone could tell, his only actual hookup was with his flat-chested high-school girlfriend. Jamie insisted their relationship was over when she blue-balled him two visits in a row, but every time the USC film student wiggled her little finger, he flew up to Los Angeles like a hummingbird on crack.

IT WAS JAMIE WHO DECIDED the guys in the OhBee house would make a manly pilgrimage to "TeeJay" – Tijuana, Mexico. The gritty, anything-goes border town, only a thirty-minute drive from PeeBee, inspired a thousand legends, started mostly by sailors from the local Navy base and spread, like a virulent strain of the clap, by college students from all over the West. In any case, Jamie figured it made more sense to take Spring Break over Labor Day weekend.

"What if you flunked out first semester?" he reasoned. "You'd miss out!"

A drinking buddy from Jamie's hardscrabble Texas hometown, who had already done a hitch in the Navy, volunteered a hot tip about a place you could get "smoked up and hooked up for one low price."

"*Las Santerías* is the name of the place," Jamie declared the first night after Summer vacation, as he laid out his big party weekend preparations. Without looking up from rolling papers, loose weed and neat piles of discarded stems and seeds on the kitchen table, he rolled joints so tight and uniformly filled, end-to-end, they looked like they came out of a machine.

"Eighteen Calle Tejada, Tijuana. You can get *anything* there, Man, any way you want it. And *totally cheap*."

"Leaving bright and early Saturday morning," Jamie announced, giving the spliff in his right hand a precise twist with his left. "All aboard for the TeeJay Express!"

"Better put that address in your Bimmer, so we don't forget it." Fred suggested, sounding helpful.

Late on the Friday night before Labor Day, Jamie received a surprise booty call. When he tried to drive up to L.A. the next morning, his car refused to start. He was desperate.

"I'm dead!" Jamie muttered as he re-entered the house, certain his sperm would back up and implode his brain.

He encountered Fred in the hallway, staggering in a ragged pair of Exeter gym shorts toward the toilet at an unusually early hour. He appeared to be conscious, mostly, so Jamie begged him for a ride to the Amtrak station. The trio's backup transportation was a barely functional Toyota with an expired California tag and a proven incapacity to pass an emissions inspection.

Fred, a typical Bostonian, used his driver's license far more often to buy booze than to operate a car. As he swerved and barely paused at red lights, Jamie flinched and clutched a seatbelt that wouldn't buckle. At the train station, Fred slowed the Toyota and Jamie slung his backpack over his shoulder and jumped out.

Back at the house, Fred awakened Tom, took him outside to Jamie's 633i and popped the hood.

"Well, will you look at that!" Fred exclaimed. He re-attached the battery cable and started the engine.

"You really can be such a dick, you know that? We coulda taken the bus."

"But does the bus driver know how to find *Las Santerías*?" Fred held up the address on the note Jamie dutifully placed in the glove compartment.

The best map of Tijuana Fred could find was a page ripped out of a 1995 AAA Tour Book. They hastily grabbed toothbrushes, antiperspirant, clean underwear and a little protection.

THEY WERE TIRED AND THIRSTY after an unexpectedly long wait in an un-air-conditioned car to buy Mexican liability insurance and to cross the border. Fred checked them into a double room at the Hotel Rey, just off the *Avenida de la Revolución*, the main drag and center of Tijuana culture, such as it was.

They spent the rest of the afternoon on the *Avenida*, haggling over trinkets they weren't planning to buy – sombreros discreetly marked "Made in China" in the headband, multi-colored serapes, maracas, dashboard Jesus figurines, and Toltec statuettes with enormous genitalia.

The September sun broiled their faces until they retreated to a shaded, breezy deck at the Cantina El Torito, in the heart of the *Avenida*. The whole place was decked out in red, green and white banners, which flapped in the occasional breeze on the deck, but hung still and heavy inside, where it was too hot for anybody to jump onto the mechanical bull or take to the dance floor, an oddly-raised platform about ten paces from a narrow, thirty-foot long bar. American dance tunes, mostly Seventies disco, blasted from speakers inside, but conversation was still possible out on the porch. A metal farmer's bucket crammed with ice and Pacifico Clara Mexican beer landed on the table the moment they sat down.

Fred's end of the conversation turned decidedly philosophical halfway through the second tin bucket of *cervezas*. "So, what do you *really* want out of life, Tomcat, other than a regular supply of tail?"

"Graduating would be nice," Tom replied honestly, his head bobbing with the music like a dashboard dog.

"Oh, great! Other than med school, that's the thing I most want to avoid!" Fred laughed and pounded a vaguely syncopated drumbeat on the table with his fists.

"*My* graduation, or *yours*?" Tom grinned.

"Either would be the end of the world as we know it. Have another beer, Amigo. Tonight we're gonna re-calibrate your ambitions."

Tom and Fred clinked their bottles together, but the sound was drowned out by an ear-shattering police whistle. A clean-shaven Mexican in his early thirties was blasting away on it, to the beat of a Bee Gees song on the sound system.

"*La silla del dentista!*" he shouted between the whistles.

Fred was confused. He wondered which girl in the bar was named "Celia." Tom was puzzled, too. He knew Spanish well enough to realize that the man was offering "the dentist's chair," never a popular place among his high school classmates.

The man hoisted a full bottle of Cuervo Gold tequila. Eight students, aged eighteen at the most, cheered and waved him over to their railside table. The Mexican motioned to one of the halter-topped girls, who gave him a barely-perceptible nod, as if she were bidding at an auction. He clutched a small bar towel to her throat and rocked her chair backward, onto its hind legs.

"*Abre la boca!*" He instructed her to open wide and started pouring tequila directly down her throat. As her companions cheered and shouted and watched the Cuervo stream ten inches through the air, the man kept blasting away on the whistle. Each of the students got the treatment in turn, paying three bucks apiece.

Tom and Fred laughed and hollered, too, until the whistling "dentist" blasted his way over to their table. He kept pointing at the bottle and they kept waving him off.

Fred gave in first, nodding his head yes and no at the same time, in a sort of circular pattern. Before he knew it, his chair was reared back on its hind legs and his tongue was pointed skyward. The whole crowd chanted "Cuer – vo!" as Fred guzzled the golden liquid. He chased it down with a swig of beer and bowed deeply to the cheering teenagers. Suddenly, he grabbed Tom, who was still unequivocally gesturing "no," by the neck and offered up his friend, a sacrifice to Fuktup, the Mayan god of inebriation.

Tom got the treatment next. He felt helpless and violated, having no control over what was showering his epiglottis. The tequila went down so fast, he didn't taste it at all. The buttery, warm sensation in his throat seemed to last half an hour. He also washed it down with more Pacifico, but was so wasted he nearly fell on his face when he bowed. Fred had to grab the waistband on the back of Tom's shorts to steady him.

When the kids next to the railing started passing out on their table, Tom and Fred decided it was time to get on with the wicked shit that brought them to TeeJay. The first order of business had to be the toilet. As they stepped inside, a surly attendant with a Pancho Villa mustache greeted them with a scowl. He jerked his thumb toward a red quarry tile trough with no water supply, other than piles of ice quickly melting down the drain in the stifling heat.

The urinal was barely long enough to accommodate two guys. Tom and Fred planted themselves in front of it, shoulder-to-shoulder. Their bladders were about to burst. Both unzipped hastily and took dead-aim at the ice.

Nothing happened. They could feel Pancho Villa eyeballing them impatiently, which made both of them even more pee-shy. By the time the attendant started cursing at them in Spanish, the guys were in pain, red-faced and desperate. Finally, Fred started laughing, nervously. In a moment, his shoulders were shaking and the ice started cracking and popping loudly. Tom laughed, too, so hard he had to use both hands to maintain his aim. The attendant cursed them even more vehemently, and kept it up until the two strode out.

Neither of them ever paid for sex before. Fred figured Tom worked too hard at it, needed it nice and easy for a change. Tom figured that Fred just needed it. It was Jamie's crazy-ass idea of adventure, not theirs. Still, like young warriors on the cusp of battle, they needed only to know what they were there to do, not why it needed to be done.

TOM'S MOTHER TAUGHT HIM TO AVOID POISON when he was just a tow-headed toddler.

"Tastes *ba-a-a-d!*" she would say, clutching her throat with both hands and making an ugly face.

"*Ack-ack!*" little Tommy would respond, clutching his own throat until his face turned alarmingly red. Despite the seriousness of the subject, Tom's mother couldn't help laughing until she turned almost as red.

Tom was turning red that night in TeeJay. He could taste that old *ack-ack* in the back of his throat, acid-sweet, slicing through the tequila and into his tonsils. As he slid behind the wheel of Bass's car, Fred slapped Tom a high-five to relieve his discomfort.

NUMERO 18 CALLE TEJADA turned out to be a squat, adobe house, sandwiched between two corrugated metal buildings, about a dozen blocks away from the hotel. A tiny, round, ancient woman came to the door. She looked more Native American than Hispanic, and she sounded so much like the troll from that old television show, "Fantasy Island," Tom and Fred nearly laughed in her face.

"Who senning you?" She stepped half out the door and looked past them, suspiciously, as they approached. When she was convinced the two young gringos were alone and might have some greenbacks to blow, she led them in to a small room with two long, cigarette-burned wooden tables with rough-hewn benches on either side. Fred and Tom appeared to be the first customers of the evening.

"Twenny dollah," she croaked at them, holding out a heavily-calloused palm.

Fred searched different pockets in his cargo shorts and fished out a pair of tens. A stocky, muscular Mexican with a wiry, close-cropped goatee motioned for them to sit at the end of the middle table. He slammed a full liter bottle of 100-proof mescal, a stronger sibling of tequila, also derived from a desert plant called the agave, down on the table, then added two extra-tall shot glasses and a small, wooden bowl of limes that looked like some lunatic had gone at them with a machete. Tom advised his Bostonian friend that the glasses were known as *caballitos*. Fred kept picking the bottle up, marveling at a worm, half the length of his little finger, with fat little Michelin-man rings, motionless at the bottom of the bottle.

An hour later, the two amigos had put a substantial dent in the mescal and were singing, badly, along with a bizarre mixture of Mexican and American pop tunes playing on a boombox buried somewhere behind the bar. Fred hovered over a full *caballito* for three minutes, while Tom held another in front of his own face, studying the dusty liquid, both elbows planted on the table. Together, as if performing some sort of religious ritual, they dumped the contents down their respective throats. It had stopped burning like hot butter after the third or fourth glass; by now, it went down like water.

Other Americans crammed one end of the table for several minutes before Tom and Fred noticed. Two burly truck drivers with tattoos on their hairy forearms sat at the far end of their table. Four Americans with genuine red necks, buzzcuts and tank tops, younger than Tom and Fred, were taking seats in the middle of the table closest to the wall.

One of the rednecks asked for "gold." It was clear he was not talking about Cuervo. The truckers left just as the room began to fill with the pungent aroma of premium Mexican weed.

Fred and Tom traded their younger countrymen shots of mescal for hits off the small, wooden pipes they dug out of the back pockets of unfashionable knee-length denim shorts that screamed "Sears and Roebuck" at Tom and Fred's "Abercrombie and Fitch." Before long, the pipes and *caballitos* were in a slow, musical rotation around the table. When the boom box began to sound almost as good as the sound system at the O&W, Tom knew he'd had enough.

Tom was so dazed after the last hit that he put his forehead down, none too gently, on the gritty wooden table. The room spun around him. As his nose started pressing flat on the table, he figured that the pot must have been laced with something. Whatever it was, he hoped it wouldn't make him blind.

"Oh, waitress!" Fred summoned the troll as Tom slowly dragged his numb face off the table. "I don't suppose you have anything warm and tasty on the menu?"

The walking-talking-Aztec-figurine poked her index finger in and out of a circle she made with the thumb and index finger of the other hand.

"Fock? You?"

Tom looked at Fred. Fred looked at Tom. They both looked at the tough old woman, not certain if she was offering her own personal services, making them a different offer or telling them to get lost.

"What's on the menu?" Fred repeated.

Suddenly, she grabbed both guys by the yokes of their nearly matching, loose-fitting safari shirts, like a nun taking two unruly pupils to the Mother Superior's office for some serious knuckle-whacking. She led them out of the building to a small wooden shack behind the adobe building. A breeze was kicking up, and the temperature inside seemed at least ten degrees cooler than in the bar, but nothing else seemed as it should be.

A shiver shot down Tom's spine as the *ack-ack* feeling filled his throat. His blood turned thick and hot and the hair on the back of his neck stood up. Tom's eyes met Fred's dilated pupils only for an instant, but he recognized a surfer dude's worst nightmare, the ice-cold, empty black stare of a frenzied shark in bloody water. His own vacant regard confessed utter capitulation to carnal instincts that devoured all aspirations, even for survival itself.

Surf's Up

"CONGRATULATIONS. YOU WON."

He doesn't recognize the woman's voice, at first, or the sterile surroundings of his hospital room.

"You got a check for a thousand bucks," Carly Bonner snaps it in front of Tom's face a couple of times and lifts the Summer Longboard Challenge first-place trophy off the tray table next to his hospital bed.

"I think they intended it as hush money, since it was a nearly-posthumous award."

Tom tries to shift positions, from his left side to his back.

"I wouldn't do that, if I were you."

Blood oozes through the gauze bandage that covers three deep gashes that run from Tom's right butt cheek, five inches up the small of his back. The anesthetic is beginning to wear off, and it feels a lot like a mescal hangover.

"Skegs," Carly says with three fingers curled downward to imitate surfboard fins. A pained expression crosses her gaunt face, as if no further elaboration were needed.

"Thanks." Tom says, recalling uncomfortably a few snippets from their mouth-to-mouth session earlier in the day.

"No problem. It would be such a pain to look for a new tenant right now!"

Tom grunts and drifts back to sleep. To Carly, it sounds a lot like his unique "*unh-unh.*"

AT DUSK on Monday, Tom decides it's time to try climbing down the stairs. He limps alone the two blocks to the beach. He sits, gingerly, on the four-foot high retaining wall in front of the O&W that separates the busy concrete pedestrian path from the PeeBee sand. Behind his wrap-around Ray-Bans, Tom scans the horizon portentously. The salt breeze makes his scalloped forelocks flutter.

Tom struggles to keep his mind blank, but it's no use. He owes Fred an answer. When the day's last sunrays submerge completely, Tom hobbles into the O&W for the "medicinal suds" Corey Collins offered.

"Kinda makes you think, don'it, Rooms?" As Tom's freshman roommate, Collins felt entitled to bask in his reflected glory and, now, in the shock of his close call. The only thing that made him more proud was winning PeeBee's Fastest Bartender Contest three years running. Collins spent most of his first and only semester at college pushing an elaborately decorative plexi-glass bong under Tom's nose, so neither of them had an entirely clear recollection of living together.

Collins deposits a full pitcher and a chilled glass on the bar in front of Tom's favorite stool, on the corner nearest the patio door. "Like, what's life all about, Man?"

"Damn near blew my chance to find out, didn't I?"

"Du-u-u-de!" Collins shakes his head, watching himself in the reflection from sunglasses perched on the bridge of Tom's nose.

Tom could always tell whether his old roommate was stoned by looking straight into his eyes. Even through polarized lenses, he sees Collins is an eleven on a scale of ten that afternoon.

"Du-u-u-u-ude!" Collins chokes out, as if *he* had been bobbing underwater, shackled to a sandbar. He regards Tom with slack-jawed awe, as if he were a ghost.

Tom is not sure how well the beer and painkillers would mix, so he abandons the greater portion of the suds and limps briskly home. When he reaches the stairs he hears his telephone ringing. Tom bounds up, putting his stitches to the test.

It's Fred.

"Surf's up, Tomcat."

"Cowabunga, Dude."

"Don't tease me, Bro."

≈≈≈≈≈≈≈≈≈≈≈

"Cowabunga!" Tom repeats.

"You'll do it? You mean it?" Fred is almost screaming, more surprised than relieved.

"Gotcha covered, Bro."

"Man, am I lucky to have you around!"

"You have no idea just *how* lucky you are this time, Kahuna." Tom winces partly because the dash up the stairs pulled one of the stitches in his ass, partly because of a sudden, distracted, odd feeling about Carly. The rescue felt like something beyond a stroke of blind luck, but Tom wasn't sure what it was, exactly, other than a debt he would have to repay some day.

Just like that, Tom is vice president of a dotcom named WebSurferUSA and the proud new owner of 400,000 shares in a company that is pissing away cash at a rate approaching a million dollars a month.

PART TWO
SHARK EYES

"The shark are all sharks, no better and no worse."

--Ernest Hemingway

Shreddin'

SHREDDIN'. That was Tom Rey's life in Boston, totally shreddin' from the moment his sand-scuffed Pumas hit the chilly soil of Massachusetts.

For the second time in his life, Tom moved in with Fred, his surfing-buddy-turned-dotcom-dweeb. He offered Tom a spare room with peeling plaster on the ground floor of a townhouse, adjacent to the Harvard University campus. Dr. Hanson bought it as an investment. Tom had no time to scrounge for his own digs in the tight Boston real estate market and the arrangement proved convenient when he had to borrow clothes from Fred to look the part of a young tech exec. Even in the "business-casual" era, faded MIT T-shirts just didn't cut it.

Tom was still contending with the gashes in his hind end, a lingering memento of his first-place showing at the Summer Longboard Challenge at Tourmaline, back in PeeBee. Each morning, he still had to apply a thick bandage over the small of his back and his right ass cheek, more for cushioning than to protect the few stitches that had not yet been removed. It did not look as weird to other people as it felt to Tom, who of course would not be caught dead trying to check out his own butt.

Fred was exhilarated and relieved by Tom's arrival. He could not resist "unveiling" his secret weapon in an impressive setting, a conference room in the downtown Boston office of Jamie Bass's law firm. It occupied the top floor of the taller tower of International Place, the one that didn't resemble an unfurling tube of lipstick.

He deliberately overcrowded the room with WebSurfer investors from the first "private placement" round. These so-called

"A Rounders," who wrote some sizzling checks, included Fred's parents' friends and some third cousins on his mother's old-money side of the family. If WebSurfer failed, there would be no hiding from this group, especially in the Caymans in January.

TOM STEPS INTO THE ROOM and has no trouble picking Jamie Bass out of the crowd. A gray pin-striped business suit hangs where a Pearl Jam T-shirt and stone-washed shorts belong and his famously hairy toes are hidden inside a gleaming pair of black wing-tips, but Jamie is still Jamie. His thick black hair is short, no longer bushy, and his hairline issues vague threats to recede. Tom is not sure whether Jamie's eyes got puffy from three years of law school, thousands of billable hours in a high-powered Wall Street firm or the pre-dawn shuttle flight up from New York. He looks fuller, Tom notices, not fat, but more filled-out, with place-holders for future jowls.

"TeeRey!" Jamie greets Tom as soon as they stood close enough together to knock knuckles on the sly.

Tom imagines Fred handing the younger, skinnier Jamie a guitar and a bong, like in the old Phi Delt days, right there in the middle of the meeting. Tom couldn't help laughing a little too loudly for the sensibilities of the gathering Brahmins.

"Dog, we're not in OhBee anymore," Jamie advises. His plain gold wedding band flashes from the hand he cupped over his mouth.

Most of the crowd regards Tom with frigid stares. They look colder than the water he could see over their heads, through the conference room window, far out in Boston Harbor. Fred's enthusiastic introduction makes the ice glisten a bit.

Some of the well-coifed, middle-aged women warm to Tom's sunny good looks and blond curls that drape to his eyebrows and over the back of his collar. Nearly all of the women's faces are expectant, as if one of their Ivy League children were about to receive an award from the Daughters of the American Revolution. Tom is not certain whether so many raised eyebrows spell "T-r-o-u-b-l-e" with a capital "T" or just "B-o-t-o-x" with a capital "B," but he subconsciously decides to establish eye contact with these ladies when it's his turn to talk.

After Fred's enthusiastic introduction, which conveniently omits any reference to Tom's appearance on *Animal Planet*, the investors begin asking questions. They are polite, Fred notes with surprise. He takes this as proof that Tom already is charming them.

"How do you intend to change the company's marketing strategy?" A male investor with nose hair streaming seamlessly into his full beard starts out with a loaded question.

"It's more a question of *speed* than *direction*," Tom ad-libs confidently, even though he knows virtually nothing about where WebSurfer is going or how fast it is getting there. "I'm hard at work learning all about that, and I'll have an answer for you the next time we get together."

"Which strategic partnerships should the company enter into with manufacturers of mobile computing devices?" a lady in classic Christian Dior, a Barbara Bush mangle of pearls and a stiff-jawed Katharine Hepburn accent asks from the back of the conference room.

"Strategic partnerships need to be truly *strategic*." Tom was not skipping a beat. "I'll have a better fix on that after a little more study."

"What opportunities are there for WebSurfer in the – what do you call them? 'Hot spots'?" another well-tended lady asks, referring to a new technology called "wi-fi," wireless high-speed Internet access points that were increasingly available in coffee shops, bookstores and airports.

Tom grins broadly, and his questioner falls in love. It appears that he is having a brilliant idea or that she asked an insightful question, but Tom actually is stifling a laugh. The only kind of "hot spot" he knows anything about is the one that would make her moan.

"I hope to be in a better position to show you what I have in mind *really soon*." Tom can't help winking at her on his way out of the room at the conclusion of the presentation.

"They seem a little restless," Tom understates as soon as he and Fred are alone in the elevator.

"Wait 'til you meet the Board of Directors!" Fred laughs, nervously. "Our most immediate problem is the burn rate. We're running short on operating cash, and it's getting hard to get anybody to cough up more. You know, good money after bad and all that."

"What the fuck am I *doing* here?" Tom was joking when he asked Fred in the elevator, but within a week it became a serious question. Tom couldn't keep all these people's names straight, much less live up to all the deadlines they tried to dump on him. Tom had to be product marketing, investor relations, media relations, government relations, issues management, advertising and what would constitute about four other fully-staffed departments in an established, Old Economy company. He didn't know where to start.

Fred, back in mentor mode, ordered Tom's priorities for him, mainly by letting him know who he could most afford to piss off and how pissed he could let them get before he satisfied their wants. Fred set him up with tutors in specific subjects, carefully selected from Boston's vast population of permanent students.

"This technoshit's givin' me a killer headache, Kahuna!"

"Just concentrate on the buzzwords and the acronyms," Fred assures him, "then we'll work up a little spiel you can switch on whenever somebody brings one of them up."

"You mean . . . ?"

"Yeah, Man, that's exactly what I mean – the investors don't really understand any of the technoshit either."

"This is nuts, Kahuna."

"There you go again."

That was as close to the subject of TeeJay as Tom and Fred dared to go. Fred made it clear he personally had no time to party, no time for any more "wicked shit," no adventures, "excellent" or "not-so-excellent" – no life, for that matter – and he no longer counted on vicarious thrills through Tom's exploits. To the contrary, he made it clear he could not afford any "bimbo eruptions" at WebSurfer.

"Better hook up with the college chicks, instead. But tell 'em your name is Dick Long."

"I'll tell 'em my name is Fred Hanson."

"Nobody'd believe you." Fred's voice betrays more sadness than irony.

THE CHOICE of a *nom-de-sword* was the least urgent task in Tom's new life. The job was not just a job. It consumed every moment of every day and night, day after day, week after week. Tom hardly found a moment to breathe, much less prowl.

He lasted almost a month before the urge was choking him instead of the other way around. Three weeks made for a new personal record, longer than that dry spell in junior year, during Fall exams, at USD. After prereq calculus and a couple of English term papers fell victim to several weeks of extraordinarily sunny weather and awesome surfing conditions, Fred came to the rescue.

In those not-so-distant college days, Tom was facing a big, fat "F." Tangents and cosigns, not the angle of the dangle, suddenly became the order of the day. After several days with his nose in the math book, Tom protested that he wanted to be *tutored,* not *neutered.* The tradeoff ultimately seemed worth it; Tom pulled a gentleman's "C" in calculus and aced English Lit.

"Good thing!" Tom declared when he got back to his dog's life, "'cause the only thing harder than calculus at this point is *me!*"

Now, four years later, the stakes were gigantically higher. Tom faced serious risk of flagging WebSurfer. The hopes and dreams of eighty full-time employees, not to mention about thirty million investor dollars, were hanging in the balance. This time, Fred arranged for an entire team of experts to get Tom up to speed on every major aspect of the business before the end of his first month on the job.

Tom wasn't scared of much, but these people terrified him. They were totally absorbed in their respective specialties, living for the obscure details in books and dissertations with titles he couldn't pronounce and subjects he didn't know existed. They reminded Tom of the mysteriously re-animated corpses in George Romero's zombie movies, except that these creatures staggered around stiff-legged, looking to gobble up knowledge instead of the flesh of the living. When they finished devouring his brains and balls, Tom feared, he would be left a "technozombie," an epithet he threw at Fred, but only once.

"Let the neutering begin!" Fred responded without the slightest hint of humor. His eyes narrowed into a piercing, critical look that scared Tom more than any horror movie could.

At age twenty-four, with a substantial amount of cash piling up in his passbook savings account back in PeeBee for the first time in his life, Tom was hardly eager to hang up his sword. All the same, something strange and raw and gnawing followed him from PeeBee.

FRED TRIED TO CRAM a lot of other stuff into Tom's head faster than Tom could hold it. He recruited a leggy, young teaching assistant, an aspiring urban planning Ph.D. from Harvard's Kennedy School of Government, to tutor Tom on WebSurfer's potential value in emergency communications services, one of the B2G, business-to-government, applications Fred hoped would make WebSurfer even more valuable in the long term.

They planned to meet at WebSurfer's office, but Tom got a familiar tingle from the message she left on his cell phone the morning of their late afternoon appointment.

"I have to let a repairman into my apartment, so we'll have to do it there."

When he sits down with her, knee-to-knee in overstuffed leather armchairs in the living room of her minuscule, Pottery-Barned apartment, the TA is incredulous that Tom has no clue what inspired Fred to invent the WebSurfer geographic reference system.

The story starts with the money.

"Fred noticed when Internet research firms started confidently projecting on-line sales to consumers would rise from $90 *million* in 1995 to $4 *billion* in 2000. He heard about a couple of other grad students in Northern California, Larry Page and Sergey Brin, who were developing a search engine that would help web surfers zero in on useful information. Content providers the world over, especially those with something to sell to the public, would pay dearly for 'Google juice' – prominent placement in the search results – and a fortune for a 'Google whack' – popping up as the only return page in response to a two-word query with no quotes."

"The Internet was swelling into a monster power curve," she tries to fit Tom's frame of reference, "and these guys were determined to surf it. All they had to do was find a way to get computers to crunch instantly a number of calculations that was so big, it had to be close to a googol, the math-geek term for a '1' followed by a hundred zeroes. Only a few investors were smart enough to bet big bucks that a new spelling of this number would some day become a verb."

"Yeah, so?" Tom's eyes speak for him.

"Fred intended to link *physical places* through the Internet as effectively as Google would link *websites*. Not every consumer could or wanted to do all their personal business in cyberspace. Why not harness the power of the Internet to help consumers find services and products in their own physical neighborhoods, get real-time information about opening hours and prices and facilitate drive-through transactions by making it easier to order, pay and navigate from a wireless computer while en route? Instead of a 'Google whack,' Fred decided, why not a 'Surfer whack'?"

She pauses long enough to sip carefully on a hot chamomile tea and to catch Tom looking into her eyes a little too intently. She could tell he planned to pick up more than buzz-words.

"Fred decided there had to be a way to assign an address to every spot on the planet, one that was unique and almost impossible to fuck up, whether it is located on a street or in the middle of a lake. It had to use the letters and numbers on a standard computer keyboard, not all the obscure symbols for degrees, minutes and seconds. Latitudes and longitudes, which are measured from completely useless places like the Equator and the International Date Line, have ruled since before the Renaissance. Fred decided we needed something simple enough for people to remember and type into a computer. He dreamed up a brilliant new way to do it."

The brainy babe admires Fred, Tom thinks, but there is no hint of romance.

"When the U.S. Patent and Trademark Office decided the system was original enough to give Fred a monopoly on it, Fred was more surprised than anybody. To him, it just seemed so *obvious*."

"So," Tom asks, hoping that the lesson is coming to an end, "what comes next?"

"You do, silly boy."

Tom is really stoked to hear that line, until she goes on lecturing.

"Having a patent and making money off of it are two entirely different matters. Somebody out there has to be willing to pay big bucks for the privilege. That's your *raison d'être*. So it's time you got moving *à très grand vitesse*!"

Talking French, talking dirty, it's all the same to Tom. As his tutor holds forth on the implications of recent federal legislation and rulemaking at the Federal Communications Commission to require "enhanced 9-1-1" emergency services for cell phone callers, Tom drops to the floor in front of her and leans forward. She hesitates, regards him with a crooked smile, then leans forward to meet his lips.

It starts out wet and wild, but she breaks the lip-lock as soon as Tom's hands start sliding up her thighs.

"Fred warned me about you!" She wags a finger at him. Suddenly, the college TA turns into an elementary school teacher, scolding a naughty second-grader.

Within a couple of minutes, she guides him up off his knees and out her apartment door.

"I don't get it!" Tom whines.

"Sorry. I'm really just not that into men right now," she shrugs him off. "But if I were, you'd be high on my list."

Tom's mouth is still agape when she gently closes the door in his face. He is angry at Fred. He should have warned him this TA was his *competition* for all the hot chicks. He suspects Fred deliberately arranged for the Tomcat to get put out, for once.

Tennis

TOM HAS GONE FROM STIFF to frozen stiff by the time he gets back to Fred's townhouse. Nirvana is cued up on Fred's primitive stereo. Tom is not sure whether Fred is still a closet grunge freak, or if he just never found time to update his music collection since his USD days. With the volume up high enough to shake the peeling plaster off the walls, Tom decides, it is good warm-up music. He solo-snake-dances around his makeshift bedroom as he changes into a heavy sweatsuit he bought at the Harvard Coop. He made sure to get one with a thick hood and a drawstring, which he ties loosely under his cold, chattering chin.

As he yanks on an extra pair of ankle socks, Nirvana's biggest hit, "Smells Like Teen Spirit," starts thrumming. Other than this tiny bit of exercise, Tom knows a good night's sleep will cure his wounded pride and prepare him for another day in Boston's deep freeze.

Tom slides into bed under three layers of moth-eaten blankets and curls up like a fetus. With the final cut on the CD still blaring, he doesn't hear Fred come home and stagger up the stairs to collapse into his own bed.

TOM WARMS UP by remembering life as it was with the summertime Phi Delt crowd on the volleyball courts south of the lifeguard tower at the foot of Grand Avenue. "Veeballers" were on PeeBee's courts all day, "roofing" and "digging" – springing up out of the sand to keep some height on the ball and diving face-first into the grit, trying for a last-second save. The scene reached critical mass every Friday afternoon.

The Phi Delts always fielded a fearsome lineup, but two of the best players were Kappa Sigs from the University of California-San Diego, up in La Jolla. They were lanky fraternal twins of Norwegian ancestry. Everybody called them Karch and Sinjin. The Phi Delts made a noisy, drunken scene every week, calling out the players' pseudonyms, plunging their knees into the sand and chanting, "we're not worthy!" The Karch and Sinjin show attracted a wide assortment of chicks in thongs who couldn't tell the buff blonds from the real-life grand-daddies of beach volleyball, Karch Kiraly and Sinjin Smith.

At precisely 5:32, Tom would always break out of the crowd on the bustling ocean-front walkway and bound barefoot down the steps into the hot sand. Without his shirt, everyone could see how precariously Tom's faded board shorts hung on his narrow hips. As he hit the beach, the Phi Delts fell on their knees, their backs to the unobstructed sun, facing red-and-white candy-cane painted net poles and prostrated themselves.

"We're not worthy!" Every TV appearance seemed to earn him the treatment they usually saved for Karch and Sinjin. The chorus scattered among the half-dozen beer-filled ice chests nestled in the sand between the courts. Pop-tops and Bic lighters punctuated the sounds of the rolling waves.

By sundown, Tom was always beyond ready for a brew. Whenever his brain got crowded with thoughts about his job, his jerk-wad boss and his need for new wheels, a quick tug on a heavy curtain in his mind would put all unpleasant subjects away. Intrusions tended to recede farther from his consciousness as the foamy contents of each pitcher disappeared.

One night, as a cool breeze was just beginning to kick in off the ocean, a couple of the bros decided it was time for an old-time dorm room celebration.

"Cores has some new *tennis equipment*," one of them announced. As captain of his high school tennis team, Corey Collins devised an elaborate set of tennis-inspired code words that came in handy when he needed to talk drugs in the presence of people who were not "cool." A "clay court" meant he had a pipe, a "composition court" meant he had a plexi-glass bong and a "grass court" meant everybody would be rolling his own. "New equipment" signified a fresh score.

ON THE LIP

≈≈≈≈≈≈≈≈≈≈≈

The younger guys had no idea "playing tennis" was code for "gettin' wasted." They looked perplexed when half the table announced they were ready for a few sets and followed Collins up the narrow stairs to the office from which he managed the O&W's delivery orders and other business.

Collins threw the rusty deadbolt on the door, then pulled a small, metal pipe and a baggy half-full of densely-packed, greenish-gold organic matter out of a file cabinet marked "sports equipment." He deftly dropped a healthy pinch into the pipe bowl, fired it up until a continuous stack of oily, thin smoke billowed toward the low ceiling.

Collins slipped the pipe to Tom, who tried to get away with simply passing it on to the guy on his left.

"Rooms!" Collins cajoled him, each word escaping in its own little puff of smoke as he tried to talk and inhale at the same time. "Guest – of – honor –" his neck muscles twitched as he stifled a cough – "takes – the – first – toke!"

The guys Collins didn't invite upstairs for smokes were still out on the deck, laughing loudly at each other's wild prevarications. They switched from beer to straight shots of tequila just as the guest of honor re-took his seat.

"Which is it?" Tom searched his foggy brain when he rejoined them, "tequila on beer, never fear? Tequila on brew, gonna spew?" He stopped worrying about it when the first shot crossed his lips.

When Tom tried to tab out, the others refused to take his money. Good thing, as it turned out, because the sandy recesses of Tom's Abercrombie & Fitches contained barely half of Tom's share of the amount due and a long-overdue parking ticket that had already made three trips through the washing machine.

He floated home, feeling extraordinarily happy, yet amazed that he hadn't swapped more than a few words with an available chick all evening. When Tom got halfway up the creaking back stairs, he felt an earthquake. This one was epicentered in his stomach. As tectonic plates in his gut moved, he doubled over on the wooden railing and spewed all over his landlord's prized hibiscus below.

≈≈≈≈≈≈≈≈≈≈≈

Tom stayed there, folded over the railing limply, waiting for the next eruption. When he finally pushed himself up, he noticed Carly, studying him from the bottom of the stairs, looking surprisingly sympathetic. She climbed up, placed his arm around her neck and led him back down the stairs.

"Now I gotta climb those all over again," Tom protested. He was loose, a rag doll on her shoulder.

"Sorry 'bout tossin' my cookies on the high biscuits," he added, little-Tommy-contritely.

"Been there, done that," Carly said. "Come on, Hot Dog. I got something special that will cure what ails you."

Tom sat in the kitchen as Carly scavenged methodically through the refrigerator and kitchen cabinets. As he sat at the old Formica kitchen table, silently tallying the rips and cigarette burns in the plastic seats, he realized he had never been in that room before.

"Chug this."

TOM REMEMBERS A CLEAR GLASS BEER MUG full of reddish liquid with large yellow globules floating throughout, like the contents of a lava lamp, just before he falls into a deep sleep, just shy of a coma.

Reality Distortion Field

AFTER THE FIRST MONTH, Fred started to regret hiring Tom. He teed up several mega-deals and turned them over to Tom, but every ball seemed to land farther from the cup. Fred's patience was growing thinner than WebSurfer's credit at the bank.

Fred didn't think it through before he started punishing Tom, nor did he level with him. First, Fred eschewed the old frat house banter, insisting on business talk between them in the office. Then he rudely ordered Tom to line up with other visitors in the "chute" outside his office instead of walking right in, the way he did from Day One. Fred tried to blame the new, arms-length SOP on Keith who, in fact, complained that Tom and Fred's frat-rat patter hurt company morale. Several of the top dogs were still in a jealous snit over the number of WebSurfer shares Fred gave Tom to lure him off the beach.

To Tom, the unapologetic change in attitude was a sharp elbow to the gut. He was doing his best with all the "primary targets" – Fred prioritized them as if they were part of a Cold War preemptive nuclear strike plan – the big cell phone service providers, the content suppliers and the Internet service providers. None of them seemed ready to reach for their checkbook. In several cases, Tom discovered, the prospect of actually "inking" a deal bore scant resemblance to the rosy picture Fred painted during his frequent pep talks to investors and employees.

WebSurfer faced a classic "chicken-and-egg" problem. Nobody offering Internet services from mobile phones or other devices wanted to be the first to sign a deal with WebSurfer. They had no idea how to price it.

Fred should at least be grateful, Tom thought, that he didn't come back to Boston and expose Fred's "reality distortion field," the equivocations, exaggerations and unvarnished lies he told to keep WebSurfer afloat. Still, with nothing to show for his efforts after several weeks, Tom felt guilty.

When Fred dropped the frat house banter at home, too, it hurt Tom more than anything he suffered at the fins of Raymond Chu's surfboard back at Tourmaline. As uncomfortable as it became to continue living under Fred's roof, Tom was glad he had not leased an apartment in Boston and that his place in PeeBee was paid up a year in advance.

It would hurt even more if Fred insisted that he bag it and go home. Cold suds and warm sunshine would eventually dull the pain, but Tom knew he could never look himself in the mirror if Fred wiped out because he trusted him, once more, with something precious.

eVILLAGE RESTAURANT AND BAR became Fred Hanson's new schoolhouse. After commuting for weeks between WebSurfer's offices in Cambridge and UOL's headquarters in Northern Virginia, Fred learned all the Internet lore the Dulles Technology Corridor could burp up.

Fred got lost the first few times he tried to navigate the burgeoning Washington, D.C., suburbs. In the process, he learned that the Tysons Corner construction boom produced an amorphous blob of concrete and congestion around an aging shopping mall. Tysons could not be avoided, Fred learned, because of its rising profile in e-commerce. Overnight, it became the unofficial center of gravity between the Old Economy, embodied in the marble monuments just across the Potomac River, and the New Economy, which was rooted in the Internet switching facilities a bunch of Beltway Bandits built with plenty of Cold War tax dollars.

With completion of gleaming twin-towered headquarters for media giant Gannett and its popular coloring-book of a newspaper, *USA Today*, including a helicopter landing pad that loomed thirty stories above tracts of Seventies split levels, Tysons took on an "Emerald City" cast. People from every corner of the globe rushed in to declare themselves the One, the Only Great and Powerful Wizard of the New Economy.

The urban blight turned Fred's stomach, and so did the little pukes that made it all possible. Fred was bitter. He felt more alone, more in danger, than ever before in his whole life – except, he hated to remind himself, for that awful night with Tom in TeeJay. The memories came back to him only when Fred could least afford a fitful night's sleep.

America Online's rags-to-riches story was his favorite. Hundreds of people who stuck with the dial-up Internet access provider back in the lean, early days in the mid-Nineties, when stock certificates and toilet paper were the company's only currency, became millionaires when their stock options vested. A guaranteed purchase or "strike" price in pennies a share and a selling or "market" price closer to a hundred bucks guaranteed every AOLer a lifetime supply of beer money, even at $6.50 a draft. Those who never *dreamed*, much less *planned*, to become rich found eVillage a good place to ponder what to do about all that cash. Plenty of other lucky folks from the string of companies with techno-babble names that lined both sides of the Dulles Access Road could afford to commiserate with them.

eVillage also gave all the shockingly new, shockingly rich and shockingly self-absorbed people a spacious place to hang out while remodeling contractors blasted out the backs of their older homes in the nearby Washington suburbs of Langley and McLean to make way for the two-story great room, the gourmet kitchen and the sound-proof in-home theater. The youngest tech millionaires, most of whom never before owned their own home and certainly weren't interested in anything "used," built all-new, two- and three-million dollar McMansions a few miles farther up the Potomac.

Leafy Great Falls was considered relatively close-in to downtown Washington, compared to a two-hour slog from Loudon, the Virginia county to the west, where ugly townhouses with color-coordinated, asphalt-shingled roofs popped up like toadstools as far as the eye could see from the air traffic control tower at Dulles. The Tech Boom also meant the start of a new "executive home" in Great

Falls every day. AOLers competed to see who could cram the most square footage – 12,000, 15,000, 22,000 – of faux-French chateau or Tuscan-style villa onto a half-acre lot, while at the same time hacking down as many mature trees as possible and replacing them with cellular telephone towers. Within a matter of months, from its perch on the edge of the fault line that separates Piedmont and Tidewater Virginia, a community known for many humble years as "Forestville" was looking down its nose and the Potomac River toward the nation's capital and the Chesapeake Bay beyond.

Fred decided this was the kind of place he could call home. A good thing, he figured, because he could tell the UOL negotiations would bring him here, to Northern Virginia's Technology Corridor, sooner rather than later.

Front Deck

FRED SHUFFLES into eVillage with depression written all over him, so Shippe dispenses with the idle chit-chat that characterized their earlier conversations.

"So, Fred, isn't it about time you told me what space you're playin' in?"

"I'm in the mobile space," Fred answers, trying to choke down a tentative tone. "Mostly telecom and hand held applications, kind of a hybrid search engine."

Fred has recited his pitch a thousand times, but it just isn't coming to mind at the moment. He pauses and focuses on the bubbles in his beer, afraid salty tears might drop in to keep them company.

"Some days I feel like a glorified Mapquest," Fred continues with a suddenly husky voice. He represses the urge to light up a cigarette.

"Sounds like you're a little late, Bud. Those punks over there –" Shippe nods toward the Early Adopters – "are from UOL.com. They just told me their company's going to buy a new outfit out of Boston, Surfer-something-or-other. Its core technology is a geographic reference system that works better with computers than street addresses and zip codes. The tall, prematurely balding guy in the middle is heading up a team that's convinced WebSurfer will get a ton of hits on their site. They think the pop-up ad revenue will be huge. The honchos at UOL are hatching even bigger plans. They're gonna put it together with enterprise applications from some other startup to leverage a whole new suite of business-to-business and business-to-government offerings."

"Also," Shippe adds, hanging one arm over Fred's shoulder and whispering directly into his ear, "I hear there's already some intense interest from a certain *special customer* over at Langley."

≈≈≈≈≈≈≈≈≈≈≈

Fred grimaces, as if his beer has turned to vinegar. He couldn't imagine why the Central Intelligence Agency would be interested in WebSurfer, and he was not keen on guys whispering Brooklynese into his ear.

After a moment, he turns on his barstool toward Shippe. It is the first time he faced away from his beer after taking refuge at eVillage from his most recent humiliation at UOL, where Fred had choked just shy of promising to sell them WebSurfer. The terms they suggested would render his own stock, the shares the George Town Angels bought with their venture capital, the shares traded for the legal work being done at Jamie Bass's law firm and the stake that turned his buddy Tom Rey's life upside down, worth exactly zero dollars and zero cents, before and after taxes. Fred would, however, salvage a trust fund he pledged in desperation as collateral for WebSurfer's most recent bank line of credit. The inheritance had remained untouched since his tool-and-railroad heiress grandmother left it to him when he was six years old.

"Are you for real?" Fred zeroes in on Shippe's coal-black eyes. They seem abnormally close to where Shippe's equally black, longish hair was swept straight back under a visible film of styling gel.

"Let's just say . . . I get around. And I listen. And I got some people really close, *really, really* close to Mike Culver. The guy's not all that bright, ya know, just got lucky, saw a band goin' down Broadway and had the alley-cat smarts to start marchin' in front of it."

Shippe grabs the last peanut out of the tiny plastic bowl in front of Fred and continues, simultaneously talking and chewing.

"Mostly, he thinks he's Gawd." Shippe's Brooklyn accent whispered in some words and bellowed in others. "Payin' too much attention to his own press releases. But he knows he'll never take AOL down without stealing their ad revenue, or at least staking claim to the market for consumers using mobile devices, PDAs, handheld computers, telematics – like in-vehicle navigation systems and other types of ITS, intelligent transportation systems."

Fred is astonished by the stranger's substantive knowledge of the mobile computing "space." It was as if Shippe had been in the sterile UOL conference room earlier in the day and heard Fred's most recent pitch for a UOL/WebSurfer strategic partnership.

"He thinks he can pick up SurferWhatsIt for a song and roll out the first UOL location-based consumer apps early in 2001. Been bragging about it for a couple of weeks. Nobody's published anything about it – yet."

Shippe has a satisfied look on his face, even as he pauses for Fred's reaction.

"No fuckin' way!" Fred shouts at him, jumping off his barstool. He looks ready to shuck his cashmere sport coat and take a swing at somebody.

"Whaddaya mean 'no fuckin' way'?" Shippe calmly raises an eyebrow.

"UOL's offer for WebSurfer is a fucking insult. It's not even in the ballpark."

"How do you know that?" Shippe asks coolly.

"Three other companies made better offers, and I turned every one of 'em down."

If you're going to tell a lie, Fred ventures, might as well make it a *really big lie*. Shooting off his mouth was one thing, but Fred realizes he is in danger of also shooting off his own foot. He hastily buttons up his heavily lined Burberry trench coat.

"But don't tell anybody, OK?" He flips Shippe his WebSurfer business card as he storms across eVillage's unadorned concrete floor toward the door.

Shippe never looks at Fred's card. He just stuffs it in his shirt pocket, looks up at the ceiling, stifles the smile beginning to creep over his nearly non-existent lips and phones in a quick report on his cell.

"No fuckin' way your boy's gonna sell out on you now – guaranteed!"

"Now, my versatile friend, there are a few things I need to know about TerraCon's 'black' contract with the boys at Langley,"

≈≈≈≈≈≈≈≈≈≈≈

the man on the line replies with a perfectly neutral Midwestern accent.

Shippe saunters toward the clump of Tech Happy Hour buzz-makers at the next corner. The digital audio recorder taped to the small of his back still has plenty of available disk space.

FRED SHOOTS OUT eVillage's front door and flies down a short flight of stairs to a makeshift wooden deck between the building and a narrow strip of blacktop in front. A blue canopy over the stairs and a red velvet rope across them announce that this is the Silicon Dominion's best approximation of "New York cool."

The canvas covers only enough of the deck to shelter the burly bouncer, who is scratching his head, trying to decide whether to admit an under-aged woman whose Virginia driver's license is as fake as the implants she is nearly pressing into his pudgy cheeks. Everybody else is out in the weather, including two dozen baby-faced techno-weenies eagerly lining up to prove they are at least twenty-one years old.

Fred quickly grows impatient, cooling his heels and other important parts of his anatomy in a damp, early-November breeze. Darkness falls on the sky even more heavily than on Fred's mood as he power-smokes a cigarette and waits for a valet to bring his rental around.

For all its techno-hipness and media hype, eVillage was nothing more than a corrugated metal barn in the middle of a suburban industrial park. It had no room for self-parking, and the valets seemed far more interested in the incoming stream of gleaming new roadsters than in the Pontiac Dogshit Fred rented that morning from Hertz. There were two hot-red and red-hot Porsche Carrera 911s and a couple of BMW Z3s, both of them iris blue.

Fred's flight back home to Boston was scheduled to depart Dulles in just a little over an hour, but he has more important subjects on his mind. Most immediately, he knows "valet" is a French word meaning "dent already there!" but he will have no time to haggle with the rent-a-turd company over any expensive surprises the eVillage valets carved into the doors and fenders.

Fred also stews about his afternoon in Herndon. In his head, he calmly explains to Mike Culver, that smug sonofabitch, exactly *how* to fuck himself sideways.

"Bastards!" Fred says it out loud and it rhymes with "fastuds." "Bragging already about stealing WebSurfer! Without so much as a formal offer on the table!"

Fred considers calling a cab. His rental car apparently disappeared into the myriad body shops and car dealerships surrounding eVillage. He doubts that the overworked grunts at Hertz would actually miss it. Finally, after several fruitless conversations with a guy in a red jacket whose only apparent function was to hold up one finger and say the word *"pronto,"* his nondescript rental squeals to a halt in front of him.

Fred's cell phone rings, as usual, at the most inconvenient moment. He flicks his half-smoked cigarette onto the blacktop, crams the ear bud in with his right hand and buckles his seatbelt with his left.

"Yeah?" Fred's dyspeptic tone surprises even himself.

"Kahuna! I finally got a ride, Man!"

Static on the line makes it difficult to hear, but Fred knows it has to be Tom Rey.

"Whaddaya mean, a 'ride'?"

"I'm in the curl, Man!" Tom screams in Teenage Mutant Ninja Turtle.

"You don't mean – "

"Fuck yeah, I mean we got the AT&T deal! They want the download for the launch application, like, yesterday, Man! We'll be surfin' the front deck of all their new, web-enabled mobile phones in just eight weeks!"

"Don't tease me!" Fred knows this means a WebSurfer icon will appear on the start screen, known as the "front deck," every time someone turns on an AT&T cell phone with wireless access to the Internet. The icon will be a "hot link" that will take the user to WebSurfer's website. It means instant "ka-ching."

"No shit, Man. This is the real deal."

"You are one totally righteous dude, you know that?"

"You're the Kahuna."

"Can we really download a usable version of the software that fast?" Fred wondered out loud.

"Toldja, Kahuna. Surfers can do anything. I got two hundred and fifty thousand up front, if that'll convince anybody to paddle out to the lineup a little quicker."

Fred's heart starts racing, burning up the beer. Tom has just solved WebSurfer's short-term debt crisis. In light of their experience in TeeJay, it should not have come as a surprise.

"I'm flyin', Dude. Catch you at home tonight."

Fred shoots through a broken turnstile onto the Dulles Toll Road without paying the obligatory twenty-five cents. Just as well, he discovers, since the eVillage valet swiped the leftover change Fred thought he hid in the cup-holder. The Pontiac groans all the way up to eighty-five as soon as Fred splits off the crowded toll road, onto the dedicated airport access road. He dashes ahead of all the suckers in the local toll lanes, mired in Washington's notorious afternoon rush-hour traffic.

"The front deck!" He screams out the car window.

Fred can see WebSurfer's prospects, and his own, straight ahead. They soar, just like the Dulles terminal that is coming into view. Still, as he studies the airport's reverse, outward-curling concrete buttresses, concave, cement bonnet and clear, glass-paneled walls, Fred reminds himself that he is not entirely certain how it all fits together.

Windows

THE NEXT SUBJECT in Tom's crash course on WebSurfer was the sacred Initial Public Offering. Jamie Bass would be the professor, with a special assist from the hottest tech maven on Wall Street.

Tom and Fred shuttle to New York early one crystal-clear Tuesday morning and join Jamie in his office. They remembered him as a loquacious beach boy who was always singing when he was not talking or studying. Jamie made a habit of falling behind in every course, then sprinting to good grades in the final few weeks. Fred often told him to forget law school and concentrate on his music, that the world was ready for some mellow acoustic beach ditties and that he could make big bucks if he went professional.

Jamie leads them on a grand tour of Kohler & Kray's elegant suite, starting with the 82nd floor reception area. Rays of morning sunshine stream into the space through the tower's narrow windows. The sunbeams create a stroboscopic effect on the lawyers and paralegals, who dash through the reception area with heavily "shmeared" bagels balanced on top of their Styrofoam coffee cups.

A spiral staircase shoots up the next two floors. Halfway up, Jamie and his star clients – in fact, the only clients he could claim for annual compensation review purposes – encounter Reginald Throckmorton, the K&K partner who introduced Jamie and WebSurfer to Samuels & Schwartzman, Ltd. – "Sammy Schwartz," to insiders.

Francine Schwartzman ran the investment banking firm her father founded forty-seven years earlier, just before she was born. In the previous five years, she turned it into the biggest, most important, most influential and most lucrative source of capitalization for emerging dotcoms in the world. *Barrons*, the stock whiz tabloid, reported that she had personally raked in more than $140 million in a series of IPOs for some of the highest-flying icons of the Internet Age.

"So sorry I won't be able to join you chaps for lunch with Francine," Throckmorton, a jaunty middle-aged man in an orange-and-black bow tie, apologizes. He is lean and distinguished and sounds like Britain's Prince Charles. "Please tell her I look forward to seeing her in the Hamptons this weekend, and I'll be *all ears*."

"Of course, Mr. Throckmorton," Jamie promises.

"Oh, please *do* call me Mortie and please *don't* call Francine 'Francie Schwartz,' like all those *loathsome* market analysts. She hated that nickname, even back in our Princeton days."

Bass knows Throckmorton used more than old school ties to persuade Schwartzman to give WebSurfer so much as the time of day. It had more to do with a favor his family did for the Schwartzmans, something about dampening an embarrassing and noisy fuss over Jews buying into their WASPy little corner of their old, old money Long Island beach community.

On any given day, Sammy Schwartz was actively studying one hundred Internet brainstorms, all of them dying for capital. With her reputation in the stratosphere and her company's fees in the ionosphere, Schwartzman needed only to decide which of them would make her richer, faster.

WebSurfer might have been last on her list of one hundred, but Schwartzman's dossier was starting to thicken. She memorized all the latest reports from Jupiter Communications and Media Metrix, outfits that projected online consumer sales and tracked how much traffic different websites got, and she could chart the progress of her top dozen candidates – she called them her "twelve prophets," but nobody was certain she spelled it that way – in her head. Schwartzman also had a gutful of intuition and a nose for money that was no worse for rhinoplasty.

Schwartzman turned her nose up at Jamie's choice of the touristy Windows on the World Restaurant but agreed to meet the young Texan and his clients there. Her numbers were beginning to suggest that WebSurfer had potential, that perhaps her good old Mortie, her favorite college eating club swing-dance partner, might actually be doing *her* a favor.

When lunchtime rolls around, the former beach housemates shuttle down a local elevator bank to a sky lobby on the 78th floor, then to the Plaza. As they pass the enormous sculpture of Planet Earth, the sunshine feels familiar, like a little touch of California. None of them admits how tempted they are to throw off their suits and go roller-blading in Battery Park. The nonstop elevator ride to Windows' reception area on the 106th floor of the North Tower makes Tom's ears pop. He was starting to get accustomed to East Coast sky-high-rises but his eardrums told him he belonged at exactly sea level.

Heads turn as three fresh-faced young gentlemen are escorted to K&K's regular table, adjacent to one of the trademark windows. Even in their serious dress clothes – Jamie in pinstripes again, Fred in his now-typical professorial tweed and Tom in a spiffy new Navy blue business suit from Filene's Basement that fit him almost like custom-made, even though it was thirty percent off – they look too young to be anybody important. The tourists turn back to their plates or continue gazing out the windows.

As Jamie starts explaining the New Economy facts of life, a busboy stops by with a polished metal pitcher. They get water but no waiter.

"Forget everything you ever learned about micro-economics," Jamie begins.

"Done deal!" Tom thinks to himself, as he takes in the spectacular bird's-eye view, looking North, over the whole of Manhattan. He notices that the restaurant windows were wider than the twenty-two-inch slits in K&K's offices. Almost three feet across, they seem more like real windows. He has no way to know that the Japanese architect who designed the World Trade Center was acrophobic, that his fear of heights meant he couldn't eat at Windows on the World without throwing up, but Tom vaguely remembers from his freshman econ class that micro-economics was "business" or "firm" economics, not all that Adam Smith, "unseen hand" stuff he learned in the "macro" class he took sophomore year.

"An e-commerce company does not have to make a profit now to make a killing in an IPO," Bass continues. "At first, web traffic – the number of people attracted to a site – was the key. Now, it's a lot more complicated. The billion-dollar question is, how fast and how much will a company grow? In the Old Economy, the traditional retail metrics were advertising-to-revenue ratios, gross sales and – last but not least – profits. Not so, not now. In the New Economy, it's 'page views' that count, 'unique visitors' and 'customer-acquisition costs.'"

"Time out!" Tom interrupts. He takes his eyes off the view for the first time and makes a "T" with his hands, like a ref interrupting the Super Bowl. "Can you, like, cut to the chase, Dude? The IPO means big bucks go into Freddy's black box, but how does anybody know they'll ever get a dime of it back out again?"

Fred smiles. Good ol' Tom, going straight to the bottom line, in something roughly resembling plain English. Fred is sure those road show performances will be *awesome*.

"I mean, like, what's worth more, my WebSurfer stock certificates or a pack of EZ Widers?"

Fred cringes. Gotta make sure that line stays out of the "road show" presentation.

"On the nose!" Jamie laughs, touching the end of his own nose with his right index finger. Like Fred, he is accustomed to explaining things to Tom.

"That's why they call Internet business the New Economy," Jamie goes on. "It's all new. We're *making* the rules, not *following* them. Sammy Schwartz has shown everybody that *actual revenues don't matter*. The value of an Internet company is determined by a multiple of *forward revenue*."

Tom remembers that Jamie liked to talk, but he didn't remember him talking so much *in italics*.

"You mean, like, 'I'll gladly pay you Tuesday for a hamburger today'?"

Jamie had forgotten that Tom's face was even more appealing in person than on television. No one ever imagined how much Tom's recent and most severe haircut, performed after much nagging by Simon Keith, would actually enhance Tom's credibility.

"Well, yeah, sort of," the lawyer stammers. "You just need to understand Internet math."

It is Tom's turn to cringe. First, economics and now, math again!

"Here's an example," Fred cuts in. "Say you got a company with $50 million capital in 2000 and you expect revenues of $100 million next year, in 2001. And say the revenue forecast for 2002 is $200 million. Then the value of the company is twice the 2002 revenue forecast – two times $200 million, so that's $400 million. And if you issue ten million shares of common stock, they should be worth $40 each."

"Excuse me, my men, but the last time I looked, WebSurfer had no revenues at all."

"That's the whole *beauty* of it, Dude!" Jamie exults. "It's not worth what it's makin' *now*, it's worth twice as much as what it's makin' in *2002!*"

Tom just grins back at both of them. He tends to grin a lot when he is sublimely clueless. After so many weeks at WebSurfer, the muscles in his cheeks are starting to cramp.

Fred knows better than anyone what the grin means, and it is getting damned irksome. He picks nervously at one corner of his linen napkin. The closest "designated smoking area," as best he could tell, was near the TKTS half-price Broadway show kiosk they passed on the Trade Center Plaza, 1,200 feet below them. He was dying for a smoke.

Schwartzman strides in late. She takes the fourth seat at their table before Jamie can stand up to make proper introductions and wags a finger high in the air at a waiter. It is a subtle threat that she will start snapping her fingers if he doesn't take her order immediately.

"You *do* have fresh tuna."

"Fresh-frozen," the waiter, a smooth young Hispanic man, replies sheepishly.

"Well," Schwartzman instructs, "tell the chef to thaw it out and just *sear* it. And bring me just *that much* wasabi and a Perrier with a lime twist."

She turns to the young trio, who look both eager and startled.

"So, tell me, Jimmy, how *is* my old friend Mortie?"

She barely gave Bass time to reply and to introduce Fred and Tom. He didn't bother reminding her he went by "Jamie."

"Ter*rific!*" Schwartzman says, and then launches into a breathless speech involving a lot of numbers, all of which she recites from memory. She speaks directly to Fred, regarding Tom sideways, as if she expects him to get up, put on a waiter's jacket and go investigate the hold-up in the kitchen.

She was not attractive by Tom's standards, but Schwartzman kept her body in excellent physical shape and draped it in the most practical and yet expensive clothes and jewelry Tom had ever seen. Perhaps, it occurred to Tom, talking so fast without taking a breath constitutes aerobic exercise.

By the time lunch arrives, Schwartzman slows down. Tom is not sure which she would run out of first, breath or numbers.

Fred finally gets a word in edgewise.

"So, you are sticking to your earlier valuation?" Fred knows $15 a share is enough to make him a millionaire several times over, without having to wait for his inheritance.

"No," Schwartzman replies, "that's not what I'm saying at all."

Fred's heart sinks.

"I'm saying it *could be* more like $25 or $30 a share, now that we have factored in the revised growth rate projections for handhelds and other mobile computing devices. The whole area of telematics could come on strong sooner than we initially expected. The foreign vehicle manufacturers are investing big in interactive guidance systems and such, and those mastodons of industry in Detroit will play follow-the-leader, as usual. This could also be important in your B2B and B2G ambitions, but that's farther out on the horizon, so we didn't factor it into the base-line valuation."

It was the first time these three frat boys got stunned together since Tom's sophomore year at USD. The only thing any of them could hear at that point was the din of plates clattering and a bunch of secretaries singing somebody "Happy Birthday" on the opposite side of the dining room.

Jamie's mouth goes so dry, he cannot speak. He convinced the partners at K&K to do WebSurfer's legal work almost entirely in exchange for an equity position in Fred's company. If the arrangement didn't pay off, the Management Committee planned to kiss Bass good-bye. This would interfere greatly with plans underway by Mrs. Bass, who recently announced in a single breath that she was pregnant, had quit her well-paying job as an assistant producer at HBO and that she found the perfect Manhattan apartment. It was a co-op located halfway between Sutton Place and the private kindergarten to which she would send the inchoate James Foster Bass III.

The partners were pushing young Bass to jumpstart the IPO so they could cash in. The firm was behind on the rent, and the Trade Center's incoming new owner, Silverstein Properties, was known to be death on deadbeat tenants, especially if they happened to be lawyers or insurance companies.

Jamie was going to save his venerable old firm from bankruptcy. His wife would not have to get her job back at HBO to meet the payments on their new coop apartment in Midtown. It was all going to work out, after all, if the firm could just hang on long enough.

Fred's heart starts pounding. He tugs at the knot in the conservative repp tie he donned for the occasion and fears he might hyperventilate and leave Windows on the World on a stretcher. Schwartzman has just told him his own WebSurfer stock could be worth $30 million.

Tom merrily chews a crunchy piece of bacon in his California Cobb salad. This seems like sunny news. If WebSurfer is worth all that much, it should practically sell itself. He has some trouble with the math, though. Too many zeros. The stock Fred gave him outright would be worth, like, $1.3 million, he figures. A million bucks! Sweet! But not quite enough to fulfill Fred's promise that Tom could spend the rest of his life on surfari.

"So," Fred finally chokes out, "you'll take us public?" Schwartzman tosses her head back and looks straight up at the ceiling.

"I didn't say that. There's a really big *if*, boys. You gotta give me some *deal grease*. You can't have any *forward revenue* until you have *revenue*! Go out and *make some deals*. The market is there for WebSurfer. I don't know how else the Internet service providers can do what they want to do without you – unless, of course, they infringe your patent and just bury you in litigation expenses."

Jamie and Fred turn to Tom, as if only he should consider this to be news. They barely notice when Schwartzman abruptly excuses herself and leaves the rock-hard frozen core of her seared tuna steak on the plate.

On the shuttle back to Boston, Fred explains why Tom's ownership stake in WebSurfer might be worth something more on the order of $13 million, not $1.3 million. He realizes this $13 million is the stock he *gave* to Tom from his own personal shares, but convinces himself he could never begrudge the guy who rescued him in TeeJay. Besides, a host of unknowns, "unk-unks," he called them, meant the stock might yet turn out to be worth nothing. There were two possible outcomes: survival or a fate worse than death. Everything depends on Tom, and time is of the essence. Again.

By the time they land at Logan, it dawns on Tom that he has officially joined the ranks of the technozombies. He sees himself staggering inexorably toward a pile of money, mouth agape, fingernails poised to dig in. It isn't purely a matter of greed, he tries to convince himself. He *has* to get his dog's life back and this looks like the quickest way to get there.

As they march lock-step off the plane in Boston, Fred catches Tom's eyes, but only for a second. He has that cold, black, shark-in-bloody-water stare that he hasn't seen in Tom since TeeJay. Fred knows the nightmares will start anew, just when he most needs restful sleep.

"Déjà vu all over again." Fred shrugs and clenches his right fist over his stomach.

Deals

AFTER ANOTHER DAY IN VIRGINIA for yet another round of frustrating UOL meetings, Fred managed to stumble back into the Cambridge townhouse without awakening Tom. Six hours later, they arose to an encouraging Beantown weather forecast – "warmer today, with a high of fifteen."

The mercury was just above zero when Fred left for work. He always rode the earliest Boston transit train, the "T," two stops to WebSurfer's office every morning and caught the last tooth-rattling train home every night. Tom arrived at the office later and went home earlier, with Fred's encouragement and approval. Fred needed time alone, to think, and Tom needed his beauty rest. He would star in the road show as soon as the two of them could concoct a convincing reason for investors to buy WebSurfer shares the moment they got listed on NASDAQ, the preferred stock exchange for new tech offerings.

"My left nut is *frozen solid!*" Tom greets Fred as he shoots past the usual early-morning queue in the chute outside Fred's office. He leaves the door open.

"You really only need *one* to procreate, Bro." Fred barely glances up from a computer screen full of e-mails, half of which were ticking time bombs.

"Like that's gonna happen. Don't you have to get *laid* to procreate?"

"Not any more, not since the invention of the turkey baster. Ya gotta start thinkin' *technology* here, Bud."

Tom is so relieved to be back on Teenage Mutant Ninja Turtle terms with Fred, he gets choked up about it for a moment. There would be no more stiff business talk between them, even in front of the underlings at the office, and he would never again have to wait outside in the queue.

Tom shivers as he gazes out Fred's window. The barren trees look tortured, standing naked in the cold, their limbs raised up in prayer for any glimmer of sunshine.

Fred divvies up e-mails across his growing stable of company subordinates with impressive-sounding titles. The prospective WebSurfer millionaires would find ticking time bombs in their "in" boxes.

Every morning, Tom and Fred started with a list of the top ten major events on Fred's calendar – conference calls, media interviews and meetings with potential "strategic partners." Most of the dotcoms seeking deals with WebSurfer were desperate to "play" in the "wireless space," but their enthusiasm always seemed to be in inverse proportion to their ability to lay any cash on the table. Jobs that required no technical background on Fred's geographic reference system previously got dragged and dropped onto Tom's calendar. Now, with the AT&T Wireless deal inked, everything is different.

"AT&T worked up a joint press release about our deal, and it looks OK to me," Tom hands Fred a single sheet of paper. "I assume you're going to make the internal announcement in person."

"Shit!" Fred suddenly spits out.

Tom looked over Fred's shoulder at today's "nastygram" from Simon Keith, flagged "urgent." At first, it looked like any other morning at WebSurfer.

"Did it occur to you that this news might be of more than passing interest to your Board of Directors?" Keith demanded. He attached an article that was posted on the eZine website and e-mailed to a thousand eager subscribers, mostly in Silicon Valley, Northern Virginia and Boston's tech corridor. It had Billy Shippe's by-line.

"*What will WebSurferUSA go for?*" read the headline, which flashed bright red on the computer screen.

Keith acted like he was still running covert political operations from his basement office in the West Wing of the Nixon

White House. His George Town Angels investment club had a lot of money riding on WebSurfer, especially after they injected another ten million dollars during the "C Round" of private investments earlier in the Fall of 2000. Keith expected Fred to be at his beck and call twenty-four-seven, and he streamed urgent advice to him on every conceivable subject, including instructions to make sure Fred's Guccis got shined before the next board meeting and that he practice speaking more from his diaphragm to give his voice a more decidedly masculine tone.

Tom Rey was a sore subject. Shortly after he arrived in Boston, Keith warned Fred he would be a "dead man" if Tom did not perform as promised. After hearing rumors about Keith's connections to the nether world of intelligence operatives, former military guys with a talent for making inconvenient foreign politicians disappear, Fred feared the old George Town Angel meant it literally. He faced more immediate worries than the prospect of someday having his knees nailed to the floor by a well-paid ex-Marine named Chuck.

Fred handled any in-house nut-cutting that became necessary when staff got too impressed with their own ideas or too distracted with hobby-horses that did not fit Fred's "strategic vision" for WebSurfer. Keith knew how to take advantage of the situation. He went around the company, setting fires at every stop. He encouraged obstreperous staffers to pursue projects and ideas that Fred killed, even when he knew they made no sense or would push the company's "burn rate" to impossible levels. Keith then made the rounds with a hose full of unctuous charm, putting out the fires whenever it suited his purpose. He always acted respectful, even deferential, toward the much younger Fred in public, which made it easier for Keith to emerge from every scrape the hero, the peacemaker, the "senior gray-hair."

This time, Keith is handing Fred a crisis of his own making.

"The battle lines are being drawn in a bidding war for WebSurfer, a Boston-based startup that promises to revolutionize location-based technology," the story began. *"Web browser upstart UOL.com is looking like an also-ran, with a bid that's too little, too late, according to a*

WebSurfer insider, who asked not to be named. UOL was banking on beefing up its B2B offerings to recover from recent price wars in residential subscription rates and a sudden drop-off in pop-up advertising revenue, but it looks like they'll have to do it without WebSurfer's innovative, computer-friendly geographic reference system."

"Will it glide on over to AOL, instead?" the squib concluded. "Going . . . Going . . . Gone!"

Fred groans and presses his fingertips against his temples. The bottle of cheap sparkling wine he downed on the much-delayed flight home the night before gave him a rotten headache.

Fred's secretary sticks her head into his office.

"Mike Culver for you, Fred."

"Speakerphone, in here," Fred points at the black and chrome starfish on the only corner of his desk that is not buried under paper.

Tom closes the door in an eager software engineer's face and stands next to the speakerphone as Mike Culver, former second-string college wrestler, failed car salesman, fabulously successful web guru and billionaire-on-paper, starts unloading on Fred.

"You . . . little . . . prick." Those were the first three words Culver ever said to him, Fred notes for posterity. With his sandy, Southern, Bill Clinton-esqe voice, Culver makes it sound oddly like a compliment. "Thought we had a deal."

"No way!" Fred tells him. "If I decide to give WebSurfer away, I'll find some deserving street person on Harvard Square."

"I thought that's how it came by its *current* ownership."

Fred is too slow with a snappy comeback, so Culver continues.

"I suppose going onto the front deck of AT&T's new web-enabled phones does change the situation a bit."

Fred's headache disappears when he snaps his head up in shock. He imagines a smug smile, connecting one side of Culver's blond crewcut with the other. How did he steal this secret from WebSurfer so quickly? Was it possible Culver knew AT&T was a done deal before Fred did?

≈≈≈≈≈≈≈≈≈≈≈≈

Tom shakes his head and turns his palms up to the ceiling to make sure Fred knows he didn't spill the beans to Culver or anyone else.

"And the royalty income off the WebSurfer patent, straight into your own hot, little pocket – that's pretty sweet!" Culver jabs at Fred. "And the fees the company will collect should go a long way toward whittling down that short-term bank debt."

"Where *don't* you have spies, Culver?"

"Only in Heaven, my friend, only in Heaven."

"What else did you call to tell me?" Fred realizes that to be on jousting terms with Culver is a quantum leap in the right direction.

"I got a lot more cash than anybody else you're talking to."

Fred is happy to see Culver bite on this one. There never were any other bidders, even though Keith and some of the board members had encouraged ugly talk about putting WebSurfer "on the block" for the past three weeks.

"And if you won't let me buy WebSurfer just yet, I want a partnering arrangement, including an exclusive license on the B2B application," Culver continues. "Get together with me on this, my friend, and the basic WebSurfer consumer application can be accessible on UOL early in '01. I'll cut you a nice little percentage of the ad revenues."

These are the words Fred was aching to hear. He drops his head in relief. Tom grins.

"I'll need the source code, of course."

Fred casts his eyes to the ceiling and shakes his head. Culver is asking for the keys to the kingdom. Fred bites his tongue just short of telling Culver what to do with himself.

"We could load up the deal to be heavy on the patent royalties, if that gets your rocks off. I know they get paid to you, personally. You won't have to share a dime of it with anybody."

"Won't matter," Fred says, dismissively, "I'm plowing every penny of the royalties back into the business."

Fred flashes a smart-ass smile at Tom. They both know Fred has yet to collect even *one* penny in royalties.

"Whatever.   Get your sorry ass back down here to Washington and we'll talk.   I'll overnight you a ticket on Greyhound." The line goes dead in the middle of Culver's nasty chuckle. He wasn't much on telephone etiquette or wasting time. An e-mail proposing a new meeting date pops up immediately on Fred's screen: November 24, 2000.

The idea of doing serious business on Thanksgiving Day makes Fred flinch. His parents always hosted a family feast at their place on Cape Cod, the last big family event before the spacious cottage got buttoned down for the winter. Tom was coming for a seaside experience vastly different from any he and Fred shared in San Diego. It was supposed to be Fred's chance to bring Tom into his world, just as Tom introduced him to the carefree life of surf'n'sex'n'suds'n'sex'n'smokes'n'sex in PeeBee. From now on, it would be deals'n'decisions'n'dollars, lots of dollars, and maybe a little depravity, too, when they finally had something to celebrate.

Meanwhile, Fred knew nothing could be more important than a revenue-positive teaming arrangement with UOL. He and Tom would spend all of Thanksgiving weekend in a hotel in the Washington exurbs, trying to avoid getting robbed by Mike Culver. That made it official. Fred had no life and Tom's was majorly at risk.

Home Page

ROUND-THE-CLOCK MEETINGS over Thanksgiving seemed a distant memory by the time Tom inked his third deal with a wireless Internet service provider. Right after the deal closed, in the second week of December, 2000, Tom also had a revelation. As he raced at full speed through the San Antonio Airport one Friday afternoon in a business suit and hard-soled dress shoes, he finally understood what happened to O.J. Simpson. Tom vaguely recalled seeing the Hertz Rent-a-Car TV commercials when he was just a little kid, the ads in which The Juice pole vaults over other passengers, sprints, hurdles, dodges and weaves his way to catch a flight.

"No wonder he turned into a homicidal maniac!" Tom decided.

At the moment, Tom wants to kill only himself. He knows better than to continue meeting with a bunch of former Southwestern Bell-heads long after it was clear none of them had authority to sign anything, including the tab for their carb-crammed lunch. Six of them, all guys, sat in the conference room the whole afternoon. Their suits ranged from heather gray to dark gray and their hairlines from gone to bad comb-over. None of them seemed to be entirely there. Each asked the same stupid questions about WebSurfer's compatibility with CDMA versus GSM-GPRS networks and the upcoming CDMA-2001X EV/DO standard. When Tom started packing up his computer to leave, they finally got to the point.

"We just can't figure out how to price this," fretted the guy with the most comical comb-over, who yawned and wrang his hands throughout the meeting.

"We're offering all the cellular-based mobile Internet providers exactly the same terms," Tom answered. "Sprint, Nextel and AT&T have already signed. You guys haven't. How much easier can it get?"

"The decision's above our pay grade." All of them nodded at each other and mumbled the names of other company executives, as if they were reciting a roster of Greek Gods.

"Then why am I meeting with you ho-dads this late on a Friday afternoon?" Tom wanted to scream at them, but he didn't. Instead, he grinned, packed up faster and dashed out the door with a final round of handshakes that looked like the perfunctory skin-slap between twelve-year-olds at the end of a Little League game.

Fred and Mike Culver put their respective stables of software engineers to work developing a user interface for handhelds that was more mobile-user-friendly, more "gooey" than what the Baby Bells had to offer, with smaller graphics. After much yelling and screaming among the code slingers and vicious haggling between the two CEOs over the revenue split, WebSurfer also added a payment processing application that made miniscule credit card transactions economical. The e-commerce functionality excited wireless access providers. It made vendors, even those who weren't sucking on a venti café latte from a drive-through Starbucks, froth at the mouth. WebSurfer's added dimension – prioritizing results according to the nearest physical location – would increase a vendor's chances of popping up as the only result of a consumer's search request – a "Surfer whack," Fred called it. With Fred's monopoly on the new geographic reference system, WebSurfer was hotter than steamed milk. They could play hardball now.

"Fuck'em!" Fred advises when Tom calls to report on the meeting as he scrambles through the San Antonio airport.

"Yeah, sideways!" Tom acknowledges.

"Hey, Kahuna, I'm totally beat. I'm comin' back to Boston by way of PeeBee – if I can get to Gate 17 in less than six minutes and catch my flight."

"Sounds like a cool idea, Man. You could use some chill-time. Wish I could join you, Man!" Fred was starting to count four hours of uninterrupted sleep as a "vacation."

"Well, that sure helps on the timing!" Tom is growing breathless, obviously moving fast.

"Wazzat, Tomcat?"

"The airport security dude was sound asleep, Man. That metal phone booth gizmo – "

"You mean the magnetometer?"

"Whatever." Tom shrugs, as if Fred could see him. "That thing was goin' off on everybody, and he was snoring so loud, you almost couldn't hear it beepin'."

Tom somehow couldn't cram his Pumas into his rolly-bag at the hotel that morning, even though they packed just fine when he left Boston, so he tied the laces together and strung them around his neck. As Tom runs the gamut of airport gates, Fred can hear the shoes smacking into each other.

"Well, at least the snoring means the security dude's *alive*," Fred offers.

"Yeah, prob'ly just brain-dead," Tom puffs. "Oh – I see my gate! Shit, they're closin' the door! Catch you at home Sunday night."

Tom switches off his phone as he boards the plane. The crew insists upon checking his bag. He is too out-of-breath to explain that he was in First Class, where there would be plenty of room in the overhead. Had they closed the hatch any faster, they would have spanked Tom's now completely-healed ass.

AFTER HE BUCKLED UP and calculated his time of arrival at the O&W, Tom remembered that he neglected to let Carly know he would be back in his apartment this weekend for the first time since he went back East. After his move to Boston, Carly called him a couple of times on administrative matters – whether to forward certain types of mail and to find out if he really had told some of the Phi Delts they could borrow his surfing gear (he did) and that they could use his apartment for their hook-ups (he didn't). The conversations were cordial, but businesslike. As Tom's pre-takeoff Bloody Mary took effect, it occurred to him what an un-businesslike parting they had.

Just minutes after Tom agreed to join Fred in Boston, Carly knocked on his door, walked into Tom's living room and handed over his prize money. He remembered the combination of sympathy and pride on her face.

"Figured you might want to buy yourself a few comfy pillows to sit on."

Tom grabbed a pen off his kitchen counter, scribbled on the back of the check and handed it back to her.

"What is this? 'Pay to the Order of Carly Bonner'? No way!"

"Way!" Tom replied decisively. "Without you, I wouldn't be cashin' checks, I'd be cashin' in all my chips."

"I said no way!" She stuck the check back in his face.

"You have a point." Tom hobbled to his bedroom and returned with his checkbook, which he balanced most recently at the end of 1998. He started scribbling again and handed Carly the prize money and a check from his own account, made out to her in the amount of $9,800.

"Did something hit you in the head? What's this?"

"Do the math. It's $10,800. That's one year's rent, in advance."

"Why?"

"I'm going away. Back East. But I'll be back."

Carly was dumbfounded. There would be no time to discuss those life-force vortices, which were obviously spinning clear out of the solar system.

"I got a sweet deal going here," Tom said evenly, hardly believing the words are escaping his lips, "and I don't want to lose it."

Carly threw her arms around Tom's neck, one check in each hand. She kissed him hard on the lips. Tom was startled at first, but he soon began to embrace and kiss her, too. Both of them were surprised by the way their hearts fluttered and the awkward entanglement seemed in danger of careening as far out of control as

Tom's chakras. For one brief moment, the ripped stitches in his ass stopped hurting.

Tom suddenly felt naked in front of Carly, even as she turned away from him and made a tat-tat-tat down the back stairs.

The memory popped into his mind, almost like a cartoon bubble, at unexpected moments. A faint feeling, just the square root of an idea, not enough to constitute a thought. It shadowed him on the plane when he set out for Boston. Mostly it was a vivid image – Carly, the woman who saved his life at Tourmaline, at the stairs below his apartment. He could still feel that strange sensation, soft, slow, platonic kisses, one on each cheek, and a careful, all-around hug, just before Carly helped carry his tattered baggage to a waiting taxi. A hand gesture, a pinky, thumb and index finger twisting at her too-thin wrist; encouragement to "hang ten," spoken softly; tears welling in her eyes, but never quite running down her deeply-tanned cheeks; an under-the-breath "TeeRey" chant as he gingerly lowered his stitches into the back seat of the cab.

Tom deliberately tried to wash these odd little fragments of memory away for good with that third glass of Jack Daniel's on the flight East. A sympathetic male flight attendant in First Class, who was paying altogether too much attention to Tom's bandaged butt, kept them coming. As it turned out, the Jack acted only as a solvent, helping bits of Carly merge into the confusing mixture of excitement and abject terror he felt over the grown-up responsibilities his old surfing buddy had thrust upon him.

Even now, so many weeks after the Boeing 777's wheels hit the runway at Boston's Logan Airport, Tom still could not find a moment to sort it out. Carly has registered in his consciousness but she shows no sign of checking out, certainly not as he settles in for his first flight back to San Diego.

He falls asleep before the wheels retract into the plane's belly. First Class is the only place he feels completely at ease.

SEX'N'DRUGS'N'ROCK'N'ROLL were staples in Carly's family. Both parents were Sixties flower children. They were not libertines, just tender-hearted liberals who talked "free love" but lived in devoted monogamy. They weren't political radicals or even pacifists, but they decided it was too much of a hassle to participate in much of anything that was going on in the world.

Carly grew up in Ocean Beach, where the Sixties lasted well into the Nineties. OhBee was a hippie haven, just rough enough around the edges to conjure up images of the Manson family, not the Partridge Family, among middle-class newcomers. Eventually, a Starbucks opened in OhBee, but nobody chained themselves to the front door or even picketed. The entire Bonner family was out of commission by then, anyway.

Carly's dad ran a coffee shop in OhBee, and the Bonners lived literally over the store. It was a popular place for beatnik-style poetry readings and offbeat musical performances. He kept it going even after Carly's mom inherited a beach house and the family moved a few miles up the Coast, across the mouth of the San Diego River, to a worn but forever popular stretch of Pacific Beach.

Carly's mother was killed by a drunk driver in 1997. She was laid to rest wearing a muumuu, covered in garlands of yellow and white daisies and pukka shells. After the funeral, Carly and her dad stockpiled jugs of the world's cheapest vodka and stayed blind drunk for two solid weeks.

She hit rock bottom in May of Y2K, less than a year after Tom signed the lease on the apartment that occupied the entire second-floor of the Bonner house. Carly's dad, who was only forty-nine, had to move into an assisted-living facility because he kept getting lost walking three blocks home from the grocery store. The doctors were unsure whether it was Alzheimer's Disease or an accumulation of bad acid in his brain.

"CAN I HELP YOU with something?"

The woman's voice is stern and strong, loud enough for Tom to hear it clearly over the racket he is making on the stairs to his apartment in PeeBee. Tom barely recognizes her, at first. Carly's high cheekbones look well-proportioned and her arms are fuller, no longer the bundles of sinews that hugged him the day he left for Boston. In place of the boyish style that some surfer girls wore because they could shake out the seawater with a quick wet dog quiver of the head, Carly's hair drapes over one ear and curls under the other. He almost drops the computer case he is rifling through in search of his door key.

"Sorry, Babe, I meant to give you a heads-up."

It is Carly's turn to be alarmed now. There, in the pitch dark, is a close-cropped narc calling her "Babe" and trying to break into her house. Or perhaps it is a cat burglar in a suit and tie with a pair of Pumas slung over his shoulder.

"Whoa! Carly, it's me, it's Tom."

"Tommy, you 'bout gave me a heart attack!" Carly's now-shapely shoulders drop in relief. "What're you doin' here?"

"Live here, remember?"

Carly smiles, pulls some keys out of the pocket of a dressy pair of pants and starts up the stairs. How well she remembered, and how nearly she had given up on ever seeing Tom again.

"So what's with the Hitler Youth thing you got going here?"

Tom shrugs and grins and Carly melts.

"Let's get you inside. Where's your bag?"

"On its way to Honolulu, according to American Airlines."

"Bummer."

"Occupational hazard," Tom explains as Carly leads him into his chilly apartment.

"The real bummer is I gotta wear *this* to the O&W tonight." Tom motions woefully at his suit pants and black leather dress shoes. "It's too cold for board shorts tonight, and they're all I left behind."

Carly looks Tom and his wa-a-a-ay Eastern establishment business suit up and down. She has never seen his skin so pale or his hair so short. She can't help laughing.

"What's so funny?" Tom asks, as he rips off his jacket and tie and casts them over the back of one of the ratty sofas in his living room.

"I've never – it's just that I've never – " Carly stammers, then collects herself. "I've never seen your *ears* before!"

Tom blushes for the first time since high school. His tan is too faded to disguise the beet red that fills his face.

≈≈≈≈≈≈≈≈≈≈≈

"Comin' home awfully late, aren't you?" Tom hastily changes the subject.

"I work down in Mission Valley on Fridays, as a counselor at a suicide prevention center. I found out about it when I was down there at the hospital, waiting for you to rejoin the living."

"That sounds really … umm … *depressing*." Tom couldn't think up a nicer word.

"*Not*." Carly's tone was not disapproving. "Sometimes, all a person really needs is for someone to help them think up just one good reason to keep on living."

"If I don't get a drink soon, I'm going to become one of your customers!" Tom put one arm over her shoulder.

Carly stiffens. Tom blushes again when he guesses why.

"Oh, hell, I'm sorry," he says. "I forgot about the – the – problem."

"They've gotta be pretty close to 'last call' at this point," Carly replies, loosening up a bit. "I can get juice or something."

As Tom and Carly walk into Orville and Wilbur's Surf Bar together, several things don't seem quite right to Tom. He doesn't like the feel of the grit under his dress shoes or the way his toes are imprisoned inside them, still drowning in the sweat he worked up sprinting through the San Antonio airport. It feels weird to enter, not exit, the O&W with a chick, and since this particular chick happens to be his landlady, it seems almost like incest. Worst of all, he doesn't like the long-haired dude who planted himself on Tom's favorite bar stool, legs splayed, takin' in "the 360" at the O&W. His faded board shorts, "Blink 182" T-shirt and iridescent, lime-green flip flops give Tom an odd feeling. He tells himself not to be jealous, that this is just some kid.

He and Carly sit down in the back, behind the foosball tables. Tom rolls the sleeves of his dress shirt halfway up his forearms and undoes the top two buttons in the front before he saunters over to the bar. He is relieved to find Corey Collins pulling the taps.

"*Ro-o-o-o-oms*! You look like an *undertaker* in that get-up!"

Two pitchers with suds oozing over their rims slide Tom's direction. He has his wallet open and sees only three dollars in cash. The nearest ATM is three blocks away.

"On the house, Bud!" Collins insists. "We gotta make up for lost time, Man. Why doncha come on up to the office a little later, after I finish the cleanup. Got some really good tennis equipment for you to try out."

"Well, thanks, Dude, uh, actually . . . can I also bum a tomato juice offa you?" Tom slides one beer pitcher back and shakes hands with the other.

Collins stands on tip-toe to peer over Tom's shoulder.

"What, you got a Mormon chick, this time?" Collins makes an obscene show of flopping a flaccid stalk of celery in the air before he slips it into a tall glass.

The sober Carly bears only faint resemblance to the wiry drunk with a butch haircut he gently ejected and asked not to come back two years earlier. Suddenly, Collins recognizes her.

"Ohhh," he draws the word out to give himself more time to think, "returnin' a few favors, eh?"

Tom blushes again, the color of the tomato juice.

"Whoa!" was all Collins could think to say.

When Tom walks back to the table, he senses Carly's intense discomfort. She looks down at the table and plays nervously with her fingers.

By the time Tom sits across from her, Carly is busting a gut to ask him about the white ribbed cloth that hides almost all of the chest hair that normally showed when he opened his top two buttons.

"Don't tell me that's a 'wife beater' I see under your narc shirt!"

"Gotta have something to soak up the sweat when I'm shreddin' to catch a flight." No way he would ever tell her it was an old Christmas gift from his sartorially-challenged dad.

Tom tells Carly the whole story, but he doesn't start at the beginning. His fruitless meetings in San Antonio earlier that day were still on his mind, but the blow-by-blow account of the seemingly asynchronous business conversation leaves Carly looking puzzled. Halfway through the pitcher of beer, Tom gets more lucid and his story becomes more chronological and less laden with every indecipherable acronym he knows how to pronounce.

Tom tells her about the dark days, when it looked like his move back East was about as opportune as a king-sized boner, smack in the middle of English 210, and that Fred's company would fail as a result. He confides how Fred reacted, how much it hurt, what an ugly hole it blew in their friendship.

"That's gonna leave a mark," Carly sympathizes.

Tom's eyes get watery. Carly never imagined Tom would ever lay his *feelings* bare to her. She decides not to spoil the moment, not to address Tom's unbalanced chakras until the morning. They have the whole weekend ahead of them.

Even before the beer gets warm, he tells her about Francine Schwartzman, the stock, the money, the millions of dollars hanging in the balance. Carly feels certain all this money stuff is just the beer talking. In the years before alcohol took over her life, before she became allergic to food, every guy she met in a bar was a millionaire by the fourth round.

"So, when do you find the time to take care of *you*?" Carly decides to lay some groundwork for the rebalancing process she plans for Tom.

Tom changes the subject. He asks Carly about her dad and her job. Collins pretends he isn't eavesdropping and doesn't throw them out until the time comes to lock up.

Landlady and tenant go back home and creak up the stairs, arm-in-arm. The moment Carly unlocks Tom's door, his cell phone sounds an alarm. A voice mail lurks inside his suit coat pocket. She watches Tom's face, his whole body, crumble as he listens to the message. Tom punches a few buttons and says into the microphone, "yeah, got it, Kahuna."

"What's wrong?"

"That was from my buddy, Fred. The San Antonio guys found out that WebSurfer is about to close a deal with Verizon – that's one of the wireless Internet providers, back East. After all that crap they put me through today, *now* they're ready to finalize a deal."

"That's great!" Carly reaches over and pats the top of his close-cropped head. It feels weird to both of them, like something important is missing.

"Yeah, except they want to finish it up in the morning."

"On Saturday? *This* morning? That's brutal!"

"I have to head to Lindbergh in about four hours and catch the first flight back to San Antonio."

"I see." Carly is breathing hard. She resolves to practice climbing those stairs more often. "You gotta get some rest."

"'Fraid so." Tom is breathing hard, too, wondering how he managed to get so out-of-shape.

"Well, g'night, Tommy."

"G'night, Carly."

Neither of them move. After what seemed like an hour, Tom takes three steps forward, throws his arms around Carly and pulls her so close, her hazel eyes are just inches from his.

"I'll get back here just as soon as I can. Fred really owes me for this one."

"Right," she says, tossing her highest hopes into the garbage. "Soon as you can."

Tom takes a decisive step back and Carly heads down the stairs at a dignified pace.

Tom starts after her. Then he plants his feet on the scuffed-up linoleum as if the floor were a surfboard and he is trying to point it in a different direction.

Board Stiff

"Y2K" BROUGHT SIMON KEITH TWO BIG SURPRISES. The world's computers did not crash at the beginning of the year and Tom Rey did not crash and burn by the end of the year. In fact, as 2000 ground to a close, Tom was still impersonating O.J. Simpson at a succession of crowded airports. There was only one problem. He was running out of mobile Internet service providers to sign up with WebSurfer. The phone companies moved in lock-step, so Tom's hardest task was to convince them that they needed to decide that somebody needed to decide who would decide to ink the deal. It was pure cat-herding.

Tom never acclimated to Boston Winter, no matter how many layers of clothing he squeezed into. It helped that Tom was on the road constantly, wearing blisters into his blisters as he ran through every airport in America that had more than two gates. These days, he had enough sense to put on his Pumas in the taxi and string the inflexible dress shoes over his shoulder before the starting gun sounded. He looked like a stubborn teenager, forced to wear one of Dad's suits to a funeral. He could care less what anybody in the airport thought, least of all the fashionably dressed metrosexuals toting thousand-dollar Italian leather flight bags.

Christmas week, Tom was in Boston barely long enough to swap dirty laundry for fresh at the Korean cleaners a half-block from Fred's townhouse. Tom was glad he still had not taken a lease on a place of his own. It would just be a waste of heating oil, he decided.

On Christmas Day, Fred was back in Virginia, still trying to finalize the financial arrangements with UOL. Every time Tom inked a new deal, it gave Fred more leverage, and he loved telling Tom how it was driving Mike Culver and his clones crazy.

"I'm gettin' really, *really close*, Man," Fred told him on the phone that morning.

"Yeah, I can tell by the way you're breathing, Kahuna. Santa must have brought you something fun to play with."

On Christmas afternoon, Tom spent more than an hour on the phone with Carly after she visited her father in the assisted living facility. She had to cut the call short to get to her job at the suicide intervention hotline. For a lot of people, Carly explained, the holiday season was the last straw.

For once, Tom did not breathe hard into Carly's ear. Ever since his *visitus interruptus*, he called her when he found a spare moment. That usually meant the thirty minutes he spent on a treadmill in a Lysol-smelling Marriott exercise room in whatever town he happened to be stuck that night.

Travel in 2001 would be even heavier, Tom predicted. Vendors who craved Fred's "Surfer whacks" were a lot easier to deal with than phone company executives, many of whom seemed to think they still had a government-protected monopoly and that marketing and public relations were somehow beneath them.

Vendors in the real world, where companies compete for global domination, knew that the best way to use the Internet to sell hot dogs or gasoline or dry cleaning was to pop up in the faces of customers who were located nearby, physically, who could pop right into the store with their cash or credit. If anyone understood the importance of making it easy for someone to act on an impulse, to deal right away with whatever popped up first, it was Tom. Corporate marketing managers ate his WebSurfer pitches with a knife and fork.

Tom made the rounds as quickly as possible, while he was still "hot." It was instinctive, just like his hook-up days in PeeBee.

ON THE NEXT-TO-LAST DAY of 2000, Tom was somewhere in Ohio, pitching Lube'n'Tube, which humbly dubbed itself "the ultimate in drive-thru convenience." Customers could choose from a wide variety of hot dogs while their cars got fresh oil and a lube job.

"Whoa!" Tom remarked to Fred when they decided to make the pitch. "We're talkin' 'bout *real* weenies!"

Just thirty seconds into his spiel, Tom steps out of the conference room and takes an urgent call from Fred.

"It's done, Tom," Fred says. His tone is flat and exhausted. Tom doesn't like the sound of it.

He turns away from his hosts, so they cannot read his face through the glass wall between them. After a long pause, Tom asks, cautiously, "wazzup, Kahuna?"

"Don't worry, don't worry!" Fred realizes Tom is expecting awful news. "It's gonna be *awesome*, Man, *totally*. It's just that it's . . . not exactly what I had in mind."

"Yeah, how'zat?" Tom is still on guard.

"Can you get home tonight?"

"You mean PeeBee?"

"Nah, Boston. Gotta talk to you, Man, *stat*."

Tom flashes a rolling gesture with his fingers at the Lube'n'Tubers and abandons the dumbstruck marketing guys with a small stack of full-color glossy WebSurfer leave-behinds.

TOM FINDS FRED POURING the finishing touches on two home-made black-and-tans over the back of a spoon in his Cambridge kitchen. He looks merry as can be, and Tom heaves a sigh of relief.

"So, who fuckin' died, Kahuna?" Tom asks as Fred takes a long, deep swallow off his beer.

"Movin'!" Fred replies between gulps.

"I meant to get my own place, anyway."

"No, Man, the *company's* movin' – to Virginia. We're gonna take office space in UOL's HQ building in Herndon, rent-free, and they are going to host WebSurfer's website. The syndicated consumer apps are pretty much ready to go live on UOL's site, but there's a shitload of work and a lot of expense ahead of us to get the B2B and B2G apps ready. UOL's gonna absorb a lot of it, so we can lighten up on the payroll."

"Lighten up?" Tom knows payroll had become the hottest flame in WebSurfer's burn rate, and the biggest obstacle to the IPO. He also knows what "cutting payroll" means.

"Fred, these boys'n'girls have worked their hearts out for you."

"I know, but I still gotta shit-can about two-thirds of the software developers and all of the website managers. The smart ones have stock, and they'll benefit from the IPO, eventually, maybe. I mean, some of them won't even *need* jobs. My secretary and other support staff will quit on their own, find other jobs here in Beantown, to avoid having to move to Herndon, Virginia. They'll assume it's like someplace out of *Deliverance,* with a banjo-pickin' albino on every front porch."

Tom feels sad for a moment, then grateful he had not spent enough time in Boston to get attached to many of his colleagues. He runs through the travel schedule in his head, to make sure he will be out of town when the blood starts soaking his office floor.

"You'll like the *good* news better," Fred goes on after another long swallow. "I'm still refusing to sell WebSurfer to UOL, but Culver personally is buying $10 million in 'early stage' shares. Franny Schwartz is dying to find some way to leak this little bit of news to the Street without leaving her fingerprints all over it."

"How much . . . ?" Tom looks dazed.

"They're gonna revise the valuation study to take UOL and all your telco deals into account. Jamie already has recruited a special-assignment team of the sharpest paralegals from all the different offices of his firm to work on the S-1 – the Registration Statement."

Tom grins.

"You remember, the document we have to file with the SEC in DeeCee before we can sell stock to the public. We gotta describe every possible way we could crash and burn, but Jamie's firm seems to be going out of its way not to consider any of our little cash-flow problems to constitute 'reportable conditions.'"

Tom is still grinning.

"Never mind. The bottom line is that we should be able to pull off the IPO in Q1 of '01."

More grinning.

"Before the first of April, next year. And it gets even better." Fred hesitates. An uncomfortable expression seems to contradict his words. "I convinced the Board of Directors to approve relocation packages for you and me, Bro. The company will loan us money to buy 'suitable executive homes,' so we can move right in when we get down there. Jamie's firm also transferred some kind of corporate law specialist out here from the Coast and she's already supervising the purchases."

Tom understands. His grin mixes with an unbelieving look.

"You mean, Bro, we don't get to *live together* any more?"

Fred laughs so hard, he has to put his black-and-tan on the cracked kitchen counter to avoid dropping it.

"Almost forgot! We're guests of honor at UOL's New Year's Eve party tomorrow night at the Ritz Carlton in Tysons Corner, Virginia. I ordered you a tux. It's in the wardrobe in your room. Classic black, all the way, totally sharp."

Fred never lacked beer money but he remembered that Tom had to work hard for his. When they were in school, he tended bar at Salk Institute receptions up in La Jolla and trade association meetings at the Hotel Del, down in Coronado. The second time he ever laid eyes on Tom, Fred was getting pleasantly potted at a heart surgeon's event, a command performance for his visiting father. He watched Tom flirt shamelessly with the older women and the less-attractive young ones, always insisting on topping off their drinks "on the house," as if he were doing them a clandestine favor. He decided on the spot to recruit Tom into the Phi Delts.

"Hope you remember from your bartending days how to tie a real bow tie. Oh, and I told 'em to sew the pants zipper closed, so don't even think about doin' any real celebratin'."

"Thanks for the vote of confidence, Bro."

"What I really can't wait to see," Fred gasps, "is the look on Culver's face when he finds out about our relo-package and the loans!"

"Why does that creep have to know anything about it?" Tom asks, still reluctant to join in the laughter.

"Because," Fred replies, between convulsions, "he's – joining – our – Board of – Directors!"

Tom's jaw drops. The look on Tom's face, like he'd just been whacked with a shovel, makes Fred tee-hee even harder.

"Freddy, where did you say you keep that stash?"

Fred opens the ugly ceramic cookie jar, shaped like a pink pig in a yellow apron holding a pot, that adorns the kitchen counter. He stuffs his arm inside it and produces a tightly rolled-up baggy containing a small amount of contraband.

"Sorry, Bro. It's gotten a little stale."

Reboot

TOM AND FRED SPENT AN ENTIRE EVENING trying to giggle away their fears and excitement about the WebSurfer news. Somehow, the "good" news was more nerve-racking than the bad. By the wee hours of the morning, they managed to munch up every chocolate chip cookie in their corner of Cambridge.

Even with his sides still splitting and his gut heavy with sugar the next morning, Tom laughs out loud when a Dulles Flyer taxi drops them off at UOL's post-modernistic headquarters building in Herndon, Virginia, just three confusing turns and a quarter mile off the Dulles Toll Road.

"This is really fucked up, Dude – or is it just me?" Tom says between guffaws, pointing up at the glass pyramid. Its alternating black-and-gold window panes shifted their color, depending upon the angle of sight. The panes were like the "1s" and "0s" at the essence of binary computer code, switching on and off in some presumably intelligent fashion. The entire structure was inverted, with the narrowest point of the pyramid seemingly buried thirty feet into the ground, so each successive story of the building angled up and out in all directions beyond the building's foundation.

"Welcome to the Perverted Pyramid, Tomcat!" Fred drapes the suit bag containing his tux over the handle extending from his rolly suitcase, then raises his arms toward the bizarre structure. "We're gonna be spending a lot of time here."

Inside, the set-up was self-consciously Information Age. A small reception desk sat at the end of a walkway that soared over some sort of cafeteria – a wine bar, perhaps? – nestled in the upside-down crown of the pyramid.

"You have an appointment with Mike?" The pretty receptionist with a punkish haircut interrupts Tom's gawkfest. Her casual manner suggests that everybody at UOL called their CEO by his first name. Another young woman collects them from the reception area and marches them to a stark, windowless room.

Their voice mail traffic is blissfully light the morning of New Year's Eve, so Fred and Tom spend most of the long wait in Culver's holding pen just looking at each other. Tom's grin bespeaks such a refreshing combination of innocence and confidence that Fred can't help breaking into a Cheshire Cat smile of his own.

Culver eventually bursts in. Tom and Fred reflexively jump to their feet.

"Dude!" Culver shouts, too clipped to sound remotely authentic. Obviously, Teenage Mutant Ninja Turtle is not his first or second language. He pumps Fred's hand enthusiastically.

"And the *sub-dude*!" Culver nods Tom's direction without offering a handshake. "Got somebody I want you boys to meet, just transferred out here from the Coast to Kohler & Kray's Northern Virginia office to help with the corporate work."

A leggy woman with pretty gray eyes, shoulder-length strawberry blonde hair and a tailored business suit strides into the conference room. Tom's eyes widen and his mouth flies open. He recognizes Gwen Stephens instantly, even with her clothes on.

She stops on a dime, just inside the room. Stephens pretends not to notice Tom as she explains, "Jamie Bass needs help getting WebSurfer ready for the IPO."

Fred cocks his head in confusion. It dawns on him that Stephens is *his* new lawyer, not Culver's.

"As I'm sure you've heard, Kohler & Kray and my firm, Jacobs & Johns, are merging, effective tomorrow. Jamie sent a firm-wide e-mail and one of the partners in San Diego thought I might be a good fit, even if I *did* go to the University of Chicago instead of the University of San Diego."

"Right," Fred cuts in, obviously pleased with what he sees. "Jamie did mention it to me a while back."

"I figured it wouldn't hurt to see how the other Coast lives, so I'm transferring to the Tysons Corner office, if that's acceptable to you, Mr. Hanson."

"Fred. Call me Fred. Please."

"My office is adjacent to the Ritz. I'll need to get some things settled there and change clothes for UOL's big party tonight – so, if you'll excuse me – "

"Right. Right. See you in a jiff."

Tom is in medically-certifiable shock. Fred has to nudge him with his elbow to generate a proper but purely mechanical handshake on Stephens' way out. She gives Tom's fingers a hard, quick squeeze.

"I need to borrow you for a minute, Fred," Culver says. He looks directly into Tom's eyes for the first time. Culver's irises are a piercing, ice blue that almost seems alien to Tom.

"Right," Fred replies, then turns to Tom.

"Gotta lay off those chocolate chips, Bro, you're lookin' downright green!" He squeezes Tom's shoulders and darts out.

Forethought

AS HE WAITED FOR CULVER AND FRED to finish their business, Tom put his head on the conference table and got lost in old memories. They weren't *old*, really, but they seemed awfully *distant*.

Tom thought about his first surfing lesson, just one week shy of his fifteenth birthday. For two years, Tom collected every surfing magazine he could lay his hands on. To his parents' dismay, he spent hours in front of their only television, watching the same two surfing videos, shifting his hands and feet to match the action, bending backwards and forwards at the waist, as if the living room floor were tilting and sliding in an earthquake clear off the Richter scale, beating down a patch of lime green shag carpet the exact, curving dimensions of a longboard.

It was no surprise when, the day he started freshman year at USD, Tom fell in love with Pacific Beach. The weather was the same but the social climate in "PeeBee" – he learned from the locals to abbreviate everything that consisted of two words – was directly opposite of San Pedro.

In his Longshoreman-dominated hometown, just up the Southern California coast, he was a mediocre student who did his homework faithfully, even after his mother died.

"Nature takes its course," she told him, halfway through his junior year, when her cancer was clearly getting the best of her. Tom buried his grief in his after-school jobs. All of his earnings went to Redondo Beach for new surfing equipment and lessons from a demanding pro.

Tom took to college life in San Diego like the proverbial wax to a surfboard. Within twenty-four hours after his grief-obsessed father dropped him off at his freshman dormitory, Tom's life consisted entirely of surf'n'sex'n'suds'n'sex'n'smokes'n'sex. Spring

Break was something that school interrupted, not the other way around.

His miraculous graduation with a degree in English occasioned no change in his attitudes or his lifestyle. He recalled a notion from one of his English classes, something about man's strange compulsion to be as carefree as a dog. Tom lived a dog's life, but he didn't see anything strange about it, especially when his buds addressed him as "Dog."

THEN GWEN CAME ALONG. She invited Tom once to her apartment, a loft in downtown San Diego's re-developing Gaslamp Quarter. An hour after their eighth (Gwen mistook it for their ninth) howling marathon, they got caught. Ike Jacobs, one of the name partners and Gwen's official mentor in her law firm, spied the pair having brunch in a tapas bar around the corner.

"Must not be much excitement in the office today," Jacobs said, approaching the tall café table where Gwen sat hip-to-hip with Tom.

"Mr. Jacobs!" Gwen greeted him, nervously hopping her stool three inches away from Tom's. The metal feet made an embarrassing clatter on the tile floor. Jacobs stood by the table silently for a full minute, until Gwen decided she had no choice but to introduce Tom.

"Tom surfs," she blurted, as if that explained everything. She hadn't bothered to learn much else about him, even as he learned a great deal about her. Jacobs expressed so much interest in Tom's surfing that he neglected to ask where or if he was employed.

"You're coming to the house tonight for the firm's luau, aren't you?" Jacobs asked them both.

"Wouldn't miss it for anything!" Gwen lied convincingly. She forgot entirely about Jacobs' big social event. It was intended as a treat for the associates, but it would inevitably turn into just another round in the increasingly brutal competition for partnership in the firm.

"Why don't you come along, too, Tom?" Jacobs left no doubt that he expected a yes. Completely misreading Gwen's face, Tom accepted.

Twenty minutes later, she had him back in her loft where, under the erotic influence of sangria and garlic and a steaming hot shower, she forgave him, loudly. He toweled her off in a gentle, respectful way. She wanted to let herself think it could always be like this, but her brain stomped the notion out of her heart.

MARY BLY STOOD at the Jacobs' front door. The firm's efficient office manager was helping the hostess bestow rings of colorful papier maché flowers on each arriving guest.

"And here's a lady in need of a lei," Bly offered Gwen with a mile-wide grin. Then she jerked it back, winked at Tom. "Ahhh . . . . Too late, I think!"

Every head in the Jacobs' spacious living room turned to check out the striking and completely unexpected couple. The stares made Gwen so self-conscious, she feared blushing.

"Haven't I seen you on television?" a second-year female associate gushed as she shook Tom's hand vigorously.

"You'd have to wake up pretty early in the morning to catch me."

"I don't doubt that for a second!" She smirked at Gwen, unafraid of her infamous, gun-metal gray eyes. "I was wondering how we landed the Zoo as a client."

"Excuse me?" Tom and Gwen asked in unison.

"Jacobs and Johns is defending that mauling case. What's the animal's name? Matawa?" The associate thought they were playing dumb.

"Makata," Tom corrected her.

"You did a fantastic job of dodging all the usual liability pitfalls. Who prepped you for the TV interviews?"

Tom gave her a blank look.

"I mean, who did your media training? I bet it was good old Gwen. She always brags about how she keeps naïve, young clients from melting down under the klieg lights and giving away the farm."

Tom and Gwen regarded at each other nervously. The surprise professional connection made Gwen's stomach cramp. Suddenly, her own personal himbo melted into a messy puddle on

Ike Jacobs' living room floor. The lawyer summarily issued herself a cease-and-desist order on sex with Tom.

TOM HEARD NOTHING from Gwen the following week. He picked up the phone and dialed her office number twice each day, but reluctantly hung up each time he got dumped into her voicemail. He could not figure out where things went wrong, but he missed seeing her. He missed the sex but, as much as he hated to admit it, he missed the sound of her voice even more. It wasn't just the coital commentary. Her confident and ambitious pillow talk intrigued him. This woman had a plan! In the circuit he traveled in, fore*play* was easily had; fore*thought* was novel, even thrilling.

Bonus Time

THE RITZ CARLTON at Tysons Corner, Virginia, hosted some awesome parties during the first Tech Boom of the Twenty-first Century, but UOL's Real New Millennium bash was the most opulent, the most crazed and the most expensive. Culver was a millennialist in the truest sense, it seemed. He was spending money like there was no tomorrow. It impressed Fred deeply that Culver knew the millennium started, strictly speaking, January 1, 2001, not a year earlier. The media insisted on making a big deal out of the change from 1999 to 2000, conveniently ignoring the indisputable fact that Christ was born in the year 1 A.D., not the year 0. Fred got tired of arguing with people about it halfway through 1999, but he gave Culver got a lot of points for doing it right.

And did he ever do it right! The evening kicked off with a private champagne reception in a top-floor suite with a jaw-dropping view of construction cranes stretching the entire dozen miles into Washington.

Technically, Tom was not invited to the VIP room. Fred was thoroughly accustomed to Culver's head games by then, so he didn't say anything until he and Tom stepped off the elevator on their way in.

"If anybody asks, you're my date," Fred says cocking one eyebrow at Tom.

"Just so you know, I don't put out on the first date," Tom answers, trying to shake off Culver's slight.

"Like hell you don't," Fred replies, flicking a speck of lint off the unnecessarily-padded shoulder of Tom's tuxedo.

"Promise you'll be gentle." Tom bats his eyes as if they are full of sand.

The two of them enter the suite howling with laughter. When they see that the crowd inside is a little older than Fred expected, they straighten up. Pepper-haired bankers, venture capitalists and politicians, mostly from Virginia's congressional delegation and the state government down in Richmond, mingle in hushed tones, as if they were in a Victorian-era gentlemen's club. The few women in attendance are there to show off their glittering gowns, not to conduct business.

Simon Keith grabs Fred and Tom by the shoulders and trots them around with lightening speed. He wants to make certain none of the honored guests mistake his golden boys for the hired help.

The wait staff, young guys with the jawlines and trim waists of *GQ* Magazine models, cruise the room. They carry silver trays laden with bubbling champagne flutes, bite-size Maryland crab cakes and bruschetta pasted with caviar and topped with little red things.

Keith looks like he was born in a tuxedo. His ruddy face glows so bright that light seemed to reflect off his lapels. Tom, with his hair cut so short, looks like a Ken Doll.

There is no need for Tom to pace his champagne consumption. He repeats the sound-bite version of his WebSurfer pitch so many times to so many people in so few minutes, he barely manages two quick sips before a formal procession to the main party begins. To Tom, it looks a bit like a conga line. He and Fred are plugged into their assigned places toward the end of the pecking order.

Culver leads the pack into the hotel's grand ballroom. None of them could be mistaken for ordinary guests, but Culver's clones rise to the most exalted level. Each wears a silk pocket square with a strong gold tint shining from his chest like the Congressional Medal of Honor, tucked in by the big guy himself. Most of the 300 young, expensively dressed and boisterous "ordinary" guests are already half in the bag, but there is no doubt who will get sucked up to at this party, and in what priority.

Culver mounts a long stage lined with live, potted palm trees. Fred chuckles when UOL's trademark-infringing logo, the hunky surfer on the notebook computer, gets projected behind Culver onto a screen bigger than the billboard at eVillage.

"This is our year!" he booms. No one in the audience dares do less than cheer and shout and clap and whistle.

Culver pulls a shovel with a golden blade out from behind one of the palms and thrusts it skyward with both hands.

"Who will help me bury AOL?" Guests are blinded as Culver shines the glittering blade at them.

More hooting and screaming.

In a far corner of the ballroom, Billy Shippe joins in the commotion, whistling with his fingers in his mouth, as if he were in some strip club in Vegas. Shippe looks respectable in a tuxedo, even with his hair slicked back more tightly than normal. Keith is in the vicinity, finishing a chat with a U.S. Senator. He catches Shippe's eye and motions his head surreptitiously toward a door in the back that stands slightly ajar. They slip unnoticed into a dimly-lit service closet, a few seconds apart.

"Your bonus for this year's eVillage work is already in the account," Keith informs Shippe.

"Yeah, I saw it. Very generous. You must be glad you bought that place."

"Without you, it would be a lot less exciting, not to mention less remunerative," Keith chooses his words carefully. He always assumed Shippe's wire was on whenever his clothes were on. He backs into the door and shoves it closed.

"I have to admit, the bait I get from your old agency friend makes it like shootin' fish in a rain barrel."

"Our former station chief in Medellín learned long ago how to put bad things to good use," Keith speaks warily.

"Enough with the shop talk, already. Are you ready for *your* bonus?" Shippe drops to one knee, then the other.

Keith raises his cummerbund and lowers his zipper.

"You bet."

CULVER *LOVES* TO HEAR HIMSELF TALK. He rages for almost an hour. The guests drain their glasses, but no one dares to go for a refill. Tom struggles to stifle a yawn just before Culver announces the WebSurfer deal.

"And last but not least –" Culver raises his voice. It was the third time he said it, so a few desperate drunks take two steps toward the nearest bartender.

"And certainly *not* the least," Culver emphasizes, "I am excited to announce a brand-new strategic partnership with WebSurferUSA.com!"

"Who?" someone near Tom mumbles into a wine glass so empty, it had gone dry.

The clones burst into athletic applause, which spreads in a wave across the ballroom. All that is missing, Tom thinks, is for them to get on their knees and chant "we're not worthy!" like the Phi Delts on the veeball court back in PeeBee.

"WebSurfer will put us squarely ahead in the mobile web space, and AOL will *never* catch us. WebSurfer's innovative, Internet-friendly addressing system will open a whole new range of B2C, B2B and B2G revenue opportunities. We will wipe AOL off the web!"

The Web-heads in the room understand all the "business-to-whatever" acronyms and are genuinely enthusiastic. Everybody else wants Culver to shut up so they can get a drink. They had serious schmoozing to do before the midnight countdown, and many planned a nightcap at eVillage to show off in front of those not invited to UOL's gala.

"Everybody please join me in raising a glass to my new best friend, Fred Hanson, WebSurfer's inventor, founder and CEO!"

A stage light darts around the ballroom like Tinker Bell before it finally lands on Fred's face and blinds him. All the guests raise their empty glasses in unison.

"Hang ten, Dude!" Culver crouches next to the microphone stand. He tries to fake a surfboard stance, but he just looks constipated.

When half the crowd makes a beeline toward Fred and swallows him, Tom considers himself free to prowl the ballroom. His sugar high has worn off and he is starved.

Culver hired the guys he called "Keith's glamour boys" for the VIP reception but, for the main event, he convinced several downtown Washington restaurants to serve up bites of their priciest dishes. In keeping with the UOL logo, each restaurant booth was supposed to look like a tiki hut.

A huge ice sculpture sits in the center of the ballroom. When Tom discovers it, he does not know whether to laugh or cry. It is a perfect replica of a longboard. The tail merges into a curling wave of ice, but the nose projects precariously over a little rubber swimming pool, the kind people use for babies. A *chaise longue*, borrowed from the hotel spa, sits just beyond the baby pool.

The ice sculpture survived Culver's hot-air pep talk, but it is melting fast. The runoff collects in the center of the board and drops a steady, pencil-thin trickle into the baby pool.

A burly man and his entourage push Tom out of the way. He sits on the chaise and drops the back of the chair from upright to flat. On the count of three, he flops his head all the way back. A red glob sluices down the center of the board and plops into the man's mouth. He jumps up. People cheer.

"*Oh, Stoli shots!*" one of the women, a devoted fan of Stolichnaya Russian vodka, exclaims. She reclines on the chaise, drops back and, on the count of three, catches the flying vodka Jello smack in the middle of her cleavage. She gets up, squeals and runs from the ballroom the instant the glob falls inside the front of her gown.

Culver drags Fred over next. The two of them make a big show of congratulating each other as they shake ice water out of their hair.

"Oh, great! TeeJay in a tux!" Tom thinks ruefully. He would give anything to be back at the O&W, ringing in the new millennium with his old buds instead of enduring one more minute of this ego orgy in the Ritz Carlton Tysons Corner.

Tom heaves a deep sigh. Then he notices that wineries from the world over are offering generous tastes of their best vintages. He discovers a sophisticated-looking blonde at one of the booths and starts chatting her up.

"So, tell me, Babe, just where would I find this 'Valley of the Moon'?" he asks, reading the sign over her head.

"I know one moon you won't find here." She waves the sizable rock on her wedding ring at him but does not seem to mind the attention. Tom speed-savors three good refills of a sturdy, flavorful, $120-a-bottle cabernet.

Culver jumps back up on the platform just before midnight to officiate over the countdown.

"Ten, eight, nine –" there is no doubt he has already overdone the Stoli shots. Some guests place bets on what would drop first, Culver or the ball in Times Square.

"Happy New Year!"

A Beach Boys tribute band hurriedly plays the first few bars of "Auld Lang Syne," then shoots jarringly into "Surfin' USA." Couples drink up, kiss and race toward the dance floor. A couple standing just inches from Tom go at it with such gusto, grinding hips, swallowing tongue, it gives him a peculiar feeling. Is he embarrassed? Jealous? He is by that point stuffed to the gills with roast lamb and crabmeat, so how can he possibly feel so – so – *empty*?

Feeling alone and more than a little dizzy in a ballroom crammed with people, Tom starts fishing through his pockets for his hotel card key and struggles to remember his room number. During his whirlwind on the road, when he often stayed in three or four different hotels in the course of a week, he tested himself for immediate recall of the room number, sort of a substitute Breathalyzer. He adopted several different mnemonic devices to avoid shoving the key to Room 386 into the door to Room 683. He was surprised at how often his key opened the wrong room, but not nearly as surprised as the people he interrupted, men with women, men with men, women with women, and women with electronics who thought their most fervent prayers had just been answered. More than once, he stood in line at a reception desk, sweat dripping into fancy hotel carpeting after an hour of foreplay-substitute on a treadmill, awaiting his chance to convince a harried desk clerk to look up his correct room number. If he isn't registered in Room 2002 tonight, Tom figures, at least this time he has some ID on him.

THE TWENTIETH FLOOR LOBBY, its mahogany sideboard and a large vase stuffed with fresh flowers do nothing to jog Tom's memory when he steps off the elevator. Even this short ascension makes his ears pop. He crams his pinky fingers into his ears and jiggles them as he follows the room number arrows around a corner.

Tom still has his fingers in his ears, as if he is impersonating a moose, when he nearly crashes into Gwen Stephens in the hallway, just outside Room 2002.

"Sorry, Babe – I – I thought this was *my* room."

"Of course it is." Gwen keeps her hands out of sight. Her bounteous breasts fill a clingy, black gown without distracting attention from her wide-open back and slenderized hips that rekindle ecstatic memories of gyrations past.

"How . . . did . . . you . . . know?" Tom speaks slowly, to avoid stuttering.

"I booked it for you myself. California king, if I remember correctly. Not just a bed, but a playground."

Tom has no idea what to say.

"Hold these," she instructs, passing Tom two crystal champagne flutes and a bottle of Dom Perignon that is dripping ice water into the carpeting. She pulls a plastic card from a black clutch purse and slips it into the lock. Tom's eyes pop wide open as Gwen backs into the door and props it open slightly.

"You're getting fucked, you know that?" Tom recognizes Gwen's deeply serious, all-business voice.

"I . . . am?" Tom's mouth stands agape.

"By your old surfing buddy, I mean. He's planning to leave you out of the stock options. And wait 'til you hear the rest of the dirt!"

"Huh?" Tom's head is swimming the English Channel.

"Come in. We're overdue for some *private conversation*." She grabs Tom's cummerbund and pulls him toward her and through the doorway.

"But first things first." She has a list and, by God, she's sticking to it.

LOCKDOWN

"A living dog is better than a dead lion."

-- Ecclesiastes 9:4

Mobile Space

GWEN STEPHENS, the newest addition to the WebSurfer legal team, supposedly worked in her firm's expensive, spanking-new offices in the core of the Tysons Corner tangle that Fred hated so much. She spent her billable time and most of her waking hours, however, near Dulles Airport, inside the Perverted Pyramid.

"Never met a bean-counter yet who could see the light of day," she remarked after persuading Fred to evict WebSurfer's cadaverously white-skinned internal auditor from the small but well lit office next to his own. "She'll be less likely to get sunburned in that cubicle down on the second floor."

Gwen would do what it took – *whatever* it took – to make certain the golden boys of WebSurfer got *exactly* what was coming to them and that she got *exactly* what was coming to her. She knew the importance of positioning, and there she was, a flimsy, non-soundproof wall away from everything going on behind Fred's closed office door.

The legal community was still oohhing and ahhing over the transcontinental and supposedly transcendent merger of the two old-line firms, Jacobs & Johns and Kohler & Kray. Everyone thought Gwen's job was to prove "Bigger *is* Better," but her operative motto in this case was "Knowledge is Power." If her colleagues back in San Diego got wind of what she knew about J&J's financial condition, their résumés would swamp every legal headhunter in Southern California.

Just one month earlier, on the first Friday in December, 2000, Ike Jacobs, the name partner who all but adopted her when she first came to the firm as a summer associate in the early Nineties, walked into her office in downtown San Diego and shut the door. Jacobs felt morally obliged to let her in on an explosive secret. J&J was broke, flat busted, or certainly would be if a handful of the firm's biggest rain-makers followed through on their repeated threats to jump ship. Partnership would win her nothing but a proportional share of the firm's debt in bankruptcy.

"There is one *ray* of hope, if you'll pardon a little word-play," Jacobs told Gwen that sunny December day.

She waited stoically for Jacobs to explain.

"Kohler and Kray – and now, accordingly, our firm – is heavily invested in a promising new Internet company, one of those – what do you call 'em? – dotcoms."

Gwen saw mischief ignite in Jacobs' clear, expressive eyes.

"This little company plans to go public soon. Our firm can sell the stock for a tidy sum. The dissenting partners aren't likely to abandon us until they know how this investment turns out."

Gwen pursed her lips.

"One reason for the exalted expectations about the stock is that one of those Internet service providers – it's called Universe Online – looks awfully interested in buying our little dotcom. Don't call your stock broker, but UOL will announce a new 'partnering arrangement' with WebSurfer sometime before this year is out. It plans to add some WebSurfer features to their basic consumer Internet service early in 2001, sort of a syndication arrangement. UOL may bid up the stock price at the public offering, then pay us a premium for enough additional shares to acquire control of the company."

UOL's TV ads were cheesy as all hell, in Gwen's thirty-year old professional woman's sophisticated opinion, but she had to admit their hunky surfer dude logo caught her eye. It made her think about her short-lived fling with Tom Rey – could it possibly have been only eight months ago? – but she would swear under oath that she chose UOL to replace AOL in her Gaslamp Quarter condo only because she got pissed off every time AOL's little Gumby guy screamed "You've got mail!" when all he really meant was, "You can get it enlarged!"

"You're not male!" she often shouted back in frustration. In all those months, no male came close to ringing her chimes the way Tom did. She scrolled down to his phone number in her cell phone twice in the Fall of 2000, but she could never bring herself to hit the green button.

Gwen's day-dreamy look faded quickly to impatience.

"And what, you may ask, has this to do with the price of chai in La Jolla?" The flash in Jacobs' eyes made it clear he was teasing her now. He reached into his custom-tailored, dark blue, pin-striped business suit and pulled out a magazine clipping, folded perfectly into thirds.

"It just so happens that I was standing in Mary Bly's office when this month's issue of *Wired* Magazine came in the mail. I had no idea Mary could squeal like that." Jacobs handed over two glossy pages.

Gwen wondered if the prospect of riding yet another law firm into bankruptcy had pushed her old mentor over the edge. Then she spied the color photo of Tom Rey next to a handsome but obviously bedraggled young man – Fred Hanson, the cut-line said – each of them in coat and tie, trying to look confidently casual. The backdrop was un-credited, but Washington insiders recognized the well-appointed library in Simon Keith's Georgetown townhouse. The headline read, *WebSurfer's Hanson and Rey: New Kings of the Internet Lay Claim to the Mobile Web Space*.

Unlike Mary Bly, Gwen did not squeal. Instead, she made a big noise sucking in her breath, a sort of backward whistle. Stranger things were known to happen in the world, but none came to mind at that moment.

"Do you know this Hanson fellow?" Jacobs asked hopefully, pointing with the rear tip of his $700 Mont Blanc fountain pen.

Gwen shook her head.

"But you *did* know this guy, Tom Rey?"

"Yes," she deadpanned. *"Biblically."*

Jacobs blanched at the confession, then got straight to the point.

"The firm wants to make absolutely certain both the IPO and the merger go forward, in that order, and sooner rather than later. I'm sure the Executive Committee would be *deeply* grateful for any assistance you could provide in that regard."

Jacobs got up and left the rest to his protégé's fertile imagination.

Gwen studied the article and stared at the photo incredulously. She did not much like Tom's shorter haircut, but the lawyer focused on more pertinent information. She ran a yellow highlighter over the three major points she figured Tom had in his favor – "not yet 25," "a major shareholder in WebSurfer" and "unmarried."

The firm advanced their star associate enough cash to prepare her precious Alfa Romeo for the cross-country drive and rented her a small, sparsely-furnished apartment in a month-to-month complex in Tysons Corner. The low-rise catered to the steady stream of defense contractors peddling weapons at the nearby Pentagon.

Gwen did some of her best thinking on road trips. The cross-country drive to Washington would be the biggest and longest in her life. With almost 3,000 miles on interstate highways and no other plans or obligations at Christmas, she had plenty of time to figure all the angles. One – and only one – of the conceivable scenarios looked like a sure thing and it did not involve reliance on the eventual gratitude of the firm's compensation committee.

Gwen carefully restrained the Alfa to the posted speed limits, even while she slogged across the wide-open Great Plains. Her mind was the only thing racing, but it was firmly pointed in the direction of WebSurfer – and Tom Rey.

Hot Swaps

GWEN WAS NOT THE ONLY SURPRISE Tom got in 2001. The year started with such a rapid-fire series of head-spinning events that the smooth-talking surfer-dude-cum-PR-man found himself utterly speechless. First, on New Millennium's Eve, Mike Culver dropped the bomb about UOL's new "partnering arrangement" with WebSurfer. Fred was eaten alive by an adoring throng of techno-zombies. The ball dropped in Times Square. Then Gwen Stephens dragged Tom into his hotel room and kept him pumping like a Texas oil well clear into the middle of the afternoon on New Year's Day.

With daylight filling his room at the Ritz Carlton in Tysons Corner, Tom awakens in time to see Gwen slipping back into her black gown and tip-toeing out into the hallway. He is late for his 4:15 return flight to Boston. He speed-showers, collects pieces of his tux from various corners of the room and wads them into his duffel bag. Blue jeans, a light sweater over a T-shirt and a black leather bomber jacket will have to do, even though the flight attendants in First always seemed more attentive when he wore a business suit. He assumes the blinking light on the hotel room phone is a message from Fred. UOL's stretch limo is under the grand porte-cochere entrance on the Ritz's "Arrivals Level" and will depart for Dulles without him. Tom knows taxis await nearby.

As usual, the aircraft door slams shut the moment Tom steps on board. Fred is dozing in the first row, his head crooked at an uncomfortable angle. Tom gently stuffs a pillow under Fred's ear, then sits across the aisle in the near-empty front cabin.

Tom is irritated to learn that his $800 ticket to Boston does not include so much as a cold snack. The flight attendant, being an old pro, scrounges up enough cashews and plies him with enough Jack Daniel's to take the edge off his appetite and his attitude, but Tom's body is missing a couple million calories after his strenuous night with Gwen Stephens.

Fred jolts to consciousness the instant cross-winds off Boston Harbor smack the plane onto the runway at Logan. He blinks at Tom.

"Where'd *you* come from, Bro?" He was sure Tom missed the flight.

"Kal-ee-for-knee-ah," Tom imitates Schwartzenegger.

"No, I mean –" Fred fears embarrassing himself. He studies Tom's face and recognizes a certain old, familiar look.

"You *dog* – you got *laid*, didn't you?"

"Gave you all the play-by-play in the car on the way to Dulles, don't you remember, Bro?"

"Huh? Oh, yeah, right." The flight attendant proffers Fred's overcoat and Tom's jacket. "So, did you – "

"Yeah, that was one *awesome* party. I had a rockin' time. Did you?"

"Did I . . . ?" Fred is having trouble keeping up with the conversation and Tom's brisk pace on the jet bridge. His own late-night antics, including unsavory events Billy Shippe organized after the Stoli shots, start coming back to him. Fred decides he'd better not ask questions lest he feel compelled to answer some. He goes straight to the Perverted Pyramid to check out his new corner office.

MIKE CULVER AND HIS CLONES never invited anyone to UOL's "corporate headquarters." AOL's rival preferred to call its peculiar, inverted glass pyramid on a tiny patch of Virginia greenery near Dulles International Airport a "campus." It was supposed to be a freewheeling environment, like Stanford and MIT and other paragons of academe, where deep and creative thought could flourish, run barefoot with reckless abandon for a while, then be sold into commercial Internet slavery for some quick cash.

Culver called all of his employees "visiting scholars," but anybody who made the mistake of thinking too long or too hard without making UOL a whole lot of money got expelled before mid-term. To make room "on campus" for the new whiz kids from

WebSurfer, Culver summarily fired the clone who was supposed to figure out a way to reverse-engineer WebSurfer's patented geographic reference system and thereby make it unnecessary to cut a deal with Fred Hanson. The clone laid all the blame on his assigned product development team, so Culver axed the whole bunch.

Culver made it a point to shit-can one of his clones every few weeks and send the poor bastard back to a standard five-foot square cubicle, seven spaces removed from daylight. Clones became clowns overnight at UOL, so all of them realized they were "hot swappable," like the floppy drive on the latest Dell notebook computer.

THE NEWLY UNEMPLOYED TECHNO-BAGGAGE never planned to make local history, but they populated the first-ever Pink Slip Party at eVillage Restaurant and Bar. It was a glum, down-in-the-mouth event until Billy Shippe, eZine's resident comfort geek, corporate spy and purveyor of government-seized contraband, accompanied the more senior guys to the men's room for a quick up-the-nose event. After their respective toots, the two early-thirty-somethings rejoined the sympathetic crowd at the large, rectangular bar. They looked like they didn't have a care in the world, as if their economic distress will excuse the bone-crushing mortgages on their hulking Great Falls McMansions. They still had student loans to pay off!

"There are plenty more tech jobs where those came from!" one of them proclaimed, and there was no more pissing and moaning into their overpriced beers.

Meanwhile, in WebSurfer's new, rent-free space on the seventh floor of the Perverted Pyramid, Fred Hanson and Tom Rey landed in executive chairs still warm from the toned glutes of the previous occupants. A majestic blue spruce stood just outside their outward-slanting office windows. Just days after the move to Virginia, WebSurfer started attracting intense media coverage from the general-interest press, not just Shippe's online *eZine*. The techno-challenged writers at the *Washington Post*, who typically pretended that nothing significant happened in Virginia since Lee surrendered to Grant in 1865, noted the UOL "partnering arrangement" with a lead article in the paper's Sunday business section.

Overnight, *everybody* wanted a piece of Tom Rey and Fred Hanson. Fred took all the attention as long-overdue recognition of his genius. Tom just kept grinning. Both knew WebSurfer would be techno-boom or techno-bust – there could be no outcome in between.

AFTER TOM SUPERVISED the movers at the townhouse in Cambridge, his flight to Dulles landed him back in Virginia just before dusk. Tom understands he and Fred will live at the WhatsIt Suites – the real name and address of which are buried inside one of his bags, or so he hopes – until the "suitable executive homes" promised in their "re-lo" packages could be procured. As he drags a jam-packed suitcase off the baggage carousel, Tom walks smack into Fred, who is standing next to Gwen.

"The multi-talented Miss Stephens graciously offered to give you a ride." Fred jokingly takes a deep bow in her direction.

"So what else is new?" Tom can't help wondering to himself, the memory of their surprise reunion at the Ritz as fresh as the rug burns on his knees. "A . . . ride?" is all he can think to say out loud.

"You know . . . a ride *home*?" Fred smiles broadly, apparently enjoying Tom's confusion and the clueless grin that conceals it from everyone but him. After he grabs Tom's duffel bag, the three walk briskly outside, into the open-air hourly parking lot that runs the length of the terminal.

"Sah-weet! Will you look at that?" Fred sits the bag down next to a gleaming, brand-new, smoke-gray Porsche Boxster S roadster, with its navy blue rag-top open to the clear, wintry sky. Someone parked it face-out in one of the spaces nearest the terminal.

"Whoa! Bro! Is that totally *hot* or *not*?" Fred can barely contain his excitement.

Tom drops his suitcase. He scratches his head slowly, admiring the four-wheeled Viagra parked in front of him.

The scoop headlights, low-slung chassis, rear spoiler and side vents just ahead of the rear wheel wells give the appearance of rapid motion, even while the car is parked. Tom studies the twin bucket seats, their high, sharply arched, headrests and integrated roll-bars and decides they would be suitable for a space mission.

"Yeah, *totally!*" Tom agrees. "But what kind of ho-dad drives around DeeCee in January with the top down?"

"Why don't you climb in and show us?" Fred dangles a set of keys under Tom's nose. "Say hello to your new ride, Ho-Dad!"

It takes Tom a full minute to get a grip on both reality and the keys to the Porsche.

"Gwen went to a dealership on Route 7, near her office, and picked out your new company car for you. Talk about your full-service lawyer!"

"Always anxious to please!" She waves at Tom coyly and starts marching toward a different row in the parking lot.

"She's bringing her own car around. It's a red Alfa," Fred explains unnecessarily. "Just follow her and she'll take you all the way home."

"Frankly," Fred says under his breath, as if he intends to hide his advice from other travelers in the parking lot, "I think when Gwen laid eyes on that car, she saw a dick on wheels and immediately thought of you. Better keep it zipped, Man!"

"You have no idea, Bro," Tom grins at Fred but says nothing. He is glad Fred caught no whiff of how he and Gwen rang in the New Year. Fred probably assumed nothing was going on because she was over-thirty, a lot more sophisticated and a lot more talkative than any "type" in Tom's shamelessly equal-opportunity repertoire.

Gwen pulls her Alfa across Tom's parking space. She is still mourning the removal of her California tags, yet there she is, with royal blue and white Virginia "Internet C@pital" plates that have a large blue half-dot with the letters *"com"* carved into it, and the vanity license number "E-LAW," gunning her engine with the clutch disengaged.

"Gotta go, Bro!" Fred says, diving into a sea of shiny, late-model cars in search of his own equally new and even more expensive fringe benefit, a banana-yellow Mercedes SLK. Fred isn't wild about the color, but it was the only hard-top convertible left on the dealer's lot.

Tom had rarely driven a stick shift. He tries to pull out of the parking space, but stalls the Porsche's muscular-sounding engine twice. Gwen throws her head back, laughs derisively and peels out. She cuts him no slack, even after they veer off the Dulles Access Road at eighty-five miles an hour, then plunge into a maze of residential streets.

NORTHERN VIRGINIA'S WINTER is far less brutal than Boston's, but Tom's ears are starting to freeze as the two roadsters shoot down a long, narrow road, the straightest Tom had seen since he left California. Within a few minutes, Gwen signals a left turn and passes two matching but unfinished stone-and-mortar monoliths that face each other across the entrance to a new development. It is getting dark, but Tom can barely make out two words, "The Preserve," chiseled into an unlit, black marble plate in the center of each wall in tasteful, small gold letters.

Uprooted scrub brush and excavation equipment litter the landscape. He could tell many old-growth pines recently fell victim to the bulldozers parked randomly about. The survivors stand in clumps, marked off by yellow crime scene tape, their lowest branches forty feet in the air.

One quick turn brings them to two enormous buildings that stand side-by-side. Each looks vertically segmented, with a series of triangular pediments across the front. The first is gray stone, three full stories tall, with six dormer windows on the top. The other, in red brick, is a jumble of different styles, with Greek columns, New England lattice-work, a Southern-style cupola and what looked like a widow's walk on one end. Tom wonders if the architect was on crack or suffered from some sort of psychotic disorder. The sight adds to Tom's boundless confusion and catatonic inability to express himself.

Gwen guides Tom into the circular, pressed-concrete driveway in front of the stone structure and parks next to the muddy hole in the center, where capped-off, white PVC pipes stick their heads up, little gopher ice sculptures peeking at the visitors.

Tom climbs out of his new Porsche and clasps his hands over his frozen ears.

"So, what do you think?" Gwen asks loudly.

"Why would anybody want to hide a couple of apartment buildings way out here in the woods?" Tom asks.

Gwen cackles, a "gotcha!" kind of laugh. She stops when Tom turns red, even though it is more from windburn than irritation.

"It's not an *apartment building*, Goofy Foot!" she mocks him with a reference to his characteristic right-foot-forward stance on a surfboard. "It's a house, and better yet, it's *your* house, as soon as you sign the stack of papers I have here in my briefcase!"

She points to the circle of half-frozen mud in front.

"And in no time that will be your breathtakingly fabulous fountain and reflecting pool." She turns back toward the muddy ruts in front of what Tom now recognizes as a formal entrance, with mahogany doors and leaded glass sidelights. "And this fabulous lawn will be so carefully tended by teams of undocumented El Salvadorans that all your guests will just *die* of envy!"

Tom looks up and down the otherwise empty street. It looks like a war zone.

"The developer originally planned to build sixty-five of these. Each sits on three-fifths of an acre, and they're listed for one-and-a-half to just under three million dollars apiece, depending on street appeal and interior design features."

Gwen rattles out more statistics. Tom is too shocked to comprehend any of it.

"What is this costing me?" Tom finally interrupts.

"This one is the model home – I mean, *was* the model home – so it's completely furnished. A bit too much of the Howard Johnson's look, I admit, but we'll deal with that after the IPO. Had the *damnedest* time convincing the developer to let it go, but I guess he must have needed the cash."

"How much?"

"It's an absolute steal at one million nine hundred fifty seven thousand."

Tom turns his head and coughs, as if a doctor has just jabbed an ice-cold finger into his groin in search of a hernia.

"Don't worry. The re-location loan from WebSurfer covers every penny of it," Gwen continues. "The company'll keep a security interest, of course, but it won't really matter. This place will be worth two and half million, easy, by the time the rest of the development is completed in 2006."

"I'm not planning to be anywhere near here in 2006. Besides, the place looks like a Napalm testing range."

"Ah, that's the best part, Tommy!" Gwen adds breathlessly. "Everything on the right side belongs to Steve Case of AOL. Rumor has it that he bought *seven lots* for just *one house* so yours will be one of the few homes adjacent to an established stand of trees."

Tom's nerves begin to shake off some of his shock. He still had not found the occasion to give Gwen his standard speech, the one about not correlating screaming, no-holds-barred, night-and-day sex with anything serious or long-term. Gwen's obvious excitement and pride in this house meant she was formulating plans the two of them had never discussed.

"What on Earth am I gonna do with all this, Babe?" Tom deliberately chooses the word "I" and he hopes she noticed.

Gwen takes Tom's hand and yanks him toward the front door.

"Oh, I'm sure we'll think of *something*." She deliberately uses the word "we" and hopes he noticed. "There are twenty-two furnished rooms, including the home theater with an eight-foot diagonal screen and cup-holders in the armrests – the DTS surround sound is to die for! – and here's the best part – four, count 'em, *four*, California king beds. I suggest we get started before frostbite sets in."

While Gwen's excited fingers fumble with the lock box on the door, Tom sneaks a look over his shoulder at the Porsche.

"Now, *that's* what I call a *ride*!" he almost shouts out loud. "I can't wait to take that baby out and really open her up!"

After Gwen finishes with him, Tom falls asleep poring over the spec sheet for his new wheels.

"Dual overhead cams and 229 foot-pounds of torque. Integrated dry sump lubrication. *Suh-weet.*"

Options

GETTING READY for WebSurfer's Initial Public Offering, Tom found, was not all that different from training for the Summer Longboard Challenge at Tourmaline or working out with Gwen Stephens. Strength, flexibility and, most of all, endurance – that's all there was to it, Tom decided.

By mid-February, 2001, Tom's "part" – even the lawyers spoke of his role in purely theatrical terms – was coming together nicely. Good thing, everyone thought, since it was eighty percent of the "road show" presentation for potential investors. All the buzzwords buzzed off of Tom's tongue at the proper speed. Now, it was simply a matter of getting them all to come out in the right order.

Fred's "founder and CEO" spiel still needed a lot of work. Unlike Tom, Fred had a lot more on his plate than to look cute and sound trustworthy in front of a video camera. He was busy explaining to Culver's guys how to make WebSurfer work optimally, but UOL subscribers still kept running into unexpected glitches. Fred had to work quadruple-time to keep the new mobile Internet features up-and-running on the website.

Tom was not only Fred's best friend, he was also his best coach. He was confident, based on their experience in the California surf, that it would all come together. Fred would get his good, long ride when it really counted. Big-dollar investors in all the major financial centers in America would soon be fighting each other hammer-and-tong for the privilege of investing a hundred million dollars in WebSurfer at the initial offering price.

With Fred planted in front of a computer screen the entire month of February, Tom became the "go to" guy at WebSurfer. With his hair on fire all day, Fred would not suffer fools or foolishness gladly. In stark contrast, the door to Tom's much smaller office was always open. He always had time to listen, stroke his chin and sympathize. Those were three things Tom learned to do exceptionally well. Most of the time, that was all his visitor really needed or wanted.

Overnight, or so it seemed, Fred started to resent Tom, to hate his glib, easy-going manner, his popularity, his good looks – the whole list of traits that convinced Fred to drag Tom into WebSurfer in the first place. Fred deluded himself into thinking he could be just like Tom, if only he didn't have the weight of the world on his shoulders. Besides, Fred decided his old surfing buddy was having way too much fun watching himself in the replays of the video practice sessions, repeating the same pitch line, like a fucking soap opera star, until it had the right "depth" and "conviction."

Fred looked forward to the magic date, March 12, 2001, for a host of reasons. That was the day Sammy Schwartz decided the sun, moon and stars would line up for the WebSurfer IPO. For all his jealousy and resentment of Tom, Fred remained confident that he made the right decision, that Tom would put the IPO over the top, make the shares Fred threw in to lure him off the beach worth a few million bucks. Tom, no doubt, would paddle blissfully back out to sea, out of WebSurfer, out of Fred's way.

Fred's debt to Tom would finally be paid, many times over. Once and for all, there would be no more nightmares about TeeJay, no more sweat dripping over his love handles at three in the morning.

GWEN STEPHENS COACHED TOM for the IPO in her own way. She considered herself on duty around the clock. *Nothing* was going to fuck up WebSurfer's public offering, not for any reason, not in any way. The moment any legal question reared its ugly head, she was at Tom's or Fred's elbow.

The first item on her checklist was to establish her dominance over her colleague, Jamie Bass. He called from New York the day before the S-1 Registration Statement, the single most crucial IPO document, was due to be filed with the Securities and Exchange Commission in Washington.

"I talked it over with Fred and we don't see any possible way around this, Gwen. Arthur Andersen considers the way WebSurfer has accounted for its revenues from the mobile Internet providers to be a 'reportable condition.'" Jamie is firm, authoritative, unequivocal. Fred is proud of him.

"Are you out of your fucking mind?" Gwen shoots back. The pressure is getting to her, too, but it still has not affected her normal office demeanor. "Are you on speaker?"

"Yeah, but my door's closed and Fred's in the South Conference Room, checkin' out the Statue of Liberty." Jamie winks at Fred, who in truth is slumped in the guest chair next to the phone. He holds a finger to his lips to shush Fred.

"Then you listen to me, Pardner. I already went over this with Francine Schwartzman. A lot of people on The Street are getting nervous about this practice of counting revenues as soon as the deal is signed, instead of waiting for the checks to arrive. If we put this crap in the S-1, Schwartzman says, it'll cut the opening price in half. You hear me? *Half.* You really want to fuck your buddy out of $15 million or so, right from the get-go? Not to mention what it would cost our law firm?" Gwen takes a breath and allows the numbers to soak in. "Schwartzman said it might even queer the IPO altogether. You know as well as I do what that means for you and me, pal, whether we like it or not."

Gwen's experience with corporate mergers and acquisitions taught her that nothing was more important than getting the deal done, even if it meant stretching a few facts now and then. It was all in a day's work. Post-deal financial *leverage* would prove far more important than the legal technicalities. This time, there is one hell of a lot more at stake than client money. It could not get more personal for her and for Jamie, whose wife was due to deliver James Foster Bass III at any moment. She would not be going back to her job in

Midtown at HBO any time soon, but the *au pair* had already reported for work and her first quarter's social security was paid in.

"The accounting firm is on the cusp of landing a huge consulting contract with one of the biggest underwriters for our IPO. Francine told these guys to give the bean counters a little career counseling, if you understand what I'm saying. So, I'm telling you they're *not* going to be a problem."

"Gwen, you can't be serious! Do you have any idea what kind of a problem this could create down the road?"

"We'll deal with any problems *down the road* when we all have plenty of money to *fix* the problems, not now, when none of us have a pot to piss in."

The line goes silent for a full minute. Finally, Jamie lets out a big-as-Texas sigh.

"Let the record show that this one's your call, Gwen. There is one logistical problem to deal with, however. Fred will not make it back to DeeCee tonight, so you have to get Tom to sign the S-1."

Fred shoots straight up in the guest chair and opens his mouth to speak. Jamie shushes him again.

"Fred's under the weather. I'm gonna take him over to Number Three –" Jamie refers to Three World Trade Center, also known as the Marriott Hotel – "to buy him some medicine. I'm writing a prescription for single malt as we speak, then I'm gonna put him to bed early. He's gotta be fit for the road show or we're all dead."

This time, it is Gwen's turn to wait and sigh. She knows Jamie is calling her bluff.

"OK," she says at last. "You take care of your boy and I'll take care of mine. Ciao, *Pardner*."

The line goes dead. Fred slumps again in Jamie's guest chair.

"Don't worry," Jamie walks around his desk and grabs Fred's shoulders. "Nobody will ever believe that Tom did this *knowingly*. That's the standard of proof the government would have to meet."

Fred sighs. "I'm ready for that medicine you promised."

"Laphroaig?"

"Yeah, if you're buyin'." Fred shrugs. "Personally, I don't have a pot to piss in."

TOM SIGNED THE S-1 that night when Gwen laid it in front of him. All he had to do was follow the trail of "sign here" sticky tags, just as he did when he closed on the purchase of his McMansion. He did not read a word of either document. All that legal shit gave him headaches.

Tom continued working brutal hours. Between road show rehearsals, he still had to fly around the country on sales calls. New contracts directly with online vendors were necessary to maintain momentum for the IPO and to make sure WebSurfer was not completely dependent on UOL for its revenues.

Gwen knew from her years in a law firm that the best way to succeed was to make herself irreplaceable in any project assigned to her. Tom was needy, so she quickly rendered him utterly dependent upon her.

Tom always looked glad to find Gwen waiting for him when he got off a plane at Dulles, but their around-the-clock relationship disquieted him. First, the merciless way she jerked the stick when she drove his Porsche made him cringe. Another concern cropped up every time he got home and opened his walk-in closet. Whenever he was away, Gwen spent a lot of her time and his money building Tom a whole new wardrobe. Her uncanny ability to pick out *exactly* the right size made him wonder if she went over every inch of him with a tape measure while he was asleep.

Tom could cope with the car and the clothes and the money. He had far more trouble dealing with those cartoon-bubble thoughts about Carly. They included memories of the day he left PeeBee to join up with Fred, sepia-toned in his mind after only a year, and of their ever-so-brief embrace just before Christmas, still as vibrant and confusing as the night he stood there in his apartment and let her go down the stairs alone. Carly pinged his mind in those few seconds between Tom finding the dry spot and losing consciousness, while he clutched a pillow over his head and Gwen continued her half of a one-sided conversation.

Gwen moved in, more or less, at Tom's McMansion. His talent for concentrating on something else during intercourse transferred well from PeeBee to the Preserve. Most of the time, when Gwen said "option," "strike price" and "board vote," he heard "more," "harder" and "faster." He was a hound, for sure, a dog that hears "treat" when his master offers a trip to the "vet." There were occasions, however, when Gwen's lectures about the stock options he needed to claim prior to the IPO pierced his consciousness. He just flipped her over and drove her face into a pile of pillows, so all he could hear was "grff," "emmpf" and "ardbrf."

IN LATE FEBRUARY, a few days before the road show was scheduled to start, Tom wanders through his 11,000 square foot "suitable executive home," cheerfully calling out to Gwen.

"Hey, Babe? Gwen? Where's a lawyer when you need one?" Tom's voice echoes off a double-spiral staircase. The carpeted risers climb the walls, right and left, then join at a well-appointed landing atop his marble entrance foyer.

For February, the weather is exceptionally warm, at least compared to what Tom suffered in Boston all Fall and half the Winter. He can already detect vague hints of Spring in the air. Tom kicks off his shoes and sox before he passes underneath the foyer landing and enters the soaring, three-story high great room that runs the entire back length of the house.

Gwen's name echoes unanswered off the thirty-foot high Palladian windows. Tom ditches his coat and tie on the room's centerpiece, a huge, white Natuzzi leather sofa with a backward-slanted base, and continues, blissfully barefoot, into the 400-square-foot kitchen. Gwen steps inside from the deck. She fastens a fluffy white bathrobe and straightens it demurely over her shapely, bare legs.

She eagerly strips off Tom's suit pants, boxers and starched white shirt. She slips an identical terry-cloth robe over him and ties the belt teasingly.

"I can't believe you've still got this thing!"

"Amazing, isn't it?" Tom blushes.

"No, I mean *this* thing." Gwen jiggles the jade donut hanging from a simple leather string around Tom's pale neck.

"Oh, *that*. My surfing coach gave me this when I was a kid. I keep it for luck, and to keep me from forgetting."

"Forgetting what?"

"My life."

Gwen immediately grabs Tom's hand and leads him to a hot, furiously bubbling Jacuzzi on the far side of the deck. He had no idea the house came with a spa.

"See! It works!" Gwen announces. Her naked breasts disappear into the bubbles, leaving large, round nipples floating on top, like Hershey's Kisses melting in a pot. "Hot stuff!"

Tom is not sure whether she was referring to the water or just ogling him when he doffed the robe. Either way, Gwen is on him immediately.

"You know," she says sternly, the moment she is in place, "you've gotta talk to Fred about those stock options *before* the IPO. That means *tomorrow*, Goofy Foot. Either you've got the *cojones* or you don't. It's as simple as that. *Ipso facto*."

For once, Tom finds no way to concentrate on something else.

"I know, Babe, I know," he mutters, softly and rhythmically several times, until his voice is overcome by the whirlpool jets and Stephens' animal cries. He keeps saying it even after he leans his head back and stares straight up at the evening stars. He doesn't realize that the freakish red brick house next door is occupied, or that its master bedroom window is almost directly above his spa. The moment he comes, it dawns on him that the figure dimly lit in the window above him is a woman, dressed head-to-toe in an ultra-conservative Muslim *burqa*, like something out of the news coverage from Afghanistan he saw on the ever-present CNN at the Perverted Pyramid. The spooky figure peers at him through an eyeslit. She drops the blinds the instant he is depleted.

"Show's over," Tom thinks. "On with the show!"

Cojones

TOM HIT THE SACK ALONE that night.

Gwen kept him in the hot tub until everything, including his fingertips, got wrinkly, then drove to her infrequently-visited apartment in Tysons Corner. She claimed she had a lot of work to do, but in truth she knew Tom would never do the painful but desperately-needed deed until he found time alone to sort it all out in his head, to screw up his courage, to find the *cojones* to confront his old friend.

Lawyer Stephens convinced him it was his due, his rightful share of the mega-fortune WebSurfer was on the verge of generating. The company was about to blast its way into the Internet Pantheon, and nobody doubted Tom's huge contributions as the voice and face of WebSurfer, the guy who cinched all the deals that produced the company's first revenues. Those figures, in turn, were the foundation for the crucial calculation of "forward revenues," the numbers from which Wall Street calculated a dotcom's worth. That figure, divided by the total number of outstanding shares, produced the public offering price per share, the starting gate for any newly-public corporation. Tom understood all that, more or less, and he also had a vague idea how issuance of new stock options can dilute the value of the already-outstanding shares.

As hard as he tugged, Tom could not close that curtain in his mind and shut out all the rights and wrongs of the situation. Fred's initial offer – a generous salary, a cash bonus bigger than a year's pay as a low-level PR manager at the San Diego Zoo and 400,000 of Fred's personal shares in WebSurfer – seemed ridiculously over-generous at the time. In the lightening-quick space of six months, how could it possibly have turned into the "dirty screw," "unconscionable rip-off" or "adhesion contract" that Gwen called it?

≈≈≈≈≈≈≈≈≈≈≈≈

Ever since Gwen voiced herself back into his life, Tom went back and forth between "whoa – get a grip!" to "whoa – wake up and smell the java!" Tom refused to believe Fred was screwing him over until Gwen showed him the corporate minutes from WebSurfer's December Board of Directors meeting, where Fred won the "re-lo" packages for himself and Tom. Gwen proved that Fred conveniently failed to mention the shitload of stock options he got solely in his own name. The "strike price," the amount for which he could purchase the additional shares, was so low that Fred was virtually certain to make a killing.

No doubt about it, Tom would never get a wink of sleep under the looming prospect of confronting Fred, his old bro, his mentor, his bud, with the multi-million dollar betrayal. Had Tom not already put up with a lot of shit from Fred the entire month of February, Gwen's revelation might not have been the last straw. The cutting remarks and pissy looks Fred gave him lately seemed beside the point. Tom understood why Fred was in a panic. February 26, the road show start date, was drawing near. Fred's attitude seemed to worsen, to become insufferably selfish and arrogant, after each closed-door visit from Billy Shippe. WebSurfer's self-appointed official historian came in to interview Fred two or three times a week.

What really kept Tom awake that night, as it had for several nights running, was Fred's wholly-unexpected compulsion to imitate Mike Culver. Fred started to use Culver-words, to embrace Culver's values, to accumulate Culver's favorite types of toys, including obscure sports memorabilia that filled a horse barn at Culver's country estate in Middleburg, Virginia. What shocked Tom most was that Fred and Culver increasingly seemed to share the same twisted notion of what it meant to be "best friends."

AFTER TOSSING AND TURNING for half an hour, Tom stumbles into the huge bathroom in his master suite, passes the unenclosed, faux-marble, orgy-sized shower, with its multiple, individually temperature-controlled jets and European hand wands, and searches all the drawers and cabinets until he figures out where Gwen stowed her economy-sized drum of industrial-strength Melatonin tablets.

She swore they worked wonders for her, that they were life-savers because they shut out all the tribulations of waking life, dropped her through a trap door, right into dreamland. Tom pops one without a chaser. Feeling no immediate effect, he cocks his head, shrugs, then washes another down with a full glass of tap water for good measure.

Within ten minutes, Tom drops into a fitful sleep. Almost immediately, a bad dream overtakes his brain. Actually, it is more of a repressed recollection, the mirror-image of Fred's recurring nightmare.

"THE WEED IS LACED WITH PCP!" Tom's cry echoes down a long hallway, bounces off the landing and rattles around the marble entrance foyer of his grand house at The Preserve. Electric flashes shoot through Tom's brain, like a PowerPoint slide show run amok. At first, all the slides he memorized for the WebSurfer road show presentation mix randomly with images of himself and Fred in TeeJay. There they are, lost under tacky sombreros, "shit-faced," as Fred would say in his New Englandese, receiving anesthetic from *el dentista*, dying to piss it out, along with all the Mexican beer they washed it down with. As if he were having an out-of-body experience, Tom hovers over himself and Fred, shaking his head in disgust, getting that "ack-ack" feeling as he watches their younger selves swill mescal, then smoke the suspect dope.

Tom sees his face land, completely numb, on the cigarette-burned table at *Las Santerías*, the infamous place where a horny sailor or a horny-sailor-for-a-night could get "smoked up and hooked up for one low price."

The look on Tom's flattened face reminds him that he had forgotten they went there to pay for play. He could barely remember his own name by the time Fred got around to asking the owner what else was on the menu and she hauled them, staggering, to a shed in the back.

A plump Mexican girl faced the guys, expressionless, barely dressed in a cotton robe that was thinner than a hospital gown and about as becoming. An oil lamp on a rough-hewn table in the corner threw off a sickly light. The only other object that could pass for furniture was a straw mattress on the floor, covered with a single, yellowed polyester sheet.

"Hunner dollahs. You hurry. Other boys come soon," the troll barked at them, then turned on her calloused barefoot heel and departed.

Tom was wasted, but not wasted enough to feel uninhibited about the proposed arrangement. With his "ack-ack" working overtime, Tom started to follow the old woman out of the shed and leave Fred to his business. The girl stepped in his path and grabbed his hands firmly.

"No time," she said. "*Los dos.*"

Fred did not understand a word of Spanish, but his eyes were open just wide enough to see what was about to happen.

"Jamie did say *any*thing."

"This is wa-a-a-ay not cool," Tom started begging off.

The girl dropped her robe and grabbed Tom's crotch roughly enough to keep him from moving toward the door, then more gently undid his belt and drawstring. She followed his treasure trail to its source, fell to her knees and captured his full attention. Tom's pockets, full of coins and overnight gear, landed with a thud on his bare toes and leather sandals.

Her touch felt strange, gentle and wet, but shock waves soon began coursing through his nervous system. It became impossible to stand. Tom saw Fred's eyes pop wide open as Tom shuddered, his knees buckled and he landed, hard, on the facing end of the mattress. Perspiration gushed off his chin and down his abs, which were exposed when he unbuttoned his shirt and threw the tails out of the girl's way. He pretended to see only the stars rotating around his head and not the sight of Fred's tan lines, distinct in the dim light, cargo shorts around his ankles, moving back and forth. Tom was at the same time embarrassed and relieved to see that Fred had the presence of mind to slip on a condom first.

There was no *mañana* in the girl's attitude. She knew from experience that the guys in the bull pen might get impatient, lose their nerve, pass out or spend the last of their jack on the grass. She dispatched Tom efficiently – for once he was unable to concentrate on anything else – and kept him firmly in her grip for what seemed a lifetime, while the panting, grunting Fred caught up. Tom stared at the grimy ceiling and tried not to pass out. He tried to imagine himself somewhere, anywhere, else.

AS SOON AS THEY FINISHED, Tom and Fred were mortified to look up and find the troll tapping her foot impatiently in the doorway. There would be no basking in the afterglow. She dragged them out the same way she brought them in, but now they were breathless and soaked in sweat. A faint breeze gave them the chills.

They passed the stocky Mexican bartender, who was guiding the other four gringos out to the shed, stumbling into one another. Tom and Fred tried desperately to look casual, to regain some semblance of pride and decency, as they struggled to hoist and refasten their pants.

When they re-entered the bar, all the tables were empty. She held out her hand again.

"Hunner dollahs."

Tom fished through his own pockets this time and counted up the requisite number of tens and twenties. She stuffed the bills into a grubby apron pocket, then turned to face Fred.

"Hunner dollahs."

"Hey, wait jessss a minute!" Tom slurred defiantly. "You never said a hunner *each*."

Fred was startled. He wasn't sure how much cash he'd brought. He realized that his ATM card was in his backpack, in the Hotel Rey. He scraped up only $25. The man returned from the shed and added his own menacing looks while Tom fished through his own pockets for more cash. He came up with another $15.

"Hunner dollars!" the woman insisted.

"Sorry Madam, and I do mean 'Madam,'" Fred said grandly. He handed her the money, turned his back on them and made post-haste for the door. "It's just gonna have to do."

She dropped the wad of fivers on the floor. The man jumped Fred from behind and flattened him face-up across the middle table.

Fred seemed to swallow his own frightened cry and choke on it as the man pinned his arms behind him.

When Tom moved in for a rescue, the Indian yanked a switchblade out of her apron. In high school, Tom learned to beat a hasty exit the instant he heard that distinctive "click." He backed off just before slashed at him viciously. She was first and foremost a business woman, and she meant business. Tom fell back, landing on his ass on the concrete floor, clutching the drawstring on his still-open shorts, inspecting his forearms, surprised to find no knife wounds.

"Be cool!" he pleaded, holding his palms out in surrender. The stars circling his head exploded, one-by-one.

Fred's mind was reeling, too. The man was choking him to keep him down, flat on the table. Fred's whole body went limp when the troll yanked his shorts back down to his ankles. As he picked himself up off the floor, Tom could see clearly what Fred could only feel. She was holding the dull side of the cold, steel blade against Fred's scrotum.

"Ah, *shit!*" Fred squealed.

"*Sus cojones son mios.*" The troll grinned mercilessly at Fred, then at Tom.

"I don' unnerstand what she jus' said, Bro, but I'd call this a fucking emergency," Fred said evenly.

"Wait! Wait!" Tom pleaded with her. "I'll go find the money. I just need a little time."

"Tom – don't leave me like this, Bro, *please!*" His Yankee reserve was suddenly gone. Fred was begging, almost crying.

"Not to worry, Bro. Gotcha covered." Tom's voice cracked. He stumbled over his own feet on the way out the door, then raised himself from the dust.

Tom trotted twenty paces to Bass's Bimmer and pulled on the driver's side door handle. It was locked. "Shit!" Tom remembered that the keys were in one of Fred's pockets, dangling at that moment around his endangered buddy's ankles.

Tom's dazed brain told him not to set foot inside again without the $60 ransom for Fred's manhood. He started running back to the *Avenida de la Revolución*, toward their hotel.

Within two blocks, his feet were leaden, his head was spinning and his metal belt buckle started thrashing his own balls because he hadn't yet found a moment to hitch up his pants properly. He managed to hit a hole in the woven-fabric belt without breaking stride.

A mangy dog jumped out from between two junk vehicles and gave chase. The dog was as old as it was ugly, and it gave up after a block and a half. Tom kept running for his life.

When he got back to the *Avenida*, Tom encountered a sober, middle-aged American tourist couple on the street. The husband consulted a map and pointed Tom in the correct direction for the hotel. He intended to retrieve and use Fred's ATM card. It dawned on him that he had no prayer of guessing Fred's PIN, strangely the only thing at this point he did not know about Fred. Tom placed one hand on a rusty street-corner mailbox, leaned over and vomited quietly. Only a sudden breeze kept him from fouling his sandals.

With much of the mescal now on the dusty sidewalk, Tom found it a little easier to collect his thoughts. The breeze became steady and the front of his shirt began to dry a little. He kept up a deliberate pace until he was half a block from the Cantina el Torito.

The *Avenida* was more crowded, now that it was dark. Tom scanned for targets. Ten minutes felt like an hour. He tried not to think about how long the time must seem to Fred. Finally, he spotted a half dozen under-age preppies, just fifteen or sixteen years old, comical stereotypes in their boat shoes and LaCoste shirts, being ejected roughly from the Cantina by angry bouncers.

"Dudes, what's the malfunction?" Tom asked, as if he'd known them for years.

"Dipshit over there pulled out the wrong ID," a stocky boy with a wrestler's build replied, nodding at a similarly-built classmate standing three feet away, with arms folded defiantly over his chest and a disappointed look across his face.

"Whoa, Dudes, getting thrown out of a bar in Tijuana for being underage, that's really *awesome*."

"Dipshit!" a third preppy threw at the offender.

"Peace, my men. All is sunshine!" Tom clasped his hands together. "You can party on, Dudes. I know where to get some totally wicked weed."

The six guileless prepsters gathered around Tom. If they noticed the sweat soaking Tom's clothes, none of them mentioned it.

"I'll get it right now, my men, and it'll last you all weekend. A mere ten bucks a head."

The youngsters looked at each other uneasily. They had already turned down offers from several Mexican vendors, who promised them dope and all-nude lap dances by their younger "seeeesters." Tom, obviously, was an American, perhaps someone they could trust to make their visit to Tijuana complete.

"It's totally awesome shit, Men, nothing like that hayfield hootch you get at home."

One at a time, after a long pause, the kids started picking through belts and shirt pockets and pants pockets and the waistbands of their underwear. Soon, they amassed the magic sum of $60.

"Maybe we should keep half of it here, until the guy gets back with the dope," suggested the kid who had gotten them thrown out of the Cantina. Sensing the group's lack of interest in Dipshit's opinion, Tom grabbed the cash and ran off.

"Ten minutes!" he called back to them.

Tom was still clutching the ransom money in his right hand when he returned, out of breath and wheezing, to *Las Santerías*. Fred was sitting up at the end of the table, looking more humiliated than scared, his hands tied behind him with a scratchy hemp rope and his shorts still dangling off his ankles.

The four younger customers were at the rear exit, sweaty and obviously spent. They seemed to be coming up a little shy of $400. The Indian kept waving her knife at Fred. She and the bartender tried to explain with the ten words of English between them what sex organs one or two of the other guys would be leaving behind unless somebody coughed up a lot more cash. When it degenerated into pure screaming, Fred looked ready to swoon and fall off the table sideways.

The troll stopped long enough to examine the proffered ransom, paying special attention to the sopping-wet ten-spot that came out of a sixteen-year old preppy's designer underwear. She held the ransom money up to the new debtors with her right hand and cut the rope from Fred's hands with a single stroke of her left.

Fred yelped as he jumped to the floor. His butt cheeks were stuck to the table. He calmly closed his shorts with the drawstring and fastened his belt. The two Mexicans eyed him cautiously as he walked toward them. Just as Tom thought he would have to tackle Fred and drag him out of the whorehouse, Fred snapped up the half-empty bottle of mescal with his right hand and walked out, the same arm around Tom.

When they piled back into Bass's Bimmer, Fred started the engine and stared through the windshield with the clutch jammed in and the gearshift floating in neutral. An hour passed, or so it seemed to Tom, before Fred spoke.

"You're my salvation, Bro," Fred paused and loudly gulped down his pride. "You can't *ever* tell *anybody* in the whole fucking world or I swear I'll *fucking die*."

"Freddy, Bro, it's me, Man, it's Tom. Toldja, I gotcha covered."

Fred gripped the steering wheel and kept staring at the entrance to *Las Santerías*.

"You know," urgency was creeping into Tom's voice, "it's time for us to think about something besides surf'n'sex'n'suds'n'sex'n'smokes'n'sex."

"Yeah, wazzat, Tomcat?"

"Shoot'n'scoot, Man."

Fred stomped on the accelerator and laughed with Tom as a layer of Bass's tire tread burned into the dusty pavement and kicked up a black rubber cloud.

Upon their return to the Hotel Rey, they polished off the mescal without saying a word to each other and split the worm. Fred puked his half into the toilet.

The entire experience was in Technicolor, right up to the moment Fred awoke at 3:00 a.m., sat straight up in bed, hyperventilating, icy sweat pouring down his chest. That part was in black and white, bathed in stark neon from the hotel's marquee, just outside their window.

AT THE PRESERVE IN VIRGINIA, Tom awakens at the witching hour in pitch dark but for the white light shining through the nearly-closed bathroom door, hyperventilating, icy sweat rolling off of every inch of his body. The "ack-ack" is so strong, Tom thinks he will choke.

The sheets are drenched. He has to slide across two feet of Egyptian cotton, to what was customarily Gwen's side of the California king. For once, that is where he finds the dry spot.

Conflicts

"I NEED 100,000 OPTIONS at a dollar and thirty cents."

Tom says it so casually that Fred reflexively responds "uh huh" in an absent-minded fashion as he continues plowing through the stack of documents on the desk in his office at the Perverted Pyramid. Fred is desperate to push a whole week's worth of paper that dreary February afternoon. In less than forty-eight hours he, Tom and the rest of the road show "players" are scheduled to hop onto a chartered jet and blanket the entire United States in less than a week.

"Say that again, Bro?" Fred drops his pen on the floor and looks up at Tom with an unbelieving expression. "Is this some kinda sick joke?"

"You heard me, Fred. I get 100,000 at a buck thirty – or I'm so totally outta here."

"What the fuck has gotten into you?" This time, Fred nearly drops a lit cigarette onto the floor instead of the ashtray he keeps hidden in a partly open desk drawer. He is furious now and sees no need to abbreviate or to explain that he needs the options to maintain voting control of the company. Without it, he cannot count on being able to assure that his and Tom's stock would still be valuable in six months, when the so-called "lockdown" period ends and they, as company insiders, will be free to begin selling their shares for cash.

"Keith put you up to this, didn't he?"

"No, *you* put me up to this. How come you never bothered to mention that you already got the Board to award you 300,000 options at that price?"

Fred looks thin, drawn and ready to hyperventilate.

"So what, Man?" Fred takes a condescending tone. "If you were paying any attention at all, you'd know that if the IPO's a bust, the options won't be worth the paper they're written on. And if it's a screamin' success –"

"Time out!" Tom resorts to referee gestures. "Gimme a little truth here, Man."

"You don't understand," Fred begins.

"Don't fuck around with me, Freddy. I know you think I'm stupid – "

"Never – "

"At least in math, I can't deny it, it's true. But in this case, I can do the fuckin' math. Sammy Schwartz is countin' on us gettin' at least thirty-five dollars a share. That's almost a $7 million bonus for you. Here's a simple equation, or maybe it's an equilateral triangle – I get a third that much, or I walk."

SIMON KEITH KNEW a golden opportunity when he saw one. At WebSurfer's emergency Board of Directors meeting, he made sure Tom's options were approved and that both of his golden boys got additional inducements for a successful road show. Since Tom was carrying eighty percent of it, he moved the Board to promote him to the position of Executive Vice President, a close second in company management behind Fred. There was no increase in salary, but the Board agreed to forgive the outstanding loans on their respective "suitable executive homes," effective one week after the IPO. It was the equivalent of a $2 million bonus for each of them.

"Divide and conquer," that was Keith's favorite game. He would find some way to wrest control of WebSurfer away from Fred. It was just a matter of time. Keith considered Tom both a short-cut and a backstop. Fred considered Tom a traitor and an extortionist.

"Thought I could trust you with my *life, Bro,*" Fred said bitterly when he walked into Tom's office, slammed the door and surrendered news of the Board's action to Tom. The words started sarcastic but ended tearful.

Tom regretted his decision immediately. Rather than rejoicing in his promotion, Tom felt miserable. He blamed himself and, to a lesser extent than she deserved, he blamed Gwen. As soon as they discovered what severe public scrutiny came along with

Tom's newly-exalted role in the company, he convinced her it would be bad for WebSurfer and terrible for her career to be seen cohabitating with her client. He also made certain they were never alone together. Gwen's workload and Tom's travel schedule were brutal, so Gwen found little opportunity to entice Tom back into the spa or one of his California king-sized beds.

Gwen did not have *stock options*, but she had *options*. She was determined to keep all of them open and to enlist allies wherever she could find them.

BILLY SHIPPE DROVE a gray Honda Civic with a creased fender. He could easily afford something sexy, but nobody was supposed to know it. He knew where all the classic cars got auctioned and would go on a buying spree the minute he made his killing from WebSurfer. The time was near; he could smell it.

Shippe laughed out loud as he parked in front of an off-brand motel near Dulles Airport. He recognized the number with a "703" area code flashing across the screen of his cell phone.

"Finally!" Shippe congratulated himself as he yanked the parking brake. "Bitch must be gettin' anxious!"

He did not take Gwen Stephens' call. He had some business to conclude with Mike Culver first. There was plenty of time, he assured himself, because Shippe was certain he and Gwen were birds of a feather.

Shippe raps gently on the motel room door, then discreetly scans the nearly-empty parking lot until he hears the chain come off the door and sees it open a crack. He slips inside.

"She's almost ready." Culver straightens his collar in a mirror between two rumpled double beds. The bathroom door is shut, but a hairdryer fills the room with an obnoxious whirring noise. Shippe stands close to Culver to give his wire a better chance to pick up their conversation.

"Where's Manassas?" Culver wants to know.

"About thirty miles and a world away from the Capital Beltway," Shippe reassures him. "Down by Bull Run, where you Southern boys had a bit of luck."

"Bull Run?" Culver laughs. He was still catching his breath from his own noontime bull run. "They got orthodontists there?"

"Yeah, but they all live in Middleburg, next to you."

"Shit-head," Culver shoots him a disgusted look.

"Oh, sorry, forgot about the divorce."

"You heard what my wife did? She clipped out that list they published in *Washingtonian* Magazine, 'The Dirty Dozen: Washington's Toughest Divorce Lawyers.' Then she plopped her ass into that little Benz I bought for her birthday, you know, that SL600, and went to *every goddamn one of 'em on the list*, every shyster divorce lawyer within fifty miles. She paid each of 'em some piss-ant fee for an 'initial consultation.'"

"So?"

"'*So?*' She conflicted out every single one of the greedy sonsobitches. She hired only one of 'em, but *I* cain't hire *any* of 'em. I'll be lucky to find a divorce lawyer who knows how to tie his own goddam shoelaces this side of Richmond. That cunt!"

"Pretty smart, ya gotta admit. She knew exactly how to do it."

"But that wasn't the worst of it. She auctioned off every stitch of clothes I had in the house in Middleburg! And my golf clubs, too, even the driver Arnold Palmer used when he won the U.S. Open. The bitch didn't even have the decency to use UOL's online auction feature. She used fuckin' *eBay*, for Chrissakes."

"So, aside from *that* Mrs. Lincoln, how ya likin' the play?" Shippe's sympathy is tinged with sarcasm.

"This WebSurfer situation's got me nervous as a cat in a roomful of rockin' chairs. My new best friend's tuggin' at the bait, but he still ain't on the hook yet."

"Mebbe it's time for some *fly*-fishin'."

"*Jeez*, and you say *I've* got a one-track mind," Culver replies, matter-of-factly. "Fred Hanson insists he's goin' forward with the IPO, doesn't like anything I put on the table. I gotta own the source code before WebSurfer's worth the kinda money he's lookin' for. He still owns it, his own personal property, just did a non-exclusive license with the company, so WebSurfer's worthless without it. I tol' him I'd save him the trouble of doing the IPO, that UOL'll pay him personally several million for the intellectual property rights and throw in a little bit o' cash for the company stock, too."

"He wants to pump up that stock price. Make his handsome pal Tom Rey a millionaire."

"Like I give a shit whether his surfin' buddy gets back on his board and rides off into the fuckin' sunset." Culver speaks more like a man behind the biggest desk in the biggest corner office, not some low-life sniffing his clothes for evidence on his way out of a no-tell-motel.

"OK." Shippe knows when it's time to dish. "The WebSurfer board gave Hanson a shitload of stock options when they approved the re-lo package. That'll make it possible for him to retain voting control of his company after the IPO without having to give up that precious source code. It also means that Moon Doggy and Simon Keith and a bunch o' lawyers will walk off with big wads of cash. Then, maybe, he'll be ready to sell the whole company to UOL."

"How come he's gotta take such good care of his surfin' buddy or butt buddy or whatever the real deal is between those two boys?"

"Haven't gotten to the *bottom* of that one, yet." Culver ignores the pun, so Shippe continues with some speculation. "Rey must have dirty pictures on him or something."

"What's the deal with that new lawyer, the woman with the perky tits?"

"Rey's bangin' her like a bongo. Hanson hasn't figured it out yet. Neither has the other lawyer from her firm, that guy Bass."

"Ooo-eee, I could go for some of that action." Culver's voice drips with envy.

"Yeah, you and me both! I can just imagine her sittin' right about here." Shippe holds his hands over his groin.

"*You?*" Culver's tone changes instantly from envy to ridicule. "Since when are you dual-voltage?"

"Hey, it's a living," Shippe responds with a big, crooked smile and an uneven shrug.

"Man's gotta do what a man's gotta do, I guess." Culver turns back to business. "D'ja know those three guys all used to live together, did a lot of inhalin' in some beach shack, back in school? That ol' Texas boy's gotta know somethin', but he's tighter than a preacher's asshole."

"Maybe you need to try more persuasive methods." Shippe wiggles his tongue obscenely but Culver ignores him.

"I got one little data point you can file away," Shippe adds with an evil grin. "Moon Doggy's last name is not really 'Rey'. It's somethin' that sounds like you're talkin' with a mouthful of hot mashed potatoes. He's a fuckin' *Polak*."

"Stupid *Polak*, eh? Howdja know that?"

A young woman, maybe twenty years old, interrupts the conversation when she steps meekly out of the bathroom. Her steady diet of biscuits and gravy fills her tight jeans and halter top with ample hips and breasts. Culver digs three one-hundred dollar bills out of his wallet and hands them to her.

"Thanks, Mister. After next week, I'll have enough to go see Dr. Brandt." She smiles a mouthful of crooked teeth.

"The john with a heart of gold, and a wallet to match!" Shippe teases. He leads the girl to his car and drives her home. The conversation en route records much more clearly than what Shippe got in the motel room.

"YOU SURE YOU DON' WANNA HOOK UP someplace a little more intimate, if ya know what I mean?" Shippe slides onto a seat at The Palm, an exclusive restaurant adjacent to the Ritz Carlton Tysons Corner and motions for a busboy to move the place-setting a quarter-turn. He is on Gwen Stephens left arm, not across from her.

"I think this is quite intimate enough, don't you?" Gwen replies with a regal expression that tells him nothing.

"I nevah have my back to the door." Gwen makes Shippe so nervous he drops all efforts to hide his Brooklyn accent. He hopes she will consider it a sign of sincerity.

"I understand perfectly."

"Yeah, I s'pose you do." Shippe scratches his left cheek and shoots Gwen a seductive grin. "That's why you tol' me where to findja."

"I eat here three days a week so I can go right back up to my office. Some guy or another invites himself to join me almost every night. They always pick up the check. So if you're feeling special, don't."

"Mebbe so, Toots, but things might be different after your surfah boy gets his big payday." Shippe's tone hardens. "I think the two of us could work out a mutually satisfyin' arrangement."

"Whatcha got?" She can't tell whether Shippe knows Tom has evicted her from the big house.

"The numbahs, that's what I got. The real numbahs and the numbahs youse guys are puttin' in the financial statements don't match. And don' try bullshittin' me. I know they're full of irrational exuberance."

Gwen silently points at the queen-size portion of prime rib and a $120 Haut Medoc Grand Cru as the waiter peers over her shoulder at the menu.

"Who are you working for, you little worm?" Gwen folds her heavy menu and hands it back to the waiter. "I'm sure Keith would pay you a pretty sum, if you can back it up."

"Ya gotta be kiddin' me," Shippe's head reels backward. "With all the dough him and his bunch got ridin' on this IPO, he'd kill me if I tol' him that now."

"I don't believe you've got the goods. Even if you did, what's it to me?"

"S'pose we swap? I keep quiet and you do some things for me, sorta friendly-like, ya know what I mean?" Shippe winks.

"You're making me lose my appetite, Billy Boy," Gwen remarks when her prime rib and Shippe's penne pasta dish arrive. She wields one of The Palm's menacing six-inch steak knives with an unmistakable Lizzy Borden flick of the wrist. Shippe winces when she attacks her rare meat and a stream of blood-red *au jus* spurts his direction. It stains the white linen table cloth within an inch of his plate.

While Shippe pads the conversation with small talk, Gwen savors the wine and studies the framed caricatures of politicians she never heard of, blanketing every wall in The Palm.

"So, whaddaya think?" Shippe breaks her concentration as she swirls the wine, studies its deep purple and breathes its fruity nose. "About you and me?"

"Give me some actionable intelligence and we'll talk again." Gwen dabs her mouth daintily, drops her wadded-up napkin next to her plate, gets up from the table and leaves Shippe the bill. He doesn't let it bother him. He'll make hay next time.

AWOL

TOM ALWAYS THOUGHT it was impossible for two people to be on top of each other for a week and never look at one another. The chartered jet for the WebSurfer road show, a Cessna Citation X with powerful engines and a tiny, tubular interior, proved otherwise. The plane was like a phone booth with two wings, stuffed with two unhappy Phi Delts, one mousy and dead-pale accountant, one senior software engineer whose presentation sounded like Urdu to Tom, and one unctuous reporter toting a steno notepad.

Culver and Keith didn't agree on much, but for some mysterious reason they both insisted that Billy Shippe, the editor and publisher of *eZine*, had to tag along. Shippe, they said, would record for posterity the birth of a new dotcom legend and the making of two new tech mega-millionaires, an ingenious, hard-working twenty-eight-year old and his sidekick, a glib, blond stud muffin just days shy of his twenty-fifth birthday. To Tom's dismay, neither of the lawyers objected.

"*Boffo!*" Shippe kept saying. It made Tom and Fred both want to slap him, but they refrained from violence because Shippe was their conduit, the only way Tom and Fred would communicate with each other, even after several days in back-to-back seats on the plane, back-to-back rooms in hotels and back-to-back presentations to potential heavy-hitter investors.

"Tell Tom . . . ."

"Tell Fred . . . ."

Oddly enough, the presentations came off more polished and professional than if Tom and Fred had been on speaking terms.

There were no "dudes" in the room, nothing was "awesome," nobody was going to get "way rich." Tom explained clearly what was so ingenious about Fred's invention, how it revolutionized location-based web services. Fred made it plain there was more genius where that came from and new inventions would soon facilitate other types of transactions. The company's financials to date bespoke even greater success in 2002 and beyond.

Shippe planned to spice up his story with lots of Teenage Mutant Ninja Turtle dialogue if the IPO turned out a success. On the other hand, if the IPO failed, it would be the tale of two callow youths who screwed the pooch from here to fucking China. Shippe already had two alternative titles picked out. It would be either "An Epic Ride on the Internet Power Curve" or "Dude, Where's My Dotcom?"

By the time the WebSurfer team gets to its last stop, the Jonathan Club in downtown Los Angeles, Tom and Fred perform flawlessly. The normally jaded Angelenos, who include stock brokers from Century City, movie moguls and more than a few of their Hollywood drug dealers, actually stand up and applaud at the end.

Tom did one thing different this time, Shippe notices. He brought his leather duffel bag to the Club and hid it behind a potted palm in the corner just before show time.

"Where ya off to?" Shippe asks when the applause dies down and the brokers start filing out. He spots Tom, clawing his tie away from his throat with one hand and grabbing his duffel bag with the other. "The plane's chock full of fuel and the tail wind might get us back to DeeCee nonstop."

"I'd rather spend the next six hours in a coffin, and you can quote me on that," Tom spits back.

Only one thing in the world could possibly cure the soul-sucking exhaustion and gut-wrenching anguish Tom feels at the conclusion of his final presentation in the WebSurfer road show. Tom does not even hear the excited applause at the Jonathan Club, nor does he notice how Billy Shippe manufactured a standing ovation by nudging an attendee seated next to him in the front row and goosing the geezer to his feet. Tom is eager to revert to his old standbys, surf'n'suds'n'smokes. Meanwhile, WebSurfer would just have to make do without him and, for that matter, without any clue where to find him.

"DU-U-U-U-U-U-U-UDE!"

Corey Collins is behind the bar and beside himself.

"Hey, Dudes, meet my old Rooms, the way rich dog I told you about!"

"Cut the 'rich' crap, Bud. Nobody'll know anything until March 12, anyway."

"How about that!" Collins holds his hands out in front and wags both of them. "Tom Rey's big day, all the way around!"

"Well, I guess we'll see about that." Tom prefers to concentrate on his own toes wiggling up at him through a comfortable old pair of leather sandals he dug hurriedly out of a closet in his apartment en route to the O&W. "You've got one hell of a memory, Cores!"

"You don't think I'd forget your *birthday*, Rooms? No fuckin' way. Hey, you guys, come over here and say hey to Tom Rey! He's gonna be a quarter-of-a-century old bazillionaire next week, on March 12!"

Tom winces. He does not want either of those facts out on the table at the O&W, especially while he was AWOL from WebSurfer.

One by one, five guys clap over in their flip-flops and offer Tom a soul-shake.

"This here's Pud, my new Rooms." Collins introduces a blond guy with a Wonder Bread tan and forelocks that come to a single point just above his left eye. He could be Tom's shorter and younger brother.

"Bud?" Tom thinks he mis-heard the name.

"No," Collins grins. "'Pud,' with a capital 'P,' you know, as in 'Pullin' Yer'."

Pud grins, too.

Tom notices that all the guys are stoned, but they are a mere four or five on a ten-scale.

"Pud just moved here from Detroit, but he's already got way awesome weed connections, dontcha?" Collins brags. "And the most tubular collection of bongs you ever saw."

Pud grins and shrugs modestly.

"In fact," Collins lowers his voice just a bit, "your timing's positively *impeckerable*, My Man."

Tom follows the group up the narrow stairs to the O&W's attic office. After the excruciating emotional turmoil Tom suffered the entire month leading up to the road show, mental anesthetic seems in order.

RAIN IN PEEBEE in March was not unheard-of, but Tom is so baked – he is at least a nine – when he walks out of the O&W that he does not know what month or what time of night it is. He enjoys the steady drizzle on his face and the way his silk Hawaiian shirt becomes extra skin as it pastes over the muscles of his chest and back. He marvels at the way the bare soles of his feet hydroplane inside his sandals.

The sea breeze picks up as he arrives at Carly's house. An oversized envelope crashes into Tom's ankle. It is a soggy greeting card.

"*May the Grace of God Sustain You in Your Hour of Loss*," the card reads. The rain washes the sender's signature away before Tom reads that far.

"Don't you have enough sense to come in out of the rain?" Tom looks up to see Carly in the main floor doorway, wearing a dry smile and a black dress with a high neck and long sleeves. He has never seen her in such formal attire and never imagined she could look so totally hot.

"What's this about?" Water flies from the card as Tom waves it.

"My Dad," Carly says. "I just got back from his funeral."

Tom feels sad, down to his core.

"I'm really, really sorry. He was one cool dude."

"Yeah," Carly agrees softly, "he was as cool as they come."

Tom looks not only stoned but bereft and pathetic, especially with the rainwater streaming off the end of his nose.

"Get in here, you fool." Carly points at the threshold. She stops Tom just inside the door.

"Off! All of it!"

Tom strips unselfconsciously and trades Carly his sodden clothes for a polyester blanket.

"In town for a little slummin'?" Carly raises an eyebrow. Even the steady rain could not wash away the metallic smell of hashish.

Tom draws his head downward, ready for confession.

"Just a little hash." Tom looks at the ceiling and giggles.

Carly shakes her head and declares a silent "chakra emergency."

"Gonna puke?"

"Nah. Didn't drink anything. Much." Tom raises his fingers to something like a Boy Scout's promise.

"Lie down," she instructs, "right there on the sofa. We'll see what kind of shape you're in tomorrow morning."

"OK." Tom keels straight over, sideways, and falls fast asleep.

CONSCIOUSNESS COMES GRADUALLY the next morning, even more than when he came out from under the anesthetic they gave him at Mission Valley Hospital the previous summer, when they stitched up the gashes Raymond Chu gave him at the Longboard Challenge.

Tom drifts in and out over the course of two hours. He feels no pain as he rolls from side to side, but the sofa is a lot more confining than any California king he's grown accustomed to. Tom gives his tackle a friendly, reassuring tug, then goes back to sleep.

A window is open. He can feel the ocean breeze and smell the sea salt. His nerve endings dance to the gentle rhythm of the downpour. Then he hears a familiar voice, the same voice he heard at the hospital all those months ago, just before he found out how lucky he was to be alive.

"Banana or blueberry?"

"Ba-nana-berry!" Tom replies slowly but emphatically, as if he were in his office in Virginia, making an important executive decision.

"You are so full of crap," the female voice shoots back at him, matter-of-factly.

"Crap," Tom says. His eyes are still closed and his face is almost pressed against the back of Carly's living room sofa.

"Crap pancakes? There's a new taste treat! Quick, I gotta call the Food Network."

Tom's eyes fly open. He spins around, sits up and modestly clutches the blanket over his chest.

Carly laughs at him. Tom's blue-green eyes are clear as day, but she can tell he has no idea where he is or how he got there.

"How do you feel?"

Tom has to think about it.

"Better than I have felt in a long, long time."

"I don't believe you."

"It's all relative, I guess," Tom confesses with a wan smile.

"We'll get you fixed up pretty quick. First, banana pancakes." Carly decides for him.

"I'm not much of a breakfast eater."

"Breakfast? It's two in the afternoon, Tommy. Consider it lunch, or early dinner."

"Oh, God!" Tom's face pinches up. After so many months on other people's schedules, he is afraid he missed a flight or an appointment or his one chance to squeeze in a workout. He sees his sleek Breitling, its red sweep hand, three rows of digits, two mini-dials and silver-and-black face, the watch Fred re-gifted to him after a forgetful aunt gave him the same thing two Christmases in a row, on a coffee table. Nearby, he sees his clothes, dried and folded neatly.

"I don't suppose you have a full schedule of Saturday morning appointments here in PeeBee?" She hands him an oversized mug brimming with espresso and steamed milk.

Tom finds situational awareness at the bottom of the first mug. The café latte warms and sooths the throat he spent an hour scorching at the O&W the night before.

Carly returns to the kitchen to start the griddle on her ancient gas stove. Tom pulls his clothes on and joins her at the old Formica table with the tattered plastic seats. His shirt shrank in the rain, or perhaps when Carly dried it, so he leaves it unbuttoned.

"That's the most fantastic meal I've had since I don't know when," Tom offers when he reaches the bottom of his plate and his third latte.

"That's just the start," Carly smiles at him. "We're going to get your chakras back into their natural balance, before it's too late."

"My – huh? – who's 'we'?"

"Me and Hugo." Her eyes sparkle.

Tom should have known. Now that Carly is sober and looking not only healthy, but downright gorgeous, of course she would have a guy. A jealous twinge flips his stomach. It makes no sense, he has no right, but he couldn't help feeling crushed.

"That's him, now." Carly dashes to the door and throws it open. Hugo was a large man, a Hawaiian, with huge hands.

"He's my wellness coach," Carly says, giving Hugo an unmistakably platonic hug. Before Tom can finish rolling his eyes, he finds himself stretched the length of a fold-out massage table. For a solid hour, Hugo bends him, twists him, jams his baton-sized fingers into "pressure points" in Tom's neck and on the soles of his feet.

"Just stay there awhile and relax, let the toxins flow out of your system," Hugo advises as he heads for the door. "I'll come back and pick up the table in the morning."

Tom is pure Jello. He isn't going anywhere, not even back to the sofa.

After several minutes, Tom speaks at the floor through a hole in the face rest.

"That thing he did with my feet?"

"Yeah?" Carly replies. She is standing next to Tom.

"Don't think I'll ever walk again. Or want to."

"Let's give it a try."

Carly swings Tom around and helps him hop off the table. They stand nose to nose.

Neither of them move. Neither of them feels uncomfortable about being so close. They look into one another's eyes for what seemed like an hour. Neither of them could see much beyond deep and abiding pain.

"Don't suppose there's a third part to this treatment," Tom says, after a long while.

"Only if you're certain it will contribute to wellness."

Carly lowers the living room blinds. As the slats sway in the chilly breeze, Tom kisses Carly and both of them turn to goose flesh. The rain picks up and establishes a steady rhythm. As Carly lowers her bedroom blinds, Tom steps behind her, puts his arms around her, envelopes her. She is a new Carly, fuller, more alive than the sun-damaged stick-figure that fished him out of the surf at Tourmaline just a few months before. Suddenly, the breeze is body temperature, warm and reassuring.

IT WAS NOT "NORMAL" SEX, at least it did not seem "normal" in Tom's considerable experience. It was not one of those wrestling matches, one of those contests of will, where the biggest thrill to be had was in figuring out whether he was expected to dominate or to submit, whether two more perfectly good neckties would get ruined from being knotted to the bed posts. It was not a surfing competition, where he had to twist and turn as soon as he popped up, to find the power curve and stay on it, to keep a ride going as long as it could last. Nor was it a whale hunt, where he had to stand watch for the first sign of a blowhole, follow in hot pursuit, wear down the resistance until he spied the perfect moment to sink in the harpoon, deep and deadly, until his prey ceased to quiver.

Carly and Tom set off on a journey of discovery. Within minutes, she knew what pleased Tom, what excited him, what shocked him, what drove him insane. There was no limit to the combinations they could find or invent, no boundary to their creativity.

Tom had long since given up any notion that there was anything new to be found in sex. It was "been there, done that," not that he ever complained. He just kept his mind somewhere else, usually focused on his first love, the sea, with her rhythm and her power and her energy. While his body pumped, his mind usually shifted and turned and drew out however much power was necessary to keep the ride alive.

With Carly, Tom found himself on a river, not the ocean. They were Lewis and Clark, punting their way together up the Missouri, seeing what they had never seen before, recording as much as possible for posterity in every synapse, breathlessly making that next turn, the excitement and danger mixing, rising, filling their nostrils. One punt followed another slowly, carefully, steadily, deliberately, each powered by anticipation.

This wasn't sex. It was two rivers flowing into each other, becoming deeper and wider and more powerful at every bend. This was making love.

TOM QUICKLY LOST TRACK of everything. He didn't know if any given day had a name or a number, just that this looked like a good day to sleep, a good day to surf. Every day was a good day to make love with Carly.

Tom went to the O&W at lunchtime, after a swim or some surfing, when Collins was too busy pushing suds and blending margaritas to suggest any combustible entertainment or other mischief. Tom stopped going there at night. Collins saw it written on Tom's face. This dog's prowling days were over.

Tom climbs the stairs to his own apartment only when he needs to grab clean clothes or look for a CD he wants to share with Carly. He is upstairs early one morning, rummaging for a long-lost but much-loved pair of board shorts, when the telephone rings. AWOL for only a few days, he feels so free, it seems like weeks. He picks up the receiver.

"'Lo," Tom says cheerfully.

"I can't believe nobody else figured out how to reach you!" Gwen Stephens howls into Tom's ear.

"Huh?" Tom holds the receiver a foot away from his ear and gives it a horrified stare.

"They've been searching for you all over the whole goddamn world!" Gwen is still yelling loud enough for him to hear every word. "And all the time, they just needed the number from the smartcard in my old cell phone."

"Yeah?" Tom's cheerful tone flies out the window with the ocean breeze.

"Don't suppose you've been reading the *Wall Street Journal* on your little sabbatical?" Gwen's tone also changes, from frantic to ironic.

Tom waits without saying a word.

"So you expect me to believe you don't know how the IPO turned out?"

"IPO?" Tom feigns ignorance of the event that had already turned his life upside down, win or lose.

"Don't be an asshole. You know it shot the moon."

"Huh?"

"It opened at thirty-five and closed at fifty-eight. Just after it started trading, it popped all the way up to seventy-nine."

Gwen assumes Tom couldn't handle the math. "That means the shares you own outright are worth almost $24 million. And your options could net you another $6 million, if you time it right."

It takes Tom a long moment to wrap his mind around it.

"I say *sell*."

Gwen pretends to laugh. "Ha, ha. Very funny. You remember, I explained the lockdown period. You are not allowed to sell any of your shares for the first six months after the IPO. By that point, they could be worth $40 million."

"Or nuthin'," Tom reminds her.

"Hush, Goofy Foot." Tom knows this news is supposed to excite him, but somehow it just isn't clicking. Gwen seems pumped enough for both of them. She is not sure what he is up to, but it never crosses her mind that Tom might decide to stay in PeeBee, to quit WebSurfer, now that he had delivered for Fred.

"If the price goes north of sixty again, you might want to exercise some of the options. But that's going to be a while, I'm afraid."

"How come?"

"Darling," Gwen purrs urgently, "you *must* come home *immediately*."

"I *am* home, Babe," Tom says.

Gwen laughs, nervously this time. "Not yet, Goofy Foot. It's Fred. You have to come back and run the company."

"Fred? What about Fred?"

"Are you sitting down, Dear?"

"Cut the crap."

"OK. Fred fell out of a gondola."

"Are you telling me he *drowned*?" Tom's pulse spikes.

"No, different kind of gondola. Culver and Fred went down to Charlottesville to celebrate the IPO with a hot-air balloon ride. They unfurled a big banner that said 'Sky's the Limit.'"

"What happened?"

"The balloonist was doing a little celebrating of his own, apparently. The banner caught on something and he crashed the fucking thing into a tree on the mountain next to Monticello. Fred tumbled out of the basket and fell almost thirty feet."

"Are you sure Culver didn't push him?"

"That's the first question everybody asks! Listen, Fred hit a couple of branches on the way down. That broke his fall, probably saved his life. But it really bunged up his left leg. He's in the University of Virginia Hospital until we can get him transferred up here to Northern Virginia."

"Shit!" Tom slaps his left palm into his forehead. "This is un-fucking-believable!"

"The company already put out a press release. It says you're taking over while Fred recuperates. Simon Keith says the stock will tank if we can't get you back here *immediately*."

Tom is silent.

"You're booked on a red-eye, tonight. Unless you intend to piss millions of dollars down the drain, you'd better be on it. I'll pick you up at Dulles bright and early. There's an emergency Board meeting at ten in the morning."

"Then I'll go to the hospital to see Fred."

"Fred says he's not taking any visits."

"Not even from me?"

"*Especially* not from you," Gwen said after an uncomfortable pause.

"OK, Babe." Tom doesn't know what else to say. He goes downstairs with a pathetic look on his face, like a man being dragged to his own execution. Carly bursts into tears before she sets eyes on him. She swears she can feel his chakras spinning backward.

Combustibles

SOMETHING SEEMS OUT-OF-KILTER that muggy summer evening when Tom sees a nondescript white Chevrolet parked in front of his McMansion in Virginia. He passes the Chevy and its two suspicious-looking, long-haired occupants slowly, then whips around to the side-loading five-car garage.

Tom makes sure the garage door closes completely before he silences his Porshe's engine and leaps out of the driver's seat.

"I'm goin' completely paranoid!" Tom mutters to himself as he enters the house and punches a secret code into the keypad on his home security system. He picks up a portable alarm with a panic button, shrugs, puts it back on the expansive granite kitchen countertop, then picks it up again before he heads to the front door to investigate his unexpected visitors.

After almost four months at the helm of WebSurfer, where he added to Northern Virginia's hustle and bustle by hiring a couple dozen additional tech workers, Tom feared the worst from just about anyone he encountered. The McMansion scared him, too, even though it was paid-for. It always felt like a hotel room without a door, a huge, scary open space where he could never feel alone. It was especially spooky at night. Every groan and pop the new building emitted as it settled onto its foundation made him jump. Tom found it especially difficult to sleep there after Gwen Stephens moved out.

They were no longer sleeping together, but Gwen loomed large in Tom's daily life. She dealt with the contractors who kept the McMansion running. She was outside general counsel to WebSurfer, having won a key role keeping the place going, advising Tom on corporate governance and day-to-day business decisions. Thanks to her ability to dive into the substance of whatever confronted the company on any given day, WebSurfer would be in one piece when Fred finally recovered from his bizarre and nearly fatal balloon accident and returned to the job. Despite the roaring success of the IPO, she knew Tom's stock and options could still end up worthless, or at least worth a lot less. Tom could not help appreciating her dedication.

Jamie Bass fought Gwen for effective control of the company at first, but he caved quickly. A couple of her earliest calls after Fred became incapacitated were dead-right, much better than what Jamie recommended. Her street-smarts probably saved the company, Jamie admitted to Fred.

Geography also favored Gwen. She was based in Northern Virginia while Jamie felt constrained to stay in New York. His wife's pregnancy had some ups and downs, so his travel was strictly curtailed.

Tom fell into the habit of following Gwen's guidance on nearly every issue. He surprised almost everyone, though, when he asked several commonsense questions that prompted even sharper advice. Everyone said they were "joined at the hip."

Tom's job as "Acting CEO" of WebSurfer consisted mostly of showing his face at an endless schedule of events inside and outside the company and following all the "sign here" sticky tags in the mounds of documents Gwen piled on his desk every morning at the Perverted Pyramid. No one was surprised that Tom was exceptionally good at both of those tasks.

By the middle of September, Tom could start selling his stock in five or six lots over several months. WebSurfer settled into a narrow trading range, between $47 and $50 after the IPO, which meant Tom's shares were worth something on the order of $20 million. If the stock climbed back to the high it hit on IPO day, Tom's holdings could get closer to $40 million. Anywhere in that range, Stephens was sure, Tom could afford to "retire" from WebSurfer and marry the woman who made it all come together for him. Fred would make a handsome and high-profile best man and her favorite paralegal, Mary Bly, would be matron of honor.

TOM KEEPS HIS THUMB poised over the remote control security system panic button as he peers through the sidelights that frame his front door of his house at The Preserve. The white Chevy looks empty. He opens the door and steps tentatively onto the stone porch in the ultra-comfortable Italian loafers Gwen bought for him. The alarm system chimes to confirm the obvious, that a door has opened.

The shout hits Tom like an electric shock. It sounds like *"rums!"* By the time Tom spots Corey Collins, who is taking a leak behind one of the newly-planted bushes in front of the house, Tom reflexively mashes the panic button. Sirens whoop and all the outdoor lights on the house flash on and off, as if someone has just blown a bank vault. Tom frantically punches in the six-digit code and cancels the alarm. The Preserve is tranquil once again, except for the sound of bulldozers knocking down old-growth trees to make room for more McMansions.

"Whoa! Dude!" Collins stuffs himself back into his jeans and extends a greeting to Tom with the same hand. Instead of slapping skin with his old roommate, Collins grabs the device out of Tom's hand and mashes the panic button. Once again, sirens scream and lights flash.

"That's *so-o-o-o-o* cool!" Collins wants to watch the show again.

Tom grabs the device back and re-enters the cancel code. The last thing he needs at the moment is a visit from the County Police. With his jaw unhinged, Tom turns back to Collins.

"Great map, Dude!" Collins congratulates Tom and unfolds an O&W requisition sheet. Tom recognizes his own neat handwriting. "You were so wasted when you told us how to get here, I wasn't even sure you'd remember we were coming to DeeCee this week for the Beer Wholesalers convention."

Pud awakens from his nap in the back seat of the rental car the second time the alarm goes off. He wipes sweat off his brow and grins at Tom through the windshield, then bounds out and pops the trunk. He heaves out two bulging backpacks.

"Yeah, right." Tom tries desperately to remember inviting them to visit, but the experience must have been recorded on brain cells that were left for dead at the O&W back in March, right after the WebSurfer road show, when Tom went AWOL. In any case, he never imagined Collins would actually step so far out of his element.

"The maid came this morning, so I'm sure there are a couple of rooms ready."

"*The maid?*" Collins mocks him. "Where is she? Lemme at 'er!"

Tom just shakes his head.

"Sure beats the Hell outta the Motel Six!" Collins exclaims when he steps inside the marble entrance foyer. Pud drops his jaw and nods his agreement. Tom tours them through all twenty-two rooms. They guffaw the whole time but the three-story great room across the back of the house instills stunned silence. Collins pronounces it "totally awesome."

The tour ends in the basement-level pub room. It is well-furnished, offering both billiards and foosball. Tom was out of town or alone in the house so much, he forgot that Stephens paid a contractor to hook up a full keg of beer when they outfitted the bar.

Collins, being a professional, notices immediately that the keg is just hours away from its expiration date.

"Ya know what that means, Dudes!"

Collins and Pud jump in the air, crashing breastbones together. Tom knocks knuckles with them and lets it go at that.

"*Keg parrrrrteeeeeee!*"

ONLY VAGUELY HUNG-OVER the next morning, Tom stretches out spread-eagle in the California king in his master suite and yawns at the top of his lungs.

"Shit!" Tom sits up when he glances at the alarm clock on the bedside table and sees that it is past ten o'clock. He tries to jump-start his brain. Did he have an appointment that morning? Was he already behind in tackling a pile of papers swamping his desk in the Perverted Pyramid? Fred was still recuperating at home, but Tom refused to move into the CEO's office, even though it was more difficult to keep the paper flowing through his own, much smaller space.

Faint pecking noises and a familiar aroma waft from the nether reaches of the house. Tom pads halfway down the entrance foyer stairs in his boxers before it occurs to him that Collins and his new "rooms" are visiting from PeeBee.

Tom passes through the kitchen and grabs a ripe banana off the fancy tree-stand Gwen installed when she was in residence. Two abandoned peels are browning on the countertop next to the remote control for the burglar alarm. Tom shudders to realize he went to bed without arming the system.

Tom eventually encounters Collins and Pud down in the pub room, attacking each other with fiendish delight over the foosball table. A roach smolders in a martini glass, their makeshift ashtray, on the edge of Tom's U-shaped wooden bar.

"Did you bring that shit on the plane?" Tom inquires without saying "good morning."

"They don't check shit at the airport," Collins replies ambiguously. He concentrates entirely on his match point.

Collins scores. Pud's shoulders drop. Tom excuses himself to go to work.

"Nope." Collins says. "Today's Saturday, Man."

Tom feels some relief, until he remembers how much more work was waiting for him than he could possibly handle on Monday. There is just enough time to remind Collins who is the undisputed king of the foosball table.

TOM IS ALARMED to find his garage open when he returns home from his office on Sunday. When he pulls into the far right space, he finds himself parked next to Gwen and gives her a "wazzup?" look. She glares back at him.

"Isn't it about time for you to straighten up and *do something* about Cheech and Chong?" Gwen felt Collins and his new "Rooms" were invading her own space. It would take more than Lysol to banish the pot smell from the pub room.

Tom never touched his guests' smokes, but he feels no obligation to tell her that. Instead, he peers over her Alfa at a brand-new car parked on the far side of his garage. Even with its top down, the candy-apple-red Porsche looks angry, like a bullet that's just been fired.

"Whoa! That's a *Nine-Eleven!*" Tom realizes the WebSurfer board has acceded to his demand to upgrade his company car, and it makes him hard before he steps out of his Boxster. As he walks around her, Gwen notices the rise in the Ralph Lauren twills she bought him, but the sight fails to soften her attitude.

"Not just a car, but a phone number!" Gwen mocks him as he caresses the grill over the rear hatch and inspects the paint for road chips. He barely realizes she is still there and hears only every third word she speaks.

"Make sure you steer clear of both the law and the emergency room, at least until Fred gets out of his cast and back to work."

"I'm cool." Tom figures she is more concerned about the liability and corporate governance than his safety. He plans to crank up the 300-horsepower engine and show his visitors some excitement on the way to Dulles.

"Actually, I've been meaning to speak to you about that, Goofy Foot. Things aren't entirely cool with the law." Tom cannot see Gwen knitting her brow in the reflection off the 911's passenger door.

"So far, so good, Counselor." She can't tell whether he is replying or providing a status report on the paint job.

"We need a little private conversation." Gwen speaks so hesitantly, Tom assumes she is propositioning him.

"Not tonight, Counselor. Gotta get my buds back to the airport."

"You can be so *fucking blond*, sometimes, you know that?"

Tom, checking out the audio system, thinks she called him "blind." Gwen slams the Alfa into gear and angrily pulls out of the garage. It feels appropriate to watch her in his rear-view mirror.

"No," Tom says out loud, "I'm seeing things more clearly than I have in a long, long time."

Clickstreams

C ARLY INITIALLY LAUGHS OFF Tom's plea that she visit him in Virginia. His idea is completely selfish, but it has a sincere, unsettling urgency.

"I swear to you, Carly, if I have to go without you for another week, I'm gonna throw myself in front of a speeding Hummer!" Tom genuinely fears his responsibilities at WebSurfer would drive him insane just days before Fred, free at last of his plaster cast, re-took the reigns.

"Oh, please." Carly's tone is more amused than scornful, even though she suspects he is deliberately pushing her buttons.

"No, Carly, I swear to you!" Tom protests in an earnest, pitiable voice. "One more financial statement, one more board meeting, I'm gonna lose it, totally."

She wonders if he could be serious. He consistently uses her name, doesn't call her "Babe" anymore, and that might signify something important.

"Tom, this is a really tough time for me to find somebody to take over my shifts at the suicide hotline. Everybody's just dying to go on summer vacation."

"Well, don't *you* deserve a vacation, too?" Tom needles her, "and do you happen to know anybody more in need of an intervention than me?"

"Than *I*," she corrects him. "Some English major!" She thinks about it, hard, for a long moment.

"Suppose I fly out Tuesday morning? I could stay a week."

"Perfect!" Tom heaves a sigh of relief. "You'll get here just in time for Fred's big coming-back party. It's on Thursday – I think that's the sixth."

Tom realizes this schedule will force him to level with Gwen, once and for all. Despite her encounter with Collins and Pud, she is already making noises about moving back into his house at The Preserve the moment the heat is off. She is not in the least subtle about claiming her "winnings" or laying a big guilt-trip on Tom about how much she gave up to come east and how Tom could not have made his millions without her.

Tom reminds Gwen he is only a multi-millionaire on paper. Stock market fluctuations raised and lowered his net worth by $2 or $3 million every day. Gwen's law firm, however, was not bound by the lockdown. On the day of the IPO, it sold half the shares it received for the work she and Jamie Bass did. The management committee was not scheduled to meet for another month to decide how much of a bonus she and her slightly younger colleague would receive for their respective roles in keeping the firm solvent. Her own bonus would seem like chump change, Gwen told herself, after the wedding.

Nobody imagined Fred's convalescence would take so long. His left leg was encased in a full cast for more than seven weeks, so it was extremely difficult for him to leave the three-bedroom Tyson's Corner penthouse apartment he chose for his "suitable executive home." To everyone's surprise, he left Tom to his own devices in running the company for an awfully long time, but Tom was not certain whether Fred intended a vote of confidence or a punishment. By September, Tom felt like he was in Purgatory.

Tom wanted desperately for him and Fred to be buds again. Tom's stock options were never taken into account in WebSurfer's financial statements and could do Fred no harm until they were exercised. After Tom held down the fort for five months, even Fred would have to admit he deserved that much and more.

In all that time, Fred and Jamie concentrated almost exclusively on the company's financials. The reporting requirements on a public company were much tougher than when WebSurfer was privately-held and he knew there was no way to leave the math to Tom.

Jamie assured Tom that all those weeks with his plastered leg hoisted in the air mellowed Fred, that he would come around, in time. To believe it, Tom would have to hear at least a few words of reconciliation directly from Fred.

TOM FLINGS open the front door of his McMansion as soon as Carly's taxi pulls into the circular drive. She holds a small, worn suitcase in each hand and looks up in doe-eyed silence as Tom hurls himself down the front steps. She would have insisted this was the wrong house had Tom not taken the bags from her, set them down and thrown his arms around her with desperate speed.

"You told me it was big," she says over Tom's shoulder, "but I know how guys like to exaggerate."

Tom laughs, holds her at arm's length and looks into her eyes. "You look great on this Coast, too! Come in and get hydrated."

Carly follows Tom to the Sub-Zero refrigerator in his spacious kitchen. It is stuffed full of bottled water, the way she likes it, still, not fizzy.

"Feel like stretching your legs after the flight?" Tom asks with a twinkle in his eye. "I have a command performance with one of my directors this afternoon. He's sending his personal limo to get us there and back and he arranged for some exercise and sightseeing along the way."

Before Carly knew it, she and Tom are jogging on the National Mall in Washington. The U.S. Capitol dome shines in front of them, the dusty gravel crackles and crunches under their feet and the Washington Monument rises in all its white phallic glory behind them, where Simon Keith's Lincoln Town Car waits to take them to his townhouse in Georgetown.

"Used to come here on weekends when I needed to escape the grind," Tom explains before he begins to get short of breath. "Buncha chicks used to sit over there, on that bench, and rate all the guys as they jogged by, held up big posters with numbers written on 'em, you know, like one to ten."

"Serves you guys right. Get a lot of tens, Tommy?"

"Doesn't matter any more. I only care what *you* think, Carly."

Her heart skips a beat and she nearly trips on a curb.

"I've gotten past the way you *look*." Carly works hard to control her breathing. "I care more about the way you *live*."

"By the time you leave here, I hope you're holding up a ten, not a two." Tom sounds anxious.

"The proof's in the pudding, they say." She and Tom jog in place as they wait for a traffic light. "But it's lookin' good, so far."

SIMON KEITH ASSURES CARLY he is glad to welcome them into his home, even though she and Tom are soaked in sweat and Lester, Keith's driver, is collecting soggy towels from the back seat of the limo. Tom never spoke of WebSurfer during the ride into town, so Lester did not bother to download the recording of his conversation with Carly.

Keith's house is on an historic street, as Colonial as they get in Georgetown, a section of Washington that predates the Capitol. The inside is amazingly modern, more Art Deco than Georgian, decorated to perfection.

"There's a bath on this floor, straight back. Lester will bring your bag from the trunk. I need your Mr. Rey for a few minutes, so I suggest you luxuriate. That's one of my favorite places to unwind after a long flight."

Carly finds a Jacuzzi tub, big enough for six people, already bubbling furiously. When she leans into an adjacent bay window to catch the view of a perfectly-tended garden, she accidentally hits a switch on the wall. Blinds built into the glass snap shut, black out the windows and assure total privacy as she slips out of her spandex jogging clothes and lowers herself into the spa.

Upstairs, Tom showers quickly and finds Keith in his library, which smells heavily of leather and furniture polish. He has not been there since the photo shoot for the *Wired* Magazine article that caught Gwen's attention nine months before.

"Ah yes, much more presentable." Keith, seated behind a mahogany library table, seems to be inspecting Tom's neatly-tucked polo and tropical-weave linen trousers. "I trust you found everything you need."

"I did, Mr. Keith, thanks."

"Simon. Please." He shuffles a short stack of documents, moves them aside and motions for Tom to sit on the opposite side of the table. "What we are about to discuss must never leave this room."

"That's cool," Tom assures him.

"Has Fred Hanson told you about TerraCon?"

"Should he have?"

"Only if he wants to live dangerously. It's top secret."

"Then no, never heard of anything called TerraCon."

"Just as well," Keith begins. "Your friend's invention has more practical uses than you might imagine."

"Fred told me that all the time, when he was still speaking to me."

"I work with some government people who would like to invest quite a lot of money into adapting it for national security purposes, for domestic surveillance, to be more specific. We're already on top of people's clickstreams."

"People's what?"

"What they click to when they use computers. Every click is a human action, and everyone's clickstream speaks volumes about them. What they like to eat or buy or screw. It tells you where they've been, but it can also tell you where they are likely to go next, what they are likely to do next, and not just in cyberspace. WebSurfer will make it possible for existing data mining software to work not only in cyberspace, but in the real, physical world. It will be a major new element of something we call 'predictive knowledge,' knowing what someone's going to do before they do it, sometimes before *they* know it."

This guy should forget the traceable clickstream, Tom thinks, and go look for his loose screw.

"WebSurfer could add a whole new dimension to tracking and surveillance of evil-doers. It will make it much easier to use information they send unknowingly when they perform a search with a mobile device or when they drive or walk past a point where hidden telematics can click automatically."

"Pretty powerful stuff." Tom understands where the conversation is going. "How can you make sure the government doesn't abuse the hell out of it?"

"Freedom is not free, Tom. There are people at large in our country who mean to do us grievous harm."

"Let me guess," Tom decides to change the subject before men in white coats came to haul his host away, "the CIA needs the source code."

"Right idea, wrong letters. You've probably never heard of the NSA. Let's just say the intelligence community would benefit greatly by feeding all WebSurfer customer data into a single computer network for link analysis on a real-time basis."

Tom exhales with his mouth barely open.

"The government would be extremely grateful for your assistance in making it available to them."

"I'll talk to Fred about it when he gets back from medical leave."

"Have you forgotten already? I said our conversation must never leave this room." Keith impassively looks Tom up and down. He doesn't flinch when Carly knocks on the library door, but Tom jumps.

THE SPECIAL GUESTS AT eVILLAGE keep the applause going the entire time it takes Fred to climb the stairs for his grand entrance on the suspended platform in the middle of the Silicon Dominion's favorite place to celebrate. Jamie Bass, who flew down from New York for the occasion, is on Fred's arm, helping him and his metal-tipped cane join the fire-code-violation-sized group of cheering WebSurfer and UOL employees. Simon Keith, ruddy-faced and impeccably dressed, beams from the far corner of the platform. The only missing person, it seems, is Mike Culver, who chose to be fashionably late out of pique that Fred still refused to sell him the WebSurfer patent.

The moment Fred makes the top step, he releases Jamie and limps briskly toward Tom. He gives Tom an old-time, two-armed, brotherly embrace, then jerks his startled buddy's right arm straight into the air, as if to crown him middle-weight champion. Carly steadfastly holds Tom's left hand.

Gwen Stephens skulks at the bar down below. She is making a new to-do list.

A heartfelt cheer seems to lift the platform higher. The outsiders around the bar below recognize the sound money makes when it whooshes in faster than people can spend it.

"I'd carry you around on my shoulders if I could, Tomcat." Fred speaks so softly, even Carly barely hears him.

"You've carried me far enough, Kahuna," Tom replies in an equally soft voice. The visit with Simon Keith convinced Tom he was out of his league, that it was time to pack it in. He would tell Fred he planned to resign from WebSurfer in a few days, once he knew for sure they were buds again.

Fred extracts Tom from Carly's grip and begins parading him around.

"Can't believe ol' Francie Schwartz had the balls to come down here!" Fred remarks and nods at the investment banker, who is holding court in one corner of the platform. "I hear she's getting a lot of heat from some of the follow-on investors."

"The who?" Tom's grin seems comfortable to Fred, like a well-broken-in pair of flip-flops.

"The IPO was oversubscribed," Fred explains. Tom grins. "She made a whole bunch of the brokers that wanted in on the IPO promise they would buy more WebSurfer stock at a higher price the day it hit the street before she would make *any* of it available to them at the IPO price. 'Laddering,' they call it. That's why it popped up to seventy-nine bucks right after it started trading."

"Is that legal?" Tom asks.

"Guess she'll find out in due course. Meanwhile, I hear she's buying an awful lot of real estate in Myanmar."

"My what?" Tom resisted the urge to stray from the point. "How much of your options did you sell at the peak price, Kahuna?"

"Coupla mills' worth," Fred admits with an equally broad smile, "minus the strike price, of course. Between that and the patent royalties, it's enough to buy a *really cool* beach house. Haven't been there, yet, but ya gotta come check it out with me, Bro." The crowd assumes their golden boys are trading surfing stories.

"Thanks for holding on to your own options, Bro." It sounds exactly like the old Fred. "I guess I owe you another one. Whoa, I'm getting that *déjà vu* thing again!"

"Not just half a fuzzy worm," Tom quotes Fred's solemn pledge in TeeJay.

While Tom and Fred are on their slo-mo victory lap, Gwen introduces herself to Carly as "WebSurfer's general counsel." She offers to fetch Carly something to drink.

"Thanks. I'll have a Virgin Mary," Carly tells her. She wants to stay on the platform to make sure Tom knows where to find her when it is time to go home and make love again. They did it for hours after they returned from Georgetown, until Tom forgot entirely about his disquieting visit with Simon Keith. Tom and Fred split up and are working the platform in opposite directions. Carly hopes Tom will finish soon.

"Two Bloodies," Gwen tells the bartender. She notices Shippe at the opposite end of the bar, twisting his fist over his nose. She realizes he is signaling her that Carly is the one, the drunk he told Gwen about, the person most responsible for Gwen's eviction from Tom's McMansion. "Make one of them a double."

Carly tastes the alcohol right off. She is thirsty, the bar is all the way down the stairs and she doesn't want to offend anybody. She will be OK if she just nurses it. Before Carly is half done, Gwen shows up with a fresh Bloody containing as much liquor as the first one. She did not plan to drink all of it until it became apparent Tom could not leave soon. Keith cornered him and they appeared in the midst of a serious conversation.

Memories of all the fun Carly had with her high school friends, back when getting drunk was a hobby and not a profession, wash over her. The buzz feels good, so familiar, so comfortable, so easy.

"Not a problem, I can handle this," Carly tells herself as she tugs nervously on an old-fashioned add-a-bead necklace she inherited from her grandmother, "but why don't they turn up the air-conditioning in this place?" Carly dabs perspiration off her brow with a cocktail napkin. What little makeup she wore starts to run.

Gwen encircles Carly with a group of WebSurfer code-slingers. "So, tell us – Carla, is it? – just how long ago did you and our Executive Vice President become an item?"

Carly got into trouble when she was drunk mostly because she would not take any shit off of anybody.

"Wait jus' a minute." Carly gets into Gwen's face. "I reco'nize that voice."

"The questions get *harder* as we go along," Gwen snickers to the assembled techno-weenies.

"That's it. I got it now. *'YES! YES! Harder, harder, ohYESohYES ohmore OHYES.'*" It is a perfect imitation of what Carly heard from Tom's bedroom for hours on end the year before. Gwen turns purple. The weenies gasp loudly and draw back from them, afraid claws will come out and slice innocent bystanders to shreds. Conversations end in mid-sentence when Gwen pokes a finger into Carly's chest.

The sudden silence attracts Tom's attention, too. Over his shoulder, he sees Carly and Gwen inches apart, squaring off for a death match. Several well-wishers and corporate hangers-on are disappointed when he turns away from them and jumps into the breach. He smells the alcohol on Carly's breath as he steps between two women with whom he had spent a lot of time in bed. He cannot believe his nose. With Gwen breathing fire, an explosion appears imminent.

"Looks like I fell off the ol' wagon," Carly slurs in an inappropriately happy tone.

"Time to go home, Carly."

"Yeah, you got that right."

Tom hears the "o-o-o-hs" and feels the startled looks from every guest on the platform. He takes a good look at Gwen's still-purple face. At first, all he sees is her familiar look of concentration, the one she got when she finished an item on her checklist. Gwen is not looking at Tom. He follows her eyes to the bar below, where Billy Shippe is applauding quietly and almost imperceptibly, his fingers just beneath his chin. She acknowledges Shippe's praise with a lightning-quick smile.

The eVillage valets always parked the 911s out front, so Tom pours Carly into his car and heads straight for The Preserve. The ragtop is down. Neither of them try to talk over the wind.

FRED AND JAMIE miss the excitement because they are in the men's room, all the way in the back of eVillage, waiting for Billy Shippe to join them in the oversized handicapped stall in the far corner. He dashes in and skillfully lays out a single, four-inch long line of cocaine on a fold-down diaper-changing platform. Fred vacuums it up in two seconds. Shippe lays out a second line and hands Bass a straw.

"Well, I see I'm not your only crutch this evening, Freddy." Jamie makes no secret of his disappointment. He wads the unused straw into a ball and tosses it into the toilet.

"They jest at scars that never felt a wound!" Fred hunches over his cane, looking more like King Richard III than Romeo.

"You promised you'd quit when you came back to work," Jamie reminds him.

"Don't let it go to waste, Man," Shippe interrupts. Fred blinks violently as the drug takes effect.

Jamie folds his arms over his chest and watches Fred and Shippe race one another to the middle of the line. They laugh when their straws meet at dead-center.

Jamie looks disgusted and nervous. He stands half out of the stall and keeps one eye on the men's room door.

"Guess I better let you gentlemen get back to business, eh?" Shippe dusts off his nostrils and merrily claps his heels on the floor as he leaves the stall and crosses the floor, toward the bathroom door. He walks in place for several paces, then dodges, silent and unseen, inside the stall nearest the door.

Jamie leans out of the handicapped stall once again for reassurance that he and Fred are now completely alone.

"Guy gives me the creeps, Freddy." Jamie hands him a handkerchief. "Here, wipe your nose, Bro."

"This is a hell of a time to tell you this," Jamie continues, "but I've got some bad news I couldn't give you over the phone, for a whole buncha reasons."

"How bad can it be?" Fred never felt more optimistic in his whole life.

"It's going-to-the-fucking-penitentiary bad, to be straight up with you, Man."

Fred gives Jamie a blank look, as if he honestly had no idea what he was talking about.

"The Feds are onto the accounting, Man. By now, they've probably figured out that WebSurfer double-counted all the revenues from Tom's deals with the wireless Internet providers."

"Easy enough mistake to make. You said so yourself, just before we each took a good, long snort and decided to take our chances."

A pained expression captures Jamie's face. "They're also looking into the ad revenue from the UOL pop-ups."

"Thought you said every dog gets one bite."

"That takes us up to two, Bro. And there's more."

"You're the lawyer." Fred's dismissive tone rattles Jamie. "Just deal with it."

"C'mon, Freddy, I got a kid to support now. I already did as much as I could for you, Man, when I kept your signature off the S-1 and the first set of post-IPO financial statements. It's Tom they're after, at least for now. Sooner or later, they'll try to get him to rat you out in exchange for a lighter sentence. Then they'll try to get you to rat other people out."

"You know full well that *the two of* us prepared those statements."

"Hey, look, Man, I'm just the piano player. I don't know nuthin' 'bout what's goin' on upstairs!" Jamie runs his finger around the inside front of his heavily-starched shirt collar.

≈≈≈≈≈≈≈≈≈≈≈

"So whaddawe do now, Bro?"

"I talked to one of our white-collar criminal defense guys – confidentially, of course, no names mentioned – and he told me the usual method is to make a firewall, make sure it stops with the guy that actually signed the financials."

"You mean Tom."

"Well, yeah. But there are a couple of problem documents, stuff with your initials, showing you reviewed and approved some of the reports. Anything that might lead beyond Tom puts extra pressure on him to sell you out, take you down with him."

"You're suggesting we cut him loose, just like that?"

"We're Major League now, Man. He's got his own lawyer and she's the one who built this house of cards in the first place when she talked Francie Schwartz into changing the accountants' opinion."

"Gwen had better be damned good at holding a perimeter." Fred's voice goes husky all of a sudden.

"She can't protect herself without taking care of Tom first."

"So I hear." Fred laughs nervously, and Jamie joins him as they walk slowly back to the party, arm-in-arm.

Shippe, still secreted in the stall closest to the door, is nervous, too. He complained to Keith several times that the acoustics in the men's room were not conducive to audio recording. He can't wait to replay this one and make a backup copy, for insurance. Shippe is sure he has finally found his pony, a Triple Crown winner – if the recording "took."

Spillin'

TOM NOTICED CARLY'S RED EYES when they arrived at Dulles Airport. She insisted on paying the extra airfare for moving her return flight up from Tuesday to Friday. The night before, Tom pleaded with her to stay for the scheduled time, but she was too emotional to discuss it.

Before they wedged Carly's suitcases behind the lone passenger seat, Tom and Carly woke up clinging to one edge of the king-sized bed. Carly kept sliding away from Tom after they made love for fear that her crying would keep him awake. Tom kept sliding toward her in his sleep, oblivious to Carly's self-reproachful sobs.

They checked Carly's bags, then found seats in the waiting area behind one of the ticket counters. Bright sunshine mixed with lively conversations in six different languages.

Tom clasped both of Carly's hands with his left and held her head against his chest. She heard his heartbeat over the din.

"Time to head to my gate."

"No." Tom was choked up and his face was red, as if he just got back from dawn patrol.

"What do you mean, 'no'?" Her eyes and Tom's face grew redder together.

"Marry me." Tom did not state it in the form of a question.

Carly rose quickly to her feet. Her eyes darted around the terminal as tears began to form again. "I am a –" she began, slowly.

Tom put an index finger over her lips. "I know *what* you are and *who* you are and that I would rather die than live without you." He put his arms around her, as if she were under arrest.

Carly pulled away from him gently before she began to cry again. She took a step away, stopped, collected herself as best she could, then turned back to him.

"Don't ask me here," she said. "Ask me someplace where I belong, and where you belong."

They embraced for a few seconds more. When she left him to get on her plane, Tom felt certain he would never again lay eyes on the only woman in the world who could pull him back from the brink of self-destruction.

"PRETTY SWANK PLACE you got here, ya know?"

Billy Shippe takes a seat in the middle of the oversized leather sofa in the great room of Tom's great house in The Preserve. Thanks to the loan forgiveness from the WebSurfer Board, he owns the place outright. He already has two un-solicited offers to buy it, each for more than two million dollars.

"What brings you out here on a Saturday morning, Shippe?" Tom demands. He wants to get rid of the reporter as soon as possible.

Tom was already tackling a pile of papers in his ground-floor home office but he had not yet bothered to dress for the day. Shippe finds him barefoot, wearing the sweatpants he bought at the Harvard Coop and a threadbare MIT T-shirt. Tom has not shaved and needs badly to clean up. Shippe's presence always gave him an intense urge to hit the shower.

"I'm finishin' up that teaser feature article for *Inc. Magazine*, 'Inside the WebSurfer IPO.'" He waves a gnawed-up steno pad at Tom. "It's gonna be *boffo*."

Tom's only reply is a blank, disinterested look.

"Naturally, your lawyers have to review and approve the manuscript before I submit it to the publisher. Can't go hangin' out any dirty laundry now, can we? Got a coupla questions for you about the financial statements, seein' as how you're the hero of the piece."

Tom lands wearily on an upholstered love seat that angles off one end of the sofa. He sits about eight feet from Shippe.

"Ya know this story's gonna win me a Pulitzer Prize, I can just *feel* it." Shippe drops his steno pad on the floor in front of the sofa, gets up and plunks his scrawny butt down on the love seat, next to Tom. "What I really need is all the *intimate* details."

From a distance of eight inches, Shippe studies Tom's face. Sensing no surprise, no hostility, he thinks he sees a whole new angle to the story, one that consumed him from the day his first WebSurfer reconnaissance mission took him to the motel balcony across from Tom's bedroom in PeeBee. Shippe reaches over and tugs playfully at the loose drawstring on Tom's sweat pants.

"I'm hoping for a most *revealing* interview."

"I don't do *revealing* interviews," Tom says flatly.

Without a word or the slightest change in his expression, Tom places his left hand between the reporter's shoulder blades. Shippe thinks Tom is guiding him into position and starts to swing around between Tom's legs. As he rises off the love seat, Tom slides his left hand down to the small of Shippe's back and grabs the body wire. He twists the card deck-sized recording device hard, so the tape that held it in place tortures Shippe's skin instead of ripping loose.

"Aaaach!" Shippe cries out. Tom immediately grabs his right arm and forces his hand up to the nape of his neck. Shippe screams in agony as his face goes down hard on the terra cotta tile floor. Tom brings all his weight down on his right knee and tries to sink the recording device into Shippe's spine. Scary determination backlights his eyes, fired by primal rage.

Shippe panics when he notices his own blood pouring onto the floor. It stings his eyes and the smell makes him want to retch.

"You're *hurting* me!" Shippe cries.

"You better spill your guts right now, asshole. *Right now,* before I rip your arm clear off and beat the shit out of you with it."

"Awright, awright, already!"

"Who the fuck is holding your leash, and what do they want?"

"It's Keith! He wants control of the company, always has, and he's been playing the two o' you like fuckin' harps!" Shippe couldn't resist adding a dig to his confession.

"What's he doing next?" Tom ads pressure to Shippe's wrist.

"Nuthin', I swear!"

"Don't fuck around!" Tom raises, then suddenly lowers his knee and jams the recorder deeper into Shippe's back, making him scream out in pain. "Tell me what's next."

"Nuthin', I toldja. When Keith finds out, he won't touch it. He'll sell it all."

"Finds out what?" Tom intensifies the pain until Shippe screams again.

"About the feds. The fuckin' feds. They're sniffin' around for accounting fraud, and the WebSurfer IPO smells like fresh dog shit."

"What about the IPO?"

"The numbahs, for one thing. The revenue numbahs. Every deal you did, all the numbahs, they all got cooked."

Tom lets up slightly on Shippe's twisted arm.

"Huh?"

"They double-counted 'em. They booked the royalties and the ad revenue when the deals got signed, then booked 'em again when the money actually came in the door. That overstated the forward-revenue multiple about 800 percent."

Tom is so stunned, he almost turns loose. It would not have mattered. Shippe is a quivering, blood-soaked mass.

"Who?"

"The lawyers and the investment bankers, mostly. They tol' the accounting firm not to ask too many questions, promised 'em a long-term consulting contract. Made sure *you* signed the disclosure statements, to protect your ol' buddy, Hanson."

"You miserable . . . lyin' . . . *son of a bitch*!" Tom is almost crying at this point, in almost as much pain, as badly crushed as Shippe. He re-establishes his rough grip on Shippe's wrist and turns it until they are both groaning.

"Who knows about this?"

"Hanson found out about it yesterday. Bass tol' him. They're both shittin' bricks, runnin' for cover. The feds are lookin' for a stoolie, somebody who'll cut a deal to avoid havin' to play wide-receiver on the prison football team, if you catch my drift."

Shippe gets quiet for a moment, catches his breath, then adds, "Hanson's settin' you up to take the fall. They're goin' up to New York on Tuesday, to Bass's office, to clean up the paperwork. Make sure you got no story to tell about bigger fish. You'll do hard time, Man, twenty years maybe, if you don't plead guilty early on, take it all on yourself." He feels Tom loosen up, then adds in an icy, taunting voice, "either way, you'll have an asshole the size of the Lincoln Tunnel by the time you're even eligible for parole."

"You lyin' bastard." Horror seizes Tom's face as he shoves Shippe's nose hard into the bloody floor. The sticky-sweet smell is starting to make Tom sick.

"Listen! Listen! Aaach, you're *killin'* me, Man. I'm bleedin' here! Don't break the goddam thing! The wire, don't break the wire! Please! Just listen to the fuckin' disk, it's all there. I got your buddies talkin' 'bout those papers you signed."

"Liar!" Tom's voice cracks as he screams into Shippe's ear.

"Just listen to it." Shippe is laughing now and trying to spit out the blood that runs freely over his thin upper lip, into his mouth.

Tom pauses to think. He keeps the pressure on Shippe's arm.

"OK, OK. Tell you what. Keep it, keep the recording, it's all yours, it's your get-outta-jail-free card, if you didn't ruin it, just don' break my fuckin' arm! Please!"

Shippe would have to find his golden pony someplace else.

TOM PITCHES SHIPPE HEAD-OVER-HEELS down his front steps and immediately agonizes about what to do next. He tells himself "cuttin' and runnin'" would be total chicken shit, that he owes Fred something better than that. Then he listens to the recording of his old housemates, his bros, plotting to send him up the river to avoid their own extended stay at Club Fed.

"*Make a firewall . . . cut him loose . . . just like that.*" Tom can make those words out clearly, three daggers, shoved into his heart, from behind.

Football is not Tom's sport and wide-receiver is not his position. He would rather die. Tom showers, digs out his favorite old clothes and sets out to fill his garage with carbon monoxide.

"If you gotta go, it might as well be in a great set of wheels," he keeps telling himself as the oxygen is chased from his lungs. Even as he finds himself *On the Beach*, the thought is nearly drowned out by the mysterious screech in his ears. When Tom stumbles into the driveway, breathing air instead of poison gas, he adopts a new chant.

"Nature takes its course! *Nature takes its course!*"

TOM'S PORSCHE is pointed outward, ready to take off like a rocket as soon as the electronically controlled door raises high enough for him to slip under it. If anybody wants to stop him, they'd better be equipped for a Hollywood-style car chase.

As he put in the clutch and started the engine, Tom runs through his own "pre-flight" checklist. His sport coat is right where he left it the night before, folded neatly in half, over the passenger seat, with his cell phone on top. His pockets are crammed with a hundred $100 bills. The plane ticket is tucked safely into the right breast pocket, in the same envelope as the written confirmation of the "sell" order he placed right after trading stopped on Monday. The broker was befuddled about how many of Tom's shares could legally be sold all at once, but Tom's instructions were clear. As soon as trading started on the NASDAQ in New York on Tuesday, sell all 400,000 WebSurfer shares and flip all the options as fast as possible. If Tom's order did not swamp the market or start a panic, he might end the day, or at least the week, with more than $20 million in cash, based on Friday's closing price.

For once, Tom memorized all the flight details. American Airlines, Flight 77, scheduled to be wheels-up, out of Dulles at 8:10, Gate C-10, due into LAX at 10:30 a.m. Pacific Time. His ticket said Tom would connect to another flight, through to San Diego, First Class all the way, but only two people in the world knew he did not, in fact, plan to change planes in LA.

In a few hours, Carly would pick up a rental car and drive it to LAX. Even though Tom would not check any baggage, they planned to meet at the baggage carrousel for his flight. The next stop would be somewhere in Baja, Mexico. They planned to stay until Tom figured out a way to get his hands on the proceeds of his

WebSurfer stock sale and, if absolutely necessary, make a home in some warm, friendly country with great beaches. If Francie Schwartz was so interested in Myanmar, it must not have an extradition treaty with the United States.

At dawn, Tom shoots past the Preserve's pretentious stone monoliths. He could tell Washington was in for a spectacular, clear, perfect day. His rearview is the last thing on his mind, so he fails to notice Gwen Stephens' Alfa in front of the peculiar brick house next door, its engine idling, its ragtop up. Both seats are occupied.

"California weather!" he exclaims to no one and shakes his head as he points the Porsche at Dulles, fires up his Bose sound system and muscles the transmission into fifth gear.

It takes a few minutes, but Tom finally finds a parking space in the short term lot at Dulles. It only takes twelve seconds to raise the 911's ragtop. He slips the ignition key under the back edge of the floor mat and manually locks the car. Somebody at WebSurfer would find the record of his American Airlines purchase on his corporate credit card and figure out where to retrieve their company car before the parking fee gets too far out of sight.

For once, Tom arrives at Dulles with plenty of extra time before his flight. Still, force of habit propels him, O.J. Simpson-like, into the terminal. The lines in the front lobby are thinner than usual, but Tom does not notice Gwen at the American ticket counter, huffing and puffing at the agent. A First Class ticket on Flight 77 to Los Angeles was more than the credit limit on her Visa card could handle at that moment. There was no Business Class cabin on this Boeing 757, so she would have to make do with mere Coach. It was "wide open in the back," the agent tells her, but the ticket printer has been on the fritz all morning. She would have to wait just another moment.

Tom recognizes both of the flight attendants busy with preflight in First that morning. They knew Coach would be almost empty but, thanks to a sudden burst of last-minute, high-dollar bookings, most of the twenty-two extra-wide leather seats up front were filling up. Tom turns off his cell phone and slips it into his cash-laden sport coat. The flight attendant teases him about how heavy it is when she hangs it neatly on a wooden hanger in a closet just inside the door.

Tom is nervous about the money – that $10,000 might have to last him a while – but at least he could keep an eye on it the entire flight. He would not doze on this trip, even after he downs the stiff Bloody Mary the other flight attendant delivers the instant he settles into his seat.

"JUST A FEW MORE MINUTES and I'm free," Tom promises himself after his reliable Breitling tells him it's 7:45 a.m. He is wide awake, still in good spirits.

Gwen boards the flight without luggage and casually takes the aisle seat next to Tom.

"You're up early," he flips at her as he casually peruses the emergency evacuation instruction card.

"Don't be an asshole." She restrains her voice, but only a little. "Do you have any idea what you're bringing down on all of us?"

"Save it, Counselor. I'm finished." Tom sounds calm, but his heart is racing. He keeps his eyes on the evacuation card. It seemed a timely choice of reading material and he always wondered how hard it would be to pop one of those emergency exit doors.

"If you sell everything at once on the first day after the lockdown period ends, they'll say it was insider trading. Tom, listen to me, you could go to prison."

"Oh, yeah? Got any insider information that I, being an insider, should be privy to?"

"As a matter of fact, I have something even better than that. I have a file that might come in handy when the feds come to see you about the financial statements."

"Are you shakin' me down?" His choices appeared to be narrowing. Prison or slavery.

"Listen to me, Tom. The whole story of how the financials got cooked and laid in front of you for signature is documented in an exchange of e-mails between Fred and Jamie. They deleted them from the firm's computers, or so they think. I have hard copies of every one of them. With these, you're home free, clean as a whistle. And your supposed buddies will be lucky to see the light of day again before they turn fifty."

"How?" Tom has difficulty getting one word out at a time. He looks horrified, not relieved.

"Let's just say it's good to have lowly friends in extremely high places."

"Where?"

"The file is in New York at the moment, but I made arrangements for it to be overnighted to me."

"So what do you want from me?" Defeat overwhelms Tom.

Stephens thinks carefully before she answers. She stares at the open cockpit door for an extraordinary amount of time because, for once, she is searching both her head and her heart. This time, perhaps for the first time in her life, both tell her the same thing.

"Come back to me, Tom. I love you with every fiber of my heart and soul and I want to help you and I know what to do to protect you." Gwen speaks each word deliberately and with unvarnished sincerity. Much to her own amazement, she means every word.

Tom has no idea what to believe. The mere possibility that she is serious scares him to death.

"You –" Tom's throat convulses and his heart races and blood pounds his temples so hard he cannot speak or hear.

Finally, Tom notices a young Arab man in casual western clothes. He reminds him of one of his USD fraternity brothers, a guy from Saudi Arabia, except he clearly lacks any sense of humor. He is pointing back and forth between his boarding pass and Gwen, without saying anything. A flight attendant shooes Gwen back into the cabin she paid for, despite all her noisy huffing and puffing.

"Come back to me, Tom," she repeats and points out an especially empty section over the wings, where they could talk privately all the way to LA.

The man next to him turns his nose up at the remains of Tom's Bloody Mary. Tom catches him nodding, almost imperceptibly, as other young Arab men board and spread out in First.

"Must be a convention," Tom joshes his neighbor, who does not acknowledge the remark.

A THICK CURTAIN across the narrow passage would soon separate civilized airline travel from mere transportation. Nobody in the cheap seats needed to know what was happening up front until one-third of the fifteen First Class passengers turned out to be terrorist hijackers. One of them knew how to fly a Boeing 757, but he never bothered to learn how to land one. American Flight 77 would soon make an unscheduled stop at the Pentagon, just across the Potomac River from the White House.

Bits

A S THE SLEEP-DEPRIVED FATHER of a colicky baby boy, Jamie Bass developed the habit of arriving at the office late, usually between 9:30 and 10:15. Despite the success of WebSurfer's IPO, Jamie knew that the appearance of resting on his laurels could jeopardize his yet-to-be-announced bonus.

He checked his watch that Tuesday morning when he switched elevator banks. It was 8:30. He knew Fred, fresh off a crack-of-dawn shuttle flight up from Washington National Airport, was anxious to get started.

When Jamie storms into the south conference room, he finds Fred on the far side of the sturdy black table, facing the doorway. He is rubbing his temples, but Jamie is unsure whether he is in pain or just trying to stimulate his brain.

"More bad news, Man." Fred says, instead of 'hello.' He is in a more serious mood than the previous week at eVillage, when he had a head full of blow.

"Now what?" Jamie knows he would rather not hear Fred's answer.

"Gwen got a call from Tom's stock broker, the guy your firm set him up with. He wanted to know if there were any restrictions on selling Tom's stock and exercising his options, now that the lockdown is over."

"I guess the Tomcat's out of the bag, huh? How much is he selling?"

"All of it."

"We are dead, you know that? Dead as doornails!" Jamie announces flatly. "Did you try to get'im'n'his cell?"

"What did you just say?" Fred leans over the huge conference room table and looks Jamie straight in the eye.

"I said, 'try him on his cell.'"

"No, you said, "*in* his cell, not *on* his cell."

"Freudian slip." Jamie breaks eye contact and bites his lip. "This is totally fucked up, Man."

"So whaddawe do about it?"

"The stock'll be in the shitter before noon." Seeing his bonus and his marriage going up in smoke, Jamie flips through the firm's telephone directory and highlights the extension for the partner who has authority to sell the remainder of its shares when trading opens in forty-five minutes.

"Here comes your fucking paper trail." Fred does not worry about his language offending the paralegal with short, deliberately easy-to-manage brown hair, who totes a stack of WebSurfer's corporate files into the conference room.

"I'm sure we've got Tom's original signature on that SEC filing and the financial statements." Jamie strips off his suit coat and rolls up his shirt sleeves.

Before the paralegal crosses the threshold on her way to retrieve the next stack of documents, a hellish vision interposes itself on top of the eight foot-long table and obscures Fred's view of Jamie's side of the room. Fred knows it's not an acid flashback. He only tried LSD once, back at Exeter, when his crazy cousin George dared him.

Fred tells himself this can't really be happening, but there it appears, plain as day – Tom, taking whatever two hardened criminals with tattoos covering their naked chests and arms can dish out. From the beaten, submissive look on Tom's face, Fred knows this is the third time this week and the one hundredth since he was incarcerated.

Fred slowly backs away from the table. He moves faster when the convicts' tattoos suddenly retract over their skin, pulling back from their wrists, as if they are vines being yanked by the roots into a hole between the rapists' shoulder blades. The men fold into themselves, disappear down separate holes, leaving Tom flat on the table, alone. Tom raises his head and looks back at Fred.

"No!" Fred cries out when he sees Tom's shark eyes. The intensity goes out of them quickly, leaving only fear and pain.

"Freddy – don't leave me like this, Bro, *please!*" Tom begs, softly.

The vision evaporates as Jamie flies through the middle of it. The terror in Jamie's face is the last thing Fred sees before he goes down, hard.

THE CRACKING SOUND IS SO LOUD when the back of Fred's head hits the window, Jamie knows his friend has just flown out of the building, eighty-two stories up. He feels his suit rip at the crotch as he leaps over the table. He is relieved to discover that Fred's face landed instead on the shiny oak flooring, just shy of the edge of an oriental carpet. Fred is breathing. Jamie is not. He rolls Fred over and cradles his head in his lap. He is not bleeding, but he can feel the lump rising on the back of his head and see another rising in the middle of his forehead.

"*Fuck!*" Jamie starts to breathe again. Fred opens his eyes, but he seems delirious.

"Can't do this, Man. Not after TeeJay."

"Fred," Jamie sounds impatient, "what the fuck are you talkin' about?"

"Told you, didn't he?"

"Who?"

"Tom. Told you what happened in TeeJay. Senior year."

"Yeah, sure. You two went to some cantina on the main drag and passed out on the table like a coupla teenage jug heads. Good thing you skipped that whorehouse I told you about. I heard some Kappa Sig got killed there after we graduated. Crazy bitch that ran the place cut the poor bastards 'nads off and he fuckin' bled to death."

A sudden lump in Fred's throat grows bigger than the bruises on his head. He opens his eyes, sees that the window he hit is intact.

He catches the reflection of Mary Lyons, the paralegal, dropping another stack of documents – and her jaw – on the table.

The scene on the floor confirms what Lyons decided the day she transferred from the San Diego office to New York, with a glowing personal recommendation from Ike Jacobs himself. Her ex-husband's fraternity brothers had gone completely off the deep end. Jamie thought she looked familiar when she was first assigned to the WebSurfer IPO, but never made the connection. The paralegal had her own reasons not to mention that she reverted to her maiden name when she got divorced.

"I'm leaving the building now," the former Mary Bly tells them.

"Leaving?" Jamie tries to pretend his client is not sprawled on the floor, passed out in his lap.

"There's a fire in the North Tower. Somebody said a bomb went off in Windows on the World a few minutes ago."

Their conversation is interrupted by an announcement on the firm's public address system. They could make out just enough from the speaker outside the open door to get the gist. The South Tower was unaffected, and it was safer to stay inside.

"See?" Jamie says.

"All the same, it's starting to look kinda bad. Go over to the other side of the building and see for yourself. People have been gathering in the north conference room. The smoke's drifting uptown. And so am I."

She turns on her heel, stops at her desk long enough to grab a heavy FedEx Pak that she has not finished addressing and makes a beeline for the sky lobby on the seventy-eighth floor.

When Fred is able to sit at the table, the first thing he sees is a sheet of paper with Tom's unmistakable, guileless, perfect, cursive signature on it.

"This document, more than any other, will put Tom in prison until he's forty?" His head is throbbing, but Fred still remembers promising Tom "surfari" until he reached that ripe old age.

Jamie nods and casts his eyes to the floor, ashamed of himself. "It's barely nine o'clock and I need a drink already, Man." He looks at the document and hands it back to Fred as if it were a cup of hemlock.

Fred weighs the papers in one hand, then in the other. He slips off the binder clip and carefully, calmly rips every sheet into confetti. He tosses the whole pile into a trash bin on his side of the conference table.

Fred never imagined Jamie would take it so hard. He watches all the blood drain from his face.

"We're dead, Man." Jamie says, looking over Fred's shoulder, toward the south-facing window.

Fred turns, just in time to see a Boeing 767 jetliner bearing down on the jacobs.kohler.kray conference room on the 82nd floor of the South Tower of the World Trade Center. They can read the "United" logo on the side of the fuselage before the plane faces them, head-on.

"Looks like 'Game Over,' Dude," Jamie says grimly.

"I love you, Man." Fred knocks knuckles with Jamie just as the window explodes.

In that single instant, Fred Hanson and Jamie Bass were reduced to bits – bits of flesh and bone and thought and genius, bits of love and hate, mischief and kindness, song lyrics and inventions, bits of memory in the minds of those who knew them, who loved them, who shared their aspirations, their futures, their lives, lives that ended too short, that were caught unawares, that still had a chance for redemption, for reconciliation, for forgiveness, for salvation – bits that soon mixed with paper and metal and plastic and Type A jet fuel, that floated, drifted, burned, mixed, formed a cloud and for a time settled over the conscience of the world, mingled with bits of humanity from the North Tower, where dozens chose to leap from windows 1,000 feet in the air, to become the vanguard into a graveyard that would in a matter of minutes swallow Fred and Jamie and almost 3,000 other people, not perfect people, not sinless people, but innocent and guilty people who fell together, like Fred and Jamie, in little bits and droplets, along with minuscule bits of papers that were important, that represented fortunes, that mattered in the world, that some people valued over other people, and bits and shards of buildings that represented something more than the steel and glass they were made of, something bigger than a nation, an aspiration to do more than survive, to keep the whole world spinning.

At bottom, in the hideous debris that smothered the streets of lower Manhattan, they were just young college buddies, a couple of Phi Delts, truly and forever brothers of one flesh, who saw the light, who found their way at the last possible moment.

ON THE MORNING OF SEPTEMBER 11, 2001, Carly got up before dawn. She was waiting at the Hertz kiosk at Lindbergh Field when the early morning crew arrived for work, and she drove their first rental of the day off the lot. She insisted on a Lincoln Town Car, big enough for her and Tom to sleep in, if it came to that.

Carly guzzled her extra-large coffee and almost finished it by the time she passed the exit for Torrey Pines and hit "The 5." No matter what buttons she hit on the car radio, it only seemed capable of finding Spanish-language stations.

"Better get used to it," she reminded herself. There was no telling how long she and Tom would be in Mexico or where they might go from there. She had no idea what language they spoke in Myanmar.

Carly gives up and turned the radio off. Nothing short of an eight-point-two magnitude earthquake would keep her from getting to LAX to meet Tom's flight on time.

When she arrives at the parking garage for Terminal 2, Carly laughs at herself for being such a worry-wart. There are plenty of parking spaces, including one big enough for the Lincoln. It was the biggest thing she ever drove and it looked like a limo, so she takes extra care to slide it squarely into her chosen space. There is plenty of time to buy more hot coffee, then leisurely check the monitors to identify the baggage claim area for Tom's flight.

The calm in the parking garage gives way to pandemonium inside the terminal. Carly feels like she has jumped from a hot sauna into an ice-cold pool. Her nerves hum and her heart skips several beats when she sees crowds gathered around the "arrivals" board and no one checking "departures."

A well-dressed, middle-aged black woman pushes Carly out of her way and gets within eyeshot of the monitor just a moment ahead of her.

"Oh, my God, my God!" the woman recoils from the board and falls backward, to a seated position on the floor. Carly instinctively crouches down next to her and helps her back to her feet.

"What's wrong?" Carly asks.

"*My baby. My poor baby.*" The woman starts sobbing and staring into space, away from the monitor. "She's on Eleven, American."

Carly finds the woman a seat, then approaches the board again. Next to American Flight 11 from Boston, flashing letters direct customers to "ASK AGENT." Carly thinks she is seeing double. The same letters flash next to the listing for another flight from Boston, UA 175. In the confusion on the monitor and among the people all around her, Carly almost turns away without identifying the baggage claim area for Tom's flight. It is not due for more than an hour, but all this unexplained mayhem might make it difficult for them to meet up.

Carly helps two other dazed women sit down before they fall down. On her third pass at the monitor, Carly elbows her way in and runs down the list. Rochester, Toronto, Tucson, there! Washington Dulles, AA 77.

"ASK AGENT . . . ASK AGENT . . . ASK AGENT."

Carly does not fall on her ass. She does not cry or scream, not like the growing number of the people around her. She is going to find out what is going on.

At the American Airlines ticket counter, she finds more pandemonium, more crying, screams loud enough to curdle her blood. Airline employees are herding together the people who came to meet loved ones on their Flights 11 and 77. Even though her ears are burning and her heart is beating out of her chest, Carly hears people say terrorists crashed Flight 11 from Boston into one of the

World Trade Center towers and that Flight 77, Tom's flight from Dulles, crashed into the Pentagon in Washington.

Apparently, other horrible things happened that morning, but Carly's mental and emotional circuits are overloaded with all the anguish and pain and horror that is right there in front of her, where she can see it, touch it, feel it and even smell it.

The "grief counselors" the airline sent in are overwhelmed.

"But, but, you don't understand. My husband was First Class!" a woman says.

"Yes, ma'm, I'm sure he was," Carly overhears the counselor's off-centered reply.

She knows there is only one way she can survive this, that she can avoid curling up into a ball on the floor, another soul reduced to bits. Carly pitches in. She gets her tortured fellow greeters to talk to her, to talk to each other, to release their emotions, to get whatever answers they could get from the airline about the passenger manifests and the arrangements for grieving families. And she prays with them, on her knees, begging God for help and comfort and forgiveness for their uncontrollable anger at the monsters who did these horrible things and at Him for letting it happen.

Carly keeps it together with the completely unreasonable and yet utterly essential conclusion that Tom is not dead. She could still feel his life-force energy. It lingers on her lips. It compels her to keep dialing an airport payphone all twenty-three times it takes to get through to her answering machine at home. Carly gets in the Lincoln and drives to PeeBee. Every station, English or Spanish, carried a special news bulletin.

Heaven and Hell

TOM REY KNOWS WHAT HEAVEN LOOKS LIKE the moment he lays eyes on it. As he zooms into the Shenandoah Valley, a row of mountains on his left – foothills, really, by California standards – are covered with trees. They are heavily laden with leaves, glistening silver and green. Somebody told him the leaves would start to turn orange and yellow and brown and put on a magnificent show when the trees finally realized that summer was gone. On Tom's right, blue peaks brood in the distance.

Tom is talking to himself a lot. He sings along with the first of the six CDs he crammed into his sound system before he left The Preserve. He harmonizes with pop music's latest discovery, Jack Johnson, a surfer Tom used to compete against on the circuit. The Hawaiian attended film school in Southern California, but people convinced him the world was ready for a whole CD of mellow, acoustic beach ditties.

That was the same advice Fred gave Jamie, his old singing housemate. After what little he could make out on Shippe's surreptitious recording of their conversation at eVillage, Tom could never think of them again without pain crackling through his brain.

In a wistful voice, Tom repeats wishful lyrics about being home when tomorrow morning comes. He can't help shouting "as if!" when the song ends and the machine silently loads the next CD.

Tom coughs up a nervous laugh when his Porsche passes a tiny green highway sign notifying him he is crossing over Dismal Hollow Road. "Dismal Hollow!" Tom chortles for just a moment until he remembers what a dismal mess he is leaving behind and how quickly it might catch up with him and take his life away.

FREAKING OUT on the airplane was not exactly Tom's idea of a fresh start, but he couldn't help himself. He had no intention of joining Stephens in the back, but he could not just settle into his comfortable seat and enjoy the flight after she told him she was in love with him and could protect him from all the horrors Billy Shippe spilled out, along with a fair quantity of blood, a couple of days before. Tom decided there was no way he could breathe the same air as Stephens for five hours, no way he could have Stephens on his heels at the rendezvous with Carly.

"No way!" Tom said out loud as he jumped up and stumbled over the Arab in the aisle seat, who suddenly reached for something in his carry-on satchel. Tom bolted for the door. The flight attendant had her arm extended, reaching for the hatch.

"I'm gonna be sick!" Tom told her, clutching both hands over his mouth.

"Take your carry-on bag with you, Sir, or we can't take off," she advised, sympathetically. "Security, you know."

Tom went back, popped the overhead, grabbed his black leather carry-on, clutched a handkerchief over his mouth and shot out the door. For once, it got slammed shut the instant he got off, not the instant he got on.

He dashed past the now-empty gate area and ran at O.J. speed across the shiny linoleum floor of the mid-field terminal toward the mobile lounge departure point. He needed to get back to the main terminal and buy a ticket for the next flight to L.A.

"Wait!" he pleaded as he barely slipped onto the people-mover before the driver locked the door. He sat his bag on the floor of the crowded mobile lounge and reached up to grab a handhold. As the ungainly vehicle lurched forward and perspiration began to soak the armpit of his Ermenegildo Zegna dress shirt, it dawned on him. His coat was hanging in the closet on Flight 77. First, he remembered the ten grand in "escape money" he crammed into the pockets. Then he realized Shippe's digital recording, Tom's "get out of jail free" card, was tucked safely into the jacket's fob pocket. Gwen surely would recognize the coat she bought him just two months ago and claim it when she got off in Los Angeles. She would own him, lock stock and surfboard.

He laughed hard enough to lose his grip on the stainless steel loop and nearly fell into the well-dressed woman in front of him. Other travelers feared being trapped in the mobile lounge with a complete lunatic.

When he finally pulled himself together, Tom counted up almost $400 in cash in the wallet in his hip pocket. It would buy enough gas to get the Porsche to California, and he would not have to leave a trail of credit card receipts. With a pair of cuticle scissors from his toiletry bag, it took Tom several minutes to slice open the cloth top, reach inside and release the latch.

He reached for his cell phone. It, too, was still in his coat pocket in the closet on the plane, which at that moment shot off the end of the runway on its way to Los Angeles, or so everyone thought.

Tom circled back to one of the Dulles Airport-area hotels and sweet-talked a chubby desk clerk into letting him use the phone. He tipped her ten bucks, promised he was calling an "800" number, then direct-dialed Carly's home number long-distance. He got Carly's answering machine and could only hope that she hadn't already left to pick up the rental car.

"Don't go to LA. I'll find you. It'll take a couple days, but I'll find you." That was all had time to say. It was time to hit the road.

The desk clerk gave him an odd look when he asked her simply, "which way is California?" Geography, oddly enough, was never Tom's favorite subject.

"OH! SHENANDO-O-O-O-AH, I long to hear you," Tom starts singing over the tune on the CD player when he first enters the Valley with his ragtop down, his face aglow in the morning sunshine and his cruise control set to avoid attracting attention from the authorities. He stops singing abruptly. He has no idea what comes next.

Tom drives on for hours. In all that time, he does not allow a single thought to enter his head.

After dark, he encounters a gas station attendant with a Cat hat and a grim look on his face.

"Are the freeways usually this empty?" Tom asks. "I've hardly seen an eighteen-wheeler for the last four hundred miles."

"Where you been, Purdy Boy?" The man steps back from his cash register and a display oinking with individual-sized bags of pork rinds. He takes off his hat, scratches his head and gives Tom all the news. The man wasn't too sure where the President was, but he figured he'd be "kickin' some Ayyyraaab butt" when he got back to "Warshington."

When Tom sees on a TV monitor hanging over the cash register that American Flight 77, where he abandoned Gwen, hit the Pentagon, he feels like his own butt has been kicked up between his ears.

Tom doesn't bother to put the ragtop up, even though it is after nightfall. He gets back in the car and keeps driving. Nobody seems to mind that he is doing ninety-five miles an hour. He stops for gas only when his "low fuel" warning light flashes.

NOBODY COULD STOP GWEN STEPHENS when she was on a roll. She heard the commotion up front and guessed what was happening. She saw it on Tom's face, just before the flight attendant pulled the curtain. He was making a run for it, and she resolved to stay on his tail.

"You have to take your seat! The captain is getting ready to push back!" A flight attendant barked as she popped out of her jumpseat.

Gwen cited three different sections of the United States Code to explain why they had to re-open the door and let her off the plane, but it was her reddened face and clenched fists that convinced the crew that Flight 77 would be better off without this particular passenger.

Comfortable shoes were always one of Gwen's trademarks, so she didn't stay too far behind Tom. She got to the departure point for the main terminal just in time to see him dodge inside a mobile lounge. An electronic sign counted down the time until the next departure. She would have to cool her sensible heels for eleven minutes and eighteen seconds. A few choice curse words came to mind, but Gwen was a professional. She pulled out her cell phone and hit a speed-dial button.

"Listen, Billy. You gotta come back. Pick me up on the curb, Arrivals Level. Tell you when I see you. Yeah, I'll make it worth your while. Oh, and watch out for third gear on my Alfa, it sticks sometimes."

TOM STUMBLES INTO CARLY'S HOUSE early in the morning of September 14. His face is fried by the sun and the wind and he is dangerously dehydrated. She embraces him immediately and kisses him more desperately than the day she resuscitated him at Tourmaline. Tom embraces her tightly and pulls her hips against his own. His designer shirt, still sweat-stained from his sprint at Dulles Airport, hits the floor just inside Carly's open door. Within two minutes, a trail of abandoned clothing marks the path to Carly's bed.

The first time Tom and Carly made love, sex was a journey, a riverboat adventure. Suddenly, it is whitewater rafting. Tom is tentative at first, then desperate, then ferocious. Carly adapts, absorbing Tom's shame, his anger, his fear and his relief. When, at last, she absorbs his essence, deep inside, it is new and frightening.

Tom rolls off and quiet tears stream into his ears, their paths interrupted by heaving sobs, spasms from a man drifting out to sea, convinced he has lost everything. Carly lightly rests her palm flat on his belly as it rises and falls. She senses no life-force energy, no more wheels spinning out of balance. Even as a thin veil of sleep covers them both, Carly keeps her hand on Tom, hoping, praying, desperate to believe he is not, after all, another victim, but instead a clean slate, on which love and hope can draw new life in their own perfect balance.

For days, Tom has little to drink and even less to eat. He stays in bed all the time, doesn't seem to notice the spectacular weather just outside his window. His fitful sleep sounds like torture. He greets Fred and Jamie in Teenage Mutant Ninja Turtle, then cries out in Spanish and other words Carly cannot recognize. Through it all, she sits beside him.

The media published remarkably complete lists of the dead and missing by the end of the week. All the newspapers were looking for facts-can-be-stranger-than-fiction stories and local angles. The San Diego *Union-Tribune* ran a front-page sidebar on Thursday about Fed Hanson, the USD graduate who invented WebSurfer, who was presumed dead at the World Trade Center.

"In a peculiar and still-unexplained twist of fate," the second paragraph began, "the second-in-command at the high-flying tech company, Tom Rey, perished in the crash at the Pentagon, and two of the company's key attorneys also died in the attacks. Each of them had San Diego connections." On page three, where the article continued, there were USD yearbook photos of Fred, Tom and Jamie, lined up like tombstones with Gwen's photo from the jacobs.kohler.kray website. Market analysts predicted that the stock would take a fatal hit on September 17, when Wall Street finally re-opened.

Carly makes sure the paper ends up at the bottom of her recycling bin. Late one night, she catches Tom reading it at the kitchen table. His face is expressionless, dead, and his running clothes are sopping wet. He went out for dawn patrol at 3:00 a.m., in pitch dark. Carly is adamant that the Tom she knew and loved would not become another statistic in the media's grim body count.

Two days later, with no sign of improvement and Tom's face growing more ashen each day, Carly tells him she is calling a doctor. The effect is like electro-shock therapy. Tom grabs Carly tight and begs her.

"They'll find me, *they'll find me*," he mutters over and over. "They're gonna put me away in a cage and people are gonna come and hurt me, bad. And they'll hurt you, too." Then he cries until he falls back to sleep.

EVERY TIME Tom seemed to regain his spirit, there were setbacks. The deepest arrived with a USD alumni magazine that published eulogies from the memorial services held back East for Fred and

Jamie. The article listed twenty-two Phi Delt brothers who flew in to pay their respects.

Thanksgiving came and went. Tom heard nothing from the FBI or the SEC. They had more urgent things to investigate, it seemed, at least for the moment. Tom did not know how many bills were piling up back at The Preserve, but the electric company somehow figured out where to send the notice that they had shut off the power.

After a huge "gap-down" in the price of its stock, WebSurfer seemed to be holding its own. The attacks killed the "sell" order Tom placed on September 11. Under Simon Keith's guidance as the new "Acting CEO," the stock price rebounded to seven dollars after hitting rock bottom, at eighty cents, the day the markets re-opened. The company stopped paying Tom's salary as soon as they heard he was dead and had no idea what to do weeks later when they learned he was, in fact, alive.

Culver sent word he was anxious to speak with Tom. Keith sent word he was even more anxious than Culver and that he had some friends in the federal government he wanted Tom to meet, guys he described as "real problem-solvers." Both of them were aware, but neither of them mentioned, that Fred's family found a photocopy of a will from 1998 in which he made a few specific bequests of heirlooms and certain trust funds and left his entire "residuary estate" to Tom Rey. Fred's stock and his ownership of the WebSurfer patent, neither of which was so much as a glint in Fred's eye in 1998, were part of the residuary estate, or at least that's what the lawyer who called from Boston told Carly. The bigger question was whether Fred had time to change his will after the falling-out with Tom in March, 2001. The Boston lawyer guessed that the original 1998 will probably was kept in Jamie Bass' office at the World Trade Center, where everyone thought it couldn't get lost or stolen. As best she could tell, it got blasted out of the sky.

Tom planned to sell his house in The Preserve, but he pulled back every time the realtors proposed a date for the closing. Tom kept having nightmares in which he and Fred were together, leaving a table full of legal documents, but when they got outside, they were at *Las Santerías*, back in TeeJay, doing a "perp walk," their hands manacled behind them, surrounded by Mexicans brandishing gleaming knives. Tom knew he couldn't put it off forever, perp walk or no perp walk, and that he at least needed to make sure Carly was on the deed, now that she was his wife and pregnant. In time, he figured he would need a whole firm's worth of lawyers, yet he did not know one he could trust.

SUPERVISORY SPECIAL AGENT "BART" BARTHOLOMEW is not sure where to start. His windowless office at the J. Edgar Hoover Building in downtown Washington, D.C., was crammed full of paper before September 11 and now it is a veritable fire trap. Any more reams of personal information on the passengers from the doomed flights, he decided, and he would have to move his chair outside and work his way back in.

A newly-minted agent with a crew cut stops in with an armload of additional files. Bartholomew remembers being happy when the kid got assigned to his team in the Federal Bureau of Investigation's Financial Crimes Unit early that summer. They were making good progress on some monkey-business involving a couple of those "dotcom" things that sold the public a crock of horseshit last spring. Those once-hot files are now buried under several layers of file jackets, over in the far left – or was it the right? – corner.

"Now what?" Bartholomew barks at the kid.

"Look what I found!"

Bartholomew abhors his assistant's eagerness to learn everything about all of the passengers on every flight, just to satisfy some paranoid higher-up that none of them were complicit with the known hijackers. It was grim business and a hell of a lot less interesting than following the financial trail left by the terrorists, the sort of job that led him to join the Bureau twenty-three years before. He opens the black file folder on top and is greeted by Gwen Stephens' law firm portrait.

"Yeah, so?"

"She should be in a *yellow* folder, not a black one. She's not dead, see? She got on American Flight 77, then got off."

"Maybe she had cramps."

"Look at this one." He hands Bartholomew another black file. Tom Rey's photo from the WebSurfer website is inside. "He got on American Flight 77, too, but he also got off."

Bartholomew shrugs. "Yeah, so what?"

"It gets better. They both worked for the same company, see, there at the bottom of the page, where it says 'WebSurferUSA.com' And they both placed huge trades in the company's stock on September 10. The guy who invented the whole thing got creamed on September 11, at the Trade Center. This other guy, Tom Rey, placed a huge "sell" order that didn't execute. The lady lawyer shorted the stock. You know what that means, right? This Stephens lady borrowed shares when the price was way high, then replaced them the day the market reopened, when the price was next-to-nuthin'. She cleared more than $3 million. That's how we found out she wasn't on Flight 77 when it hit the Pentagon."

"All these weeks and we're just now figurin' this out?"

"Well, 'R' and 'S' are pretty far down in the alphabet."

"Find 'em. Find 'em yesterday! But don't tell anybody what we know about this."

Bartholomew makes a note to start digging for that file on the WebSurfer IPO. First, he would have to remember which corner it landed in.

Headquarters assigned agents Samuels and Barkowski from the Chicago field office to interview the two passengers who somehow knew Flight 77 and WebSurfer stock were both extremely bad picks. However, two days earlier, both agents were dispatched to Hamburg, Germany, where the terrorist plot was organized. Somebody neglected to update the system.

Aerial

CARLY PICKS OUT A PRIME STRETCH OF SAND at Tourmaline Surfing Park and lays claim to it with a bright red beach umbrella that is almost too big for her to carry. She grunts a bit as she sits down under it and laughs at herself. These days, it seems difficult to get up or sit down without making some kind of ugly noise.

The sky is perfect, bright and clear, the waves were strong and steady. Carly slathers a thick coat of SPF-50 lotion over her exposed face, forearms and legs. She is prepared to stay out there for however long it might take.

Carly went there to watch a twelve-year old boy's surfing lesson. He is a handsome kid, tall for his age, with hair that looks blond even when it is wet. He has a natural talent and seems at ease on the big board. He plainly likes his coach and pays close attention to his instructions. Carly can't help laughing at some of the coach's exaggerated arm motions and fancy footwork on the nose of his brand-new nine-footer.

At the end of the hour, the boy and his coach exchange soul-shakes and flash upraised thumbs at one another. The boy carries his rental longboard onto the beach until he has to drop one end and drag it. Carly watches his parents kick off their shoes, run onto the beach, pat the back of his junior-sized wetsuit, throw a beach towel around him and wave their thanks at the instructor, who remains at the lineup, fifty feet out, sitting upright on his own board.

As soon as the student and his parents are out of sight, a powerful wave starts rolling in. Carly sees the coach pop up and stretch his not-quite-six-foot tall frame and form-fitting wetsuit into a muscular crouch. He heads straight for the "lip" of the wave, the spot where the curl starts.

Under her umbrella, in the deep shade, a streak of white, almost luminescent, hair glows from Carly's widow's peak all the way back and down to her shoulder blades. Friends urged her to color her hair and make the white disappear, but Carly refused. To hide a war wound just wouldn't be right. Besides, the bearded man on the surfboard in front of her seems determined to give her another exactly like it.

TWO MINUTES AFTER Carly planted her umbrella at Tourmaline, a bilious green, two-door Chevrolet pulls up outside her house. Billy Shippe shuts off the engine. His right arm is no longer in a sling, but it still hurts to turn the key.

"You got the goods?"

"Right here." Gwen Stephens thumps a thick, soot-smudged FedEx Pak with her middle finger. It contains a file folder with "jacobs.kohler.kray" printed in small block letters on the front.

"His ass belongs to us, now!" Shippe is joyful. "Wish I could be there to see the sonofabitch read it, to see him figure out he's got no choice but to sign all of it over to us."

"Billy Boy, I guarantee you don't really want to be in the same room with Tom when he reads what's inside here." Gwen waves the FedEx Pak in his face.

Shippe huffs. Gwen closes the door gently and saunters to Carly's front door. Just as she thought, the package is too big to slip through the mail slot. While Shippe keeps lookout, Gwen slips unseen behind the house and climbs the stairs to the top floor apartment. She finds the door unlocked and the California king-sized bed where Tom first drove her crazy stripped to the bare mattress, obviously unused for a long time.

"Goofy Foot," Gwen writes neatly on the front of the Pak with a black Sharpie and draws a smiley face. She stands it up against the headboard, where it could not be missed. It contains the complete exchange of e-mails establishing Fred and Jamie's culpability for the WebSurfer accounting fraud, Shippe's backup copy of their tape-recorded confessions in the eVillage men's room and the original, signed, Last Will and Testament of Frederick Ames Hanson, dated October 12, 1998, four weeks after his and Tom's "Not So Excellent Adventure" in TeeJay. The will, in effect, left Tom a controlling interest in the battered company, plus ownership of the WebSurfer patent and the software source code that Mike Culver and Simon Keith were so desperate to snatch away from one another.

"Are we done?" Shippe asks cheerfully when Gwen returns to the ugly car he rented that morning upon his arrival in San Diego.

Gwen was ready for the question. The day before the flight back to California, she did some independent research in a hardware store and was certain she knew the quickest way to jam a car door shut.

"You can say that again!" Gwen nonchalantly crams a toothless, blank key deep into the lock on the passenger door and tugs on it, hard. When she is confident the door cannot be opened, and before Shippe realizes what is happening, she crosses to the driver's side and shims it, too.

"Don't get me wrong," she explains through the open car window, "I really do appreciate that stock tip, Billy, but even the *thought* of sex with you makes my skin crawl."

Shippe looks ready to jump out of the car and pounce on Gwen with his fists, but his panic-stricken fingers try without success to open either car door.

"Here comes Tom, now!" Gwen says with a devilish smile. Shippe catches sight of her Alfa in his rear-view mirror and peels out so fast she could not hear him cursing and threatening her.

Gwen's roadster skids to a halt in the exact spot Shippe occupied a moment before. It's a woman with short, brown hair, not Tom, behind the wheel.

"Perfect timing, as always," Gwen congratulates her favorite accomplice. "Scoot over, Girlfriend, I'll drive the first leg."

Mary Bly or, as she was known after she transferred to her law firm's New York office, Mary Lyons, eagerly jumps to the passenger seat. She is stoked for a road trip, especially since she has never been to Vegas before, or to a medical convention.

"Two M-R-S-M-Ds, coming right up!" Gwen checks one more item off her list and flips a mental page to a new chapter in her life. She throws her head back and howls as she jerks the shift lever and screeches out of PeeBee forever.

Pacific Beach, California
March, 2002

TOURMALINE'S MOST POPULAR surfing coach senses another perfect curl and heads straight for the lip. Carly hopes it will be his last attempt of the day.

The surfer's newly-sprouted facial hair glistens in the sun. Those eyes, those intense blue-greens, synchronizing with the ocean, take Carly back to simpler, more certain days. He races to the lip as fast as he can make the board go. When he hits it, the longboard leaves the water, flips laterally in a perfect cork-screw and lands back on the face of the wave. The young man's feet stay glued to the board from beginning to end.

"All right!" Carly claps and jumps up so fast, she bangs her head on one of the wooden umbrella ribs.

"Dog!" Several people on the beach cheer along with her. This aerial counts, even under California rules.

He rides the wave the rest of the way in, then lopes effortlessly up the beach wearing a grin as wide as the Pacific. He flexes his muscles like a circus weightlifter to acknowledge the cheers from all his witnesses. When he stops at Carly's feet, she scrunches the blond whiskers sprouting on his chin.

"I can shave now."

"And *then* what will you do?"

"There is only one thing *to* do. Let nature take its course."

Carly smiles at him as he plants his board in the sand.

Tom Rey kisses his wife and holds her expectant belly against his wetsuit until the last crimson slice of sun sinks into the Pacific.

Acknowledgements

I AM DEEPLY INDEBTED to Ginger Foglesong Guy and Dennis Wholey, dear friends and accomplished, best-selling authors, for their support and guidance from the earliest drafts. Their kindness and encouragement kept the pages coming and the oxygen masks from deploying on Ginger's flight from Seattle.

I can never adequately thank the friends who pitched in as "advance readers" with so much good cheer and candor. Special thanks go to Jay Hamilton, who makes an excellent one-man focus group, and to Mary Gwyn Allard for her limitless enthusiasm.

My teachers also deserve much gratitude: George Garrett, acclaimed novelist, poet and creative writing professor, for the discipline to keep putting "words on paper, words on paper;" Pulitzer Prize winner Haynes Johnson, who looked at the first draft of my senior thesis at Princeton and warned me away from "running backwards sentences until reels the mind;" and award-winning journalism teacher Ron Clemons, who taught me to look at every sentence I write and ask, "who cares?"

Finally, a loving tribute to my wife, Victoria, at once my most inspiring fan and most insightful critic, who cheerfully suffered through innumerable drafts and many foregone billable hours.

www.ingramcontent.com/pod-product-compliance
Lightning Source LLC
Chambersburg PA
CBHW050513260626
47157CB00004B/1308